Judge Not
by Lee Lowry

JUDGE NOT

For more information about this and other books by Lee Lowry, contact the author's website:
www.leelowryauthor.com

iUniverse books may be ordered through booksellers or by contacting:

iUniverse
1663 Liberty Drive
Bloomington, IN 47403
www.iuniverse.com
1-800-Authors (1-800-288-4677)

ISBN: 978-1-4917-7202-7 (sc)
ISBN: 978-1-4917-7204-1 (hc)
ISBN: 978-1-4917-7203-4 (e)

Library of Congress Control Number: 2015910883

Print information available on the last page.

iUniverse rev. date: 8/25/2015

In loving memory of Terry & William

Prologue

The pilot announced that Greenland was visible from the starboard side of the plane, but Bibi Birnbaum kept her gaze on her friend and seatmate, Jenny Longworth. Bibi was fully focused on Jenny's decision to upend her life in Boston and move to Geneva – a decision made just twenty-four hours previously, as Jenny concluded a visit to David Perry, a newly widowed friend, long-ago classmate, and former lover who had made his life in Europe for the past three decades.

"Okay, you and David have known each other since college. And okay, you've loved each other in your weird way all these years. But his grief is really intense. I don't see him getting over Sandie's death any time soon. Moving in with him may seem like a noble gesture, but frankly, it's not a good idea. Certainly not at this stage."

"This is precisely the stage where he needs me most," Jenny countered.

"Jenny, the man isn't living on a desert island. He has lots of friends in Geneva. Both his kids are close by. Look, I'm really glad I came on this trip and got to know him better. I can see why you care about him so much. But you need to look at him with your brain, not your heart. By your own reckoning, he's been deeply depressed ever since Sandie died. You're a terrific problem solver, but grief can't be 'fixed,' and even with your Puritan heritage, you're not cut out to be a martyr. Keep in touch with him, yes. Visit him often, yes. But move in with him? For an otherwise practical person, you're putting a lot of faith in romance."

"I don't think it's a question of faith in romance," Jenny replied. "I can't fail this man just because the leap is a scary one. He needs me. He really needs me. As long as that's the case, I'll figure out a way to take care of him. It's not romance, Bibi. It's love."

For Sandie's birthday

"She just forgot to breathe,"
The doctor said,
Shaking my hand gently
At the bottom of the hospital stairs
Some fifteen months ago
That autumn evening when,
For both our sakes,
I wanted her to go.
I haven't forgotten the moment
Or more importantly the feeling
That she'd adventures waiting elsewhere,
Maybe in that domain of light
Near-death accounts relate
And maybe not, maybe somewhere else.
And what if, here and there,
The hurt her images in me procure
Still represents a tie to show
Our love for one another rests secure?

D.P. – January, 2002

Chapter 1

"You survived the day?" Bibi asked when Jenny answered the phone.

Bibi was calling from California, but the connection to Geneva was so clear she might as well have been next door.

"Hi, Bibi. Yes, I survived the day. We got through the wedding more or less without incident. It wasn't exactly cheerful, but, happily, the luncheon afterwards was really splendid. David managed to discreetly surround me with English speakers while we were eating, so I didn't have to struggle with French or sit there quiet as a mouse."

The two women had met thirty years earlier, in Boston, just after Jenny earned her CPA credentials and started a small accounting firm. In the early days of Jenny's friendship with Bibi, David Perry's name rarely came up in their conversation. On the few occasions when Jenny mentioned him, she described David simply as a former classmate who, after graduation, fell in love with Paris, found a job teaching English, and married a dark-eyed Parisian beauty named Sandrine Caillet.

As far as most people knew, he and Jenny led separate lives with an ocean between them. Over time, however, Bibi came to understand that despite the distance, David and Jenny quietly sustained a very special friendship. A poster-sized photograph featuring a youthful David and Jenny had hung for years in Jenny's office, attesting to David's continuing presence in her heart.

"I have half an hour before I have to head out," Bibi announced, "so give it to me in detail, from the beginning."

"Bibi, just describing the luncheon menu would take half an hour!"

"You're telling me the wedding started with lunch? The menu you can send me. It's the other details I want with my coffee. What did you wear?"

"I'm not very good at shopping in French, so I didn't get anything new. I have a nice camel-colored suede outfit I got a few years back, and that's what I wore."

Jenny thought back to her morning preparations. She had done nothing out of the ordinary beyond double-checking her appearance in the mirror as she fastened on a simple gold necklace that once belonged to her mother. The dark brown eyes peering back at her were her best feature, but they were past their heyday, so she added some eyeliner and touched up the sparse outer edges of her eyebrows. And that was it.

"We didn't want to do anything fancy," Jenny explained, "especially in light of the children's ambivalence. Marc and Dellie still mourn their mother deeply, and it's hard for them to figure out where my happiness with David fits into all that. In any event, the dress code wasn't important. David's not much for wearing a jacket and tie, although he did manage a touch of class with his blue cashmere sweater."

Despite the casual attire, Jenny thought David looked very handsome in his wire-rimmed glasses and his fresh haircut. In their student days, she would have used the word cute. Back then, David had a mane of sandy hair, deep dimples, and a warm smile that could burst into a spectacular grin given the slightest provocation. Now his visage attested to his fifty-seven years. The grin had been eclipsed by the grief suffered with his first wife's death. It was slowly making a comeback, but Jenny had seen no sign of it that morning as they readied themselves for their wedding.

"Dellie was the real fashion plate," Jenny continued. "She wore a long denim skirt with a turtleneck top, a paisley scarf, dangly earrings, and a pair of oversized *baskets*, as the French call serious athletic footwear." In Jenny's view, David's daughter could wear anything and look good. Even in her eclectic wedding outfit, Delphine displayed her mother's casual elegance.

"So there was no last minute resistance from Dellie's corner?"

"She wasn't thrilled, but no. She handled it well. The worry was weeks back, when we weren't sure either Dellie or Marc would participate. As you know, neither of the kids wanted us to get married to begin with. They're glad their father won't be alone any longer, but they're still protective of Sandie's 'rightful place.' Fortunately, when Dellie realized I couldn't get a residency permit without the marriage, she accepted the legal necessity."

"So she didn't mind coming back from Paris for the event?"

"I think she saw her participation as a gesture of support for her father. It would have cut David to the quick if she had refused to serve as a witness."

"And Marc came on board as well?"

"Yes. David got Dellie's okay first, so he was able to tell Marc that Dellie had agreed to be a witness. I think that made it easier. I strongly doubt Marc would have signed on if Dellie had declined to participate. The two of them have become much closer since their mother died, and they sort of stick together. Marc hasn't found his balance yet, and his emotions are volatile. Even though Dellie only just turned twenty and is two years Marc's junior, she's better at stepping back and being objective than he is."

"Okay, so back to the day itself," Bibi said, pushing to keep the account on track.

"The ceremony was at the *Mairie* – the town hall – with the Swiss equivalent of a Justice of the Peace."

"What's the *Mairie* like? To me, a town hall has all the appeal of a police station," Bibi commented.

"Actually, ours is quite nice – classic nineteenth century Swiss architecture. We gathered in a large chamber that reminded me of a library reading room – high ceilings, intricate moldings and pastoral paintings. There was a conference table in the center, and chairs were set around the wall for guests."

"Did any of your family come?"

"No. Bad time of year and too far to travel for such a minimal ceremony. David even discouraged his local friends from attending. 'The wedding's gonna be as entertaining as getting a goddamn driver's license,' he told them. 'The real celebration is the luncheon.' I think he wanted to downplay it because of Marc and Dellie's discomfort." *And that of several others*, Jenny added mentally. Ambivalence about David's swift remarriage was not limited to his children.

"We ended up having three other couples, starting with Michel and Josette DuPont. They're the fellow teachers who coaxed David and Sandie into leaving Paris and joining the staff at l'Académie Internationale. David includes the DuPonts in almost everything he does.

"Josette is normally perky and bustling, but she seemed withdrawn as we waited for things to begin. She was wearing a bright scarf that I recognized as one that used to belong to Sandie.

"The second couple, our neighbors Mehrak and Manuela Pashoutan, arrived a minute behind the DuPonts, and the guest list was completed by another set of David's school friends, Edie and Jeremy Duval. It was a small gathering, but it reflected the international flavor of David's life here. Michel, Josette and Jeremy are French. Mehrak is Iranian. Manuela is Spanish. Edie's a New Yorker. I'm a Bostonian. David is Swiss and American. Dellie is Swiss, American and French."

Jenny paused. "And Marc, unfortunately, is somewhat unreliable. There we were, a mini United Nations waiting to start our session, and Marc was nowhere in sight."

"Wait a minute. Why didn't he come with you?"

"Marc lives in the city with his girlfriend – over near the University. There was no point in having him come by the house first. And it's just as well we didn't ask him to, or we would *all* have been late. Perhaps there was a legitimate reason for his tardiness, but with Marc it's hard to tell. I really don't know how to deal with him. He was sweet and impish as a little boy, but he turned into a sullen, scowling teenager. I know that's not unheard of, but he's nearly twenty-two now, and he has yet to get past that adolescent persona. His mother's death seems to have frozen his development."

"Jenny, I hear you. I had some real challenges with my Daniel before he straightened out. It's worth a long conversation, but I gotta go in about ten minutes. Let's save Marc for another day."

"Well, anyway, David apologized to the JP for Marc's absence, citing his age and his tendency to stay out late on Friday nights. She graciously allowed a little leeway. I saw David glance at Michel as the minutes ticked by. The DuPonts were primed to fill in as our official witnesses if either Marc or Dellie suddenly reneged.

"The atmosphere was definitely subdued. There wasn't a smile in the room. Jeremy used the lull to take some pictures, but there was no happy chatter among the guests as we waited. I wanted to blame the quiet on the early hour, but I knew everyone was thinking about Sandie. About ten past nine, Marc arrived, rumpled and still half-asleep. He mumbled an apology and slouched into the seat next to me.

"The JP opened the ceremony by citing the cantonal statutes regarding marriage. She verified the data on our application forms, line by line. It was very precise and very Swiss. The whole process took fifteen minutes. At the end, I was given a dainty bouquet of roses and daisies, courtesy of the taxpayers, and we went outside to have a formal photograph taken in the courtyard. It was cold out, but the sun was shining. I could feel the mood lighten. I think everyone was glad it was over."

"Did Dellie catch the bouquet?" Bibi asked.

"I didn't toss it," Jenny answered.

"What did you do with it? Isn't it back luck to keep it?"

"I didn't keep it. I gave it to Sandie."

"You gave it to *Sandie*?"

"Yes, I gave it to Sandie. We went back to the house for a late breakfast with the attendees, and I set my bouquet on the entry table, next to Sandie's photograph. You know David views our wedding as Sandie's birthday present. That's why we did a private ceremony at home last month, the day after her birthday, with just David and me and a ring. It's important to him to see it that way, and under the circumstances, it seemed appropriate to give Sandie the *Mairie's* flowers."

"Jenny, sometimes I think you're certifiable, but your *ménage-à-trois* is yet another conversation, for yet another day," Bibi commented dryly. "Meanwhile, I gotta go."

"Okay. I'll send all the lunch details in an e-mail."

After they hung up, Jenny retreated to her computer and began to type.

De: J W Longworth
A: Bibi
Envoyé: 23 février, 2002
Objet: Wedding luncheon

As promised: The luncheon was held at a small *auberge* with an excellent chef and, equally important to me, a powerful exhaust system to keep the air relatively smoke-free.

David was in and out of his chair, working the crowd like a professional politician, but I stayed put. I felt a little shy even though I had met all the guests at one time or another.

Edie Duval sat directly across from me. When she first moved to Geneva, she had no conversational French. She now speaks it fluently. I asked how long it took her to learn.

"About five years to feel comfortable," Edie answered, "and I was lucky. At l'Académie Internationale, I was thrown into giving lessons to French-speaking children. That was far and away my most valuable learning experience and much better than taking some class."

"Unfortunately, I'm here on a spousal permit only," I explained. "I'm not allowed to work, so lessons are likely to be my best bet."

"David is completely bi-lingual. You could speak French at home," Edie suggested. She was trying to be helpful so I declined her suggestion as diplomatically as possible.

"David and I have a well-seasoned relationship," I told her, "but it's still a very new marriage, complicated by grief over Sandie. I want to know right away when David's stressed or sad. I don't want to miss the tiniest nuance. Even if I had a good grounding in French, English has five times as many words as French does. That allows for a lot more shading in terms of meaning."

Edie immediately understood and backpedaled. "So, you'll have to get your exposure other ways. Do you go out when David's at school? Take the bus into town? Go shopping?"

"No, not without David. To be honest, I'm somewhat agoraphobic," I admitted. "I take no pleasure in venturing out on my own in a strange city. I'm also not a shopper by nature. I don't need more clothes, and David does all the grocery buying because he's the one who cooks. I tag along to the farmers' market, but he's the one who negotiates with the vendors."

My tablemates chimed in with suggestions, but as I listened, I realized that I wasn't ready to sign up for the lengthy immersion programs they recommended. My primary focus will be on David through the rest of the academic year and summer vacation too. Lessons can wait until the fall.

There was one somewhat dramatic moment. While David was up having a cigarette with the smokers, Edie asked me, "Does it ever make you uncomfortable to be completely surrounded by people who were so close to Sandie and miss her so very much?"

Everyone within hearing turned to look at me. There are times when I long to be with people who have never even heard of Sandrine Perry, but this wasn't one of them. "I wanted this group precisely because of that connection," I told them. "I know how painful Sandie's loss was to everyone here, but it's not uncomfortable to be surrounded by her friends, because your presence is a testament to your affection for David and your hopes for his happy future."

That last sentence was a bit of a white lie – the part about not being uncomfortable. But I really meant what I was saying about their affection for David.

The meal lasted almost four hours. The menu and wine list are attached. The event was a success, but I'm glad it's over.

Love, J.

Sunday morning, David and Jenny took Delphine to the train station for her return to Paris and her classes. "Have a safe journey, Dellie," Jenny said, giving her a hug as the train pulled in.

Then it was David's turn. In the French tradition, he and Delphine kissed on both cheeks. "Thanks for being my witness," he told his daughter. "Thanks for being you."

"Sure, Dad," she replied as she mounted the steps of the train car. "No problem for being me," she added, turning back to look at her father, her lower lip beginning to tremble. "You and Mom made me like that." And she was off.

"You must be very proud of her," Jenny commented as they retrieved the car.

"Yup," was his reply. Jenny waited for more, but David changed the subject and spent the drive back noting the disruption being caused by the expansion of the Geneva trolley lines. Jenny was not surprised. David was well-practiced at covering complex feelings with casual banter.

When they got home, David composed a report for his friends and family. He minimized the wedding itself and touched only lightly on his "inner state."

De: David
A: Family & friends
Envoyé: 24 février, 2002
Objet: C'est fait

It's done. Jenny and I are now married legally as well as spiritually. Can't say I feel the difference in status, although henceforth I'll have to tick a different box on bureaucratic forms, married instead of widower. Doesn't have much to do with my inner state. However, it will permit Madame to avoid living as an illegal immigrant and me to forego having to manage our domestic affairs. Even as I write, all the bills have been paid (Jenny has taken over,) all the household projects organized (again, Jenny,) and the crocuses are blooming in the precocious pre-spring weather. That I take at least some credit for, although Jenny is quickly surpassing me in gardening. She actually likes to weed.

Best to all, David

Jenny's friends and family had already received communiqués describing her move to Geneva and their "first wedding" – the spiritual vows she and David had exchanged at home while observing Sandie's January birthday. Jenny's generic report on the official wedding was brief, upbeat, and supported by attachments featuring the menu, the wine list and photographs of her new family. "FYI," she added at the end, "I'm happy to use David's name in social situations, but I'm keeping Jennifer Longworth as my legal identity, so don't change me in your address books."

For some of David's far-flung circle of friends, the announcement of the *Mairie* wedding was the first news they had of Jenny's move to Geneva. Where appropriate, Jenny added what David dubbed "the feminine details" to the various replies David sent, generating further correspondence.

From: Claudine Miller
To: David Perry, Jenny Perry
Date: March 7, 2002
Subject: Re: Thanks from Jenny
My Dearest Perrys –

David, it just boggles the mind that an ornery old coot such as yourself could get the undying love of not just one woman, but two! There is absolutely no accounting for taste.

Jenny, welcome aboard, and thanks for filling me in on the history. You have lived so long in a triarchic relationship it strikes me that your challenge will be to learn to live as two. In my painting of the universe, Sandie would bless your union if she weren't so busy doing other things like talking to birds and taking huge long drags off cigarettes made out of bright purple light that make her think amazingly profound thoughts.

Living, on the other hand, is a trickier business, and none of us should do it alone. I am thrilled that you and David, who have known each other so well and for so long, are together now.

Much love to you both, Claudine

Jenny's side of the aisle chimed in too. She was especially pleased by a note from Ross Barrett, her attorney, brotherly confidant and dearest friend in Boston. Ross was her link to Ramon Delgado, the college classmate responsible for her introduction to David over three decades before. In their youth, Ramon had served as a catalyst for a number of important friendships. He was also Jenny's first adult experience with grief.

Ross had been Ramon's lover and companion in the final decade of Ramon's life, and had nursed him throughout his long battle with AIDS. After Ramon's death, Ross came up from New York to see Jenny in Boston. Ross knew little of Ramon's youthful days. Jenny knew little of Ramon's last years. They spent a week trading tales, visiting Ramon's old haunts and celebrating his memory with laughter and tears.

A year later, Ross moved to Boston. Still steeped in grief, he wasn't ready for a new romance. In the lingering hurt from her divorce, neither was Jenny. They were sufficiently content in one another's company that people who didn't know Ross was gay assumed they were dating. Ross called her Jewel, the nickname Ramon had created from her initials, JWL. It made Jenny smile every time she heard it.

From: Ross
To: Jewel
Date: March 11, 2002
Subject: Re: Wedding, Part II
Thanks for sending the pictures of your new family. David looks happy, and you look positively radiant, as

befits our precious Jewel. Tell me about the portrait on the wall behind you. Is that a painting of you, or is it Sandie? If it's Sandie, there seems to be a remarkable resemblance.

Your condo has survived the winter thus far. Every time I go down to the Dedham Courthouse, I pop over to Shawmut to check on it. Boston misses you. When will you grace our shores again? I have someone I want you to meet.

Best always, Ross

Jenny was delighted when she read his words. *I do miss that man,* she thought as she answered his e-mail.

De: JWLongworth
A: Ross
Envoyé: 12 mars, 2002
Objet: Re: Re: Wedding, Part II

Someone you want me to meet? Does this mean what I hope it means? I keep saying that Sandie would have wanted David to find love again. For sure and for certain, Ramon would have wanted that for you. Details please! Don't make me wait. I won't be gracing your shores until my high school reunion in late May.

Regarding the portrait on the wall, it's a painting David did of Sandie for her fiftieth birthday. According to David, Sandie's first reaction was, "It looks more like Jenny than me." When I visited them in Geneva that summer, Sandie marched me over to the painting and asked what I thought of it. I said honestly that she was much prettier than the picture, but that it captured her vivacity. She covered the mouth and nose with her hand. "Whose eyes are you seeing?" she demanded.

They weren't Sandie's. Sandie's eyes were almond shaped and slanted down at the outside corners, giving her an exotic look. Her brows were carefully shaped to emphasize the slant. The eyes in the portrait were level, closer together than Sandie's, and topped by the perfect arcs a child would employ when drawing eyebrows. Still, I didn't get it until David pointed out that everyone who knew me thought the eyes looked much more like mine than like Sandie's.

It's interesting that you see the similarities. Long ago, when David got engaged to Sandie, he mailed me a picture of her. Ramon took one look at the photo and said, "He's marrying a French version of you!"

Take good care. Please send me a picture of this "someone" you want me to meet.

Much love, Jenny

PS - As soon as I have the reunion schedule, I'll let you know so we can set up dinner or something.

Bibi sent a wedding present with a sweet note wishing happiness to the bride and groom. Though she often teased Jenny mercilessly, Bibi was at heart a sentimentalist.

De: JWLongworth
A: Bibi
cc: DavidP
Envoyé: 15 mars, 2002
Objet: Wedding gift

Your lovely hexagonal plate made it all this way from Sausalito in one piece! Despite your card expressing "reservations about giving so decorative an item to so practical a person," the gift is perfect. And here is why:

Sandie loved decorative items and filled this house with them. She had an austere childhood, growing up fatherless in post-war Paris, and I think her many collections – mirrors, demitasse cups, creamers, pill boxes – reflected a need for bright, pretty items that were beyond reach in her youth.

What has this to do with your plate? Well, of course, Sandie had a collection of serving plates. I asked David if it would be okay to display your plate with Sandie's collection. "I should hope so!" was the response. So now, there it sits.

The integration of my things with Sandie's, of my life with Sandie's, continues to progress in unexpected ways. David constantly points out how similar we are, how close in taste, attitude and behavior. According to him, we even share the same shortcomings. We were at the farmers' market last week, and since I was busy looking at the stalls, I failed to spot a dip in the pavement and lost my balance. David grabbed me just in time, so I didn't fall, but you should have heard him.

"Goddamn!" he sputtered. "I've only known two women in the entire world who could trip on a flat stretch of sidewalk, and I married both of them."

Anyway, I digress. David joins me in thanking you for the gift and the thought behind it.

Much love, Jenny

From: BIBirnbaum
To: Jenny
Date: March 16, 2002
Subject: Re: Wedding gift

It makes me a little tearful to know that my plate has joined Sandie's collection. I missed getting to cry at your wedding, so this is good. I have watched you find ways to add *you* to David's life without "subtracting Sandie," as you once put it. You've taken on a tough balancing act, but if anyone can make this work, it's you. You are the Queen of Problem Solvers. Mazel tov!

Love, Bibi

Married life wasn't much different from the unmarried life David and Jenny had led since her move to Geneva the previous fall. The alarm still went off at 6:00 a.m. The cats still prowled around the bed covers if David didn't get up promptly to feed them. The coffee machine still made rude noises. David regularly accused Jenny of being a busybody when she fussed over him and insisted he take his vitamin pills.

In addition to the daily domestic chores, Jenny devoted time to learning her way around Sandie's old financial records. True to her professional CPA training, she found quiet satisfaction in monitoring the budget and filing the paperwork.

In the early evenings, she perched on a stool at the counter that divided the kitchen from the dining room, sipping a glass of wine while David worked his culinary magic. "Can I help with anything?"

Jenny asked one night as David set out two potatoes that he planned to dice and sauté in butter. "Maybe I could peel those potatoes for you?"

"Woman, you stay outta my kitchen," he replied, narrowing his eyes at her in an effort to appear stern.

"Yes, Dear," she said with mock meekness.

"Goddamn busybody!"

"Yes, Dear," she repeated, enjoying their unorthodox fencing match.

"Hmpff," he growled.

"I like being married to you," Jenny said sweetly.

"Hmpff," he muttered again, turning away from her so she wouldn't see the grin he could no longer suppress.

There were still dark shadows, however. Some were predictable, but David was frequently caught off-guard by little things. One evening he answered the phone, and his face immediately went rigid.

"*Non*," he said in a taut voice, "Madame is not here. May I help you?" After listening for a few seconds, he then declared, "No, we are not interested."

It must have been a telemarketer, asking for Sandrine Perry, Jenny inferred. The household accounts were still in Sandie's name. David wasn't ready to designate Sandie as *décédée*. Jenny was confident that the transition would ultimately happen, but in the meantime, the commercial world still asked to speak with Sandie, leaving David moody and tense.

One of the clouds that shadowed their domestic life was the underlying tension between David and Marc – and by extension, between Marc and Jenny. David's reluctance to confront his son's behavioral issues, and Jenny's uncertainty as to her step-parenting role, made productive communication difficult on all fronts. *At least he's not living under the same roof*, Jenny reminded herself when relations became strained.

Marc shared a tiny studio apartment with his girlfriend, Valerie, not far from the University of Geneva. He and Valerie stopped by the house three or four times a month, bringing their laundry, availing themselves of the washing machine, and staying for lunch or dinner. Marc, who had twice backed away from attempting a college degree, had a dead-end job as an errand boy at a bank. Valerie was a full-time student with a part-time job on weekends.

Jenny liked Valerie. She was petite and peppy, with an infectious laugh. Valerie was eager to practice her English, and she was patient with Jenny's French. Mixing the two languages, they managed reasonable conversations. Talking with Marc, however, was difficult for Jenny.

"It's hard for me to explain," Jenny said, sharing her unease with David after Marc's departure one afternoon. "There's a barrier, and I don't know how to get past it. Sometimes Marc clowns around, but I sense a pervasive anger and defensiveness. I feel a responsibility toward him, but I have no idea how to execute it. Frankly, his bad manners and thoughtless behavior really get to me."

"They get to me too," David conceded, "but I've been living with his screw-the-world attitude since he landed in his teens. I'm used to it. And in the days before you knew me, I had a pretty rebellious youth of my own. Provided we don't shoot him first, Marc should eventually get past his emotional problems. He's somewhat adrift, but I have hope."

"Life would be easier if you occasionally called him on his manners. 'Please' and 'thank you' are totally absent from his vocabulary in either French or English. You're always doing nice things for him, like cooking too much or buying too much at the market so there'll be leftovers he can take back to Valerie's apartment. Your patience is laudable, but I think we're remiss when we don't insist on a certain level of civility."

"The change has to come from inside him, Jenny. Marc resents and resists authority. If I start enforcing strict rules, we'll never see him."

Jenny took a deep breath. *David's way of handling parental concern is to cross his fingers and hope everything will work out in time. I could follow suit, but that feels like taking the path of least resistance.*

"Surely there is some middle ground?" she countered. "He's so prickly. Even Michel and Josette remarked on it. Remember the other night when Josette observed that Marc was 'so uncomfortable in his skin'? She really hit the nail on the head. Marc always seems itchy when he's here. It's the best word I can come up with. I sometimes suspect he only comes by when there is laundry to be done, or when he needs money."

"He's still adjusting to our marriage," David sighed, "so I see it as positive that he comes by at all."

"Dellie has the same adjustment to make, and she at least handles it politely."

"She also has the advantage of distance, and the distractions of Paris. Marc's bound to find his footing at some point," David offered. "Delphine has always been a step ahead of him in terms of poise and self-confidence, and from what I see in my classroom, that's natural. Girls routinely mature earlier than boys. He'll get there. Different hormones, but same mother, same father, same household, and same school."

"I certainly hope that he'll achieve a similar balance," Jenny responded, "but I've seen a lot of siblings whose personalities are dramatically different, despite the same mother, same father, and all the rest. I don't think we can automatically assume Marc will turn out fine just because Dellie seems to be on a positive path."

"Well, maybe Valerie will whip him into shape," David said. "The love of a good woman and all that," he teased, giving Jenny a knowing look. "Meanwhile, I'm going to start making dinner," he announced, closing the discussion.

Valerie does seems to be a good influence on Marc, Jenny observed the next time the young couple stopped by. Valerie had been deeply touched by Marc's sorrow over losing his mother. "He still cries," she told Jenny, "and his sadness has the great influence on how he is," she explained.

Such comments softened Jenny's view of her stepson, but she also listened carefully to Valerie's complaints, which increased over time.

"Marc is impossible!" Valerie fumed when she appeared by herself one day with a bulging laundry bag slung over her shoulder. "He has promised for three days that he will bring this washing to your house, but it stays always in our hallway, and now I have no clean tops. He is so often late, and he doesn't do the things at which he has agreed."

Jenny didn't doubt the legitimacy of Valerie's criticism, but chose to express only reassuring sentiments. "I understand your lament," she told Valerie, "but it may take a long time for Marc to get past Sandie's death. David still has a lot of rough days, and as you yourself pointed out, grief can really interfere with effective functioning."

"Ah, but the death of his mother does not stop him when there is something he wants to do. Only when it is something he doesn't want to do. He talks the big game about how he will go to university in San Francisco, but then he says he doesn't finish his application because he is too sad about his mother. I have told him he is wrong how he thinks. If he really loves his mother, he must stop to use her as an excuse. He must start to honor her and do what she has wanted – that he will get a college education."

"What was Marc's reaction when you told him that?" Jenny queried.

"He was angry. 'You don't know how my life hurts,' he said, and told me I must not tell him how to be. For Marc, everything is bad and everything is wrong, and it is always someone else who is the reason."

Jenny silently concurred with Valerie's observation, but her response was neutral. *I have to be careful*, she realized. *Valerie may repeat anything I say right back to Marc.* "There is an expression in English," Jenny offered, "that says, 'Time heals all wounds.' David seems to think that may be the best cure for Marc's problems."

"*Eh bien*, but I wish time will hurry with it," Valerie replied with a pout.

Fortunately, time was not the only benign influence. Although fully occupied with her new life as a student at the American University of Paris, Delphine came back to Geneva for a long weekend in early April. Marc was visibly more relaxed during her visit, and her cheerfulness and courtesy set a standard of behavior that clearly had a positive impact on the family dynamic.

Jenny considered this all the more remarkable because of the Delphine's initial difficulty in accepting the marriage. Jeremy Duval had sent David the candid snapshots he took at the *Mairie* while waiting for the wedding ceremony to begin. Most were of David and Jenny, seated side by side, but two of the pictures had captured Delphine as well. Unaware she was being photographed, her face was a study in sorrow. "I am afraid to lose my mother's scent," Delphine had sobbed the first time Jenny hung her clothes in the bedroom closet that had once been Sandie's.

She's come a long way in a short time, Jenny felt.

Beyond the family, people in David's social circle were generally kind and welcoming to Jenny, but there were some who were uncomfortable with her presence. They still sought Sandie's face and Sandie's voice. Jenny was jarring and painful proof that Sandie was forever lost to them.

Jenny understood their resistance, and initially, she didn't let it worry her. *I'm sure I'll develop my own network here at some point*, she reassured herself. In the meantime, e-mail was her social lifeline, and she occasionally treated herself to an overseas phone call. One gray afternoon, feeling a need for live conversation, Jenny called Bibi.

"Hi, it's me. Is it too early to call?"

"Jenny! Hiya! No, it's almost 8:00 a.m. here. I've had my coffee. What's up?"

"I've been exchanging e-mails with Ross. He's met someone, and it sounds serious. I finally got the details out of him yesterday."

"Well, it's about time. Who's the guy? What did he tell you?"

"His name is Kevin McGarry. He's an architect and developer. Ross's law firm is expanding, and they've invested in a brownstone over on West Canton Street."

"That used to be a tough neighborhood back in the days when I lived in Boston."

"Not any more. It's serious real estate now. Anyway, the firm is gutting the place and redesigning the interior. Kevin is the lead architect on the project."

"Sounds Irish. Here's to miscegenation! Are they living together?"

"I'm not sure. Ross just said that after they met, they 'went out for coffee, got to talking, and there you have it.' Ross isn't strong on details unless he has his lawyer's hat on. I'm going to Boston in May for my high school reunion, and we're planning to get together while I'm there."

"Well, get the full scoop when you're in Beantown, and lemme know what you think of this guy. Meanwhile, how's your own love life doing? Are you still operating as a *ménage-à-trois*? Is Sandie still right there, front and center, in the middle of everything?"

"That's not something that's going to change any time soon," Jenny replied. "Yesterday evening, as I was getting ready for bed, I could hear David rummaging around in the kitchen. After a few minutes, he called up the stairs. 'Sandie? – uh, Jenny?' he began. He was looking for our appointment calendar. When he came up, he said nothing of the slip. I'm not sure he even noticed it."

"Did you call him on it?"

"No. What would be the point? He doesn't do it intentionally. And it doesn't really bother me. He's constantly saying how much I remind him of Sandie. Not a day goes by when there isn't some reference to it. Last night, for example, Minuit, our black cat, was all settled and comfy on the bedcover when David walked in. David wanted to put him outside, but I like having a cat snuggled against my feet so I asked him to let Minuit stay.

"'Damn cat's gonna wanna go out in the middle of the night,' he warned.

"'I don't mind getting up to let him out,' I told him.

"'You and Sandie!' he snorted, shaking his head. And that's typical," Jenny continued. "I could give you a dozen similar examples."

"But doesn't that drive you nuts?" Bibi asked.

"No, it really doesn't. I want David to be clear that he doesn't have to hide his thoughts from me. He still has some really bad spells," she noted candidly. "I'm certainly not going to make him feel guilty because he still loves Sandie and still thinks about her. And, Bibi, Sandie's still in my thoughts a lot too. I'm surrounded by things that once were hers. Right this minute, I'm sitting in the little home office that used to be Sandie's. There's a framed photograph on my desk of the two of us, taken on our last holiday together. Our past friendship and Sandie's trust in me were surely factors in David's inviting me to move to Geneva so soon after her death. I owe her. We keep a long-stemmed rose in a vase on the fireplace mantel, in her memory. And I do mean *we*. All of which is to say, this is not a simple situation. We're all feeling our way, and it's still really important to the kids that Sandie remain 'present' in the house and in our conversations."

"So, the pre-nuptial emotional issues are still bouncing around," Bibi observed bluntly. "Well, I've said it before, and I'll say it again. I worry that your relationship is lopsided. You deserve a man who loves you completely and shows it. I'm waiting for David to say, 'Okay, that's it. I loved Sandie, and I'm sorry she's gone, but I'm glad you're here. You're wonderful, Jenny. You're amazing. I love you, I've always loved you, and I always will.'"

Jenny laughed. "I'm waiting for David to say that too, but I'm not holding my breath, and neither should you. David doesn't emote. Never has. He isn't someone who seeks – or needs – feedback from others to reinforce his feelings. On the subject of romance, he's definitely taciturn and not given to what he calls mush. If we'd only just met, if this were a new relationship, the fact that he's so private might make me nervous, but over the years, David and I have shared our thoughts and experiences with total honesty. Specific topics may take a while to percolate through, but my trust in him is absolute.

"Anyway, I certainly don't expect a Hollywood wrap-up, with all conflict resolved and everyone living happily ever after. Sandie is always going to figure in our lives to some degree. I accept that David and I don't necessarily love each other in exactly the same way at the same time. I'm not sure that's even possible over the course of a marriage. But where is it written that each party has to feel the same level of intensity about the relationship? Does it diminish its validity?"

"No, I'm not saying that," Bibi countered. "I just don't want to see you sacrificing your other options and settling for helping an old friend if it doesn't really make you happy."

"Being this far from Boston doesn't make me happy. Trying to communicate in French doesn't make me happy. But David? Trust me. David makes me happy."

"If you say so."

"I do say so. What's your weather like?" Jenny asked, changing the subject.

"Our weather is what it's always like. This is sunny California, remember? We don't do cold. Listen, I'm off to work. Keep me up to date, and call me when you get to Boston. May, right? Have a great time at your reunion, and say hi to Ross and whatsisname for me."

Koans

The teapot broke.
  What happened to the tea?
    The filament snapped.
      What happened to the light?
        She turned off the radio.
          What happened to the news?
            He scratched his head.
              What happened to the time?
                She filled the vase.
                  What happened to the space?
He read a book.
  What happened to the words?
    She forgot.
      What happened to the thought?
        He remembered.
          Where did it come from?
            Their marriage faltered.
              What happened to the bonds?
                They turned their backs.
                  What happened to the love?
He dropped the Breton jug he loved.
  It shattered. Does it matter?
    What happened to the water?
      What happened to the love?

D.P. – November, 1995

Chapter 2

From: J W Longworth
To: Family & friends
cc: DavidP
Date: April 10, 2002
Subject: Progress report

Hi, All. My new computer is up and running, with an English keyboard, browser and help menus. To assuage my guilt at insisting on my native tongue in cyberspace, I've started working seriously on my French. Every morning, I wade through the newspaper with dictionary in hand, and in the evening, I watch the news with David.

I keep hoping some of my high school French will surface, but I studied French long before the era of language labs and interactive teaching tools. We never spent much time on actual conversation. The teacher wanted us to read French literature and poetry in its original language. She also wanted to ensure that we could pronounce properly any item on the menu at a French restaurant.

One result is that my pronunciation is better than most Americans, but this actually works to my disadvantage. When I speak a simple sentence, people assume that I'm fluent, and off they go, a mile a minute. Despite my good accent, my vocabulary is non-existent, my grammar is spotty, and I've forgotten how to conjugate verbs. I feel like a real dunce, but David is being sweet about it. "No one expects you to learn French overnight," he keeps saying. "No one is going to grade you. Just do your best and let it come naturally." May it be.

In other news, David is talking about going to Florence for spring vacation. It's sort of amazing to think that we can get in the car, drive through the Mont Blanc Tunnel, and come out the other side in Italy! I promise a full report.

Let me know what's happening on your side of the world.

Love, Jenny

Despite David's supportive advice, Jenny found that "letting it come naturally" was an uphill struggle. One weekend, a group of David's colleagues invited David and Jenny to join them at a cabaret theatre production. The show didn't start until 9:00 p.m., which was normally when Jenny began thinking about bed. The ubiquitous cigarette smoke made her nose run and irritated her throat. The music was loud and the French dialogue was beyond her, so she missed the story line. She wanted David's friends to like her, and accept her as one of them, but it was physically and emotionally exhausting to pretend for two and a half hours that she was having a good time. *This is not my kind of evening,* she agonized, *and David's friends can probably see that. Sandie was always socially at ease. They probably expected David to choose a second wife who was equally outgoing. Quel disappointment!*

She was silent during the drive home.

"Tired?" David asked.

"Mmm," she mumbled.

The next morning, David was up ahead of her and had her tea ready when she walked into the kitchen. "Sorry if last night was boring," he said, handing her the steaming mug. "I thought you'd be able to follow the story on the strength of the characterization. I didn't realize the plot would be so dependent on the dialogue."

"It's not a question of boring," she replied. "Frustrating is more accurate. Or even discouraging."

"Jenny, you've got to be more patient about the language. I know you're a perfectionist, but you're being too hard on yourself."

"It's more than the language, David. It wasn't just the play I didn't get. I couldn't understand what your friends were saying. There were too many people, and everyone was talking at the same time. I couldn't begin to separate one person's words from the next. I can't filter simultaneous conversations. I have trouble with it even in English. And the smoke is a killer. I don't see how I'm going to manage any kind of social life here when almost everyone you know lights up every half hour."

Several years before, Jenny had undergone radiation for thyroid cancer. It saved her life, but also damaged her saliva glands. Her mouth and throat were perpetually dry, and her respiratory system was sensitive and short of protective moisture. David, a smoker since his teen years, always made an effort to keep his cigarette smoke outdoors or at least at some distance, but the vast majority of adults in Geneva smoked. A smoke-free social environment was an oxymoron.

"Why didn't you speak up?" David asked. "I'm so used to it that I don't notice when the air gets thick. You need to sound an alarm when you're in trouble. We didn't have to stay. I'd rather have you home safe than out being asphyxiated!"

At the mention of smoking, David reflexively shook a cigarette out of his pack of Gauloises and flipped on the heavy-duty exhaust fan over the stove. "But this works for you, yes? Don't want you keeling over in the kitchen either." He picked up his lighter, but didn't flick it until she nodded.

"The exhaust fan works," Jenny allowed.

"Okay," he said. "Problem solved. We'll just avoid smoky congested settings. Or I'll go alone and explain. Everyone will understand."

Everyone will think you've married a prickly candidate for "The Princess and The Pea," she thought. *I don't exactly fit into the normal flow of things.*

Even with the DuPonts, their most frequent visitors, Jenny sometimes felt out of place. Michel and Josette were warm and thoughtful people, full of energy and always ready for adventure. They had been a critical support system for David during Sandie's illness and in the dark months after her death, and they were generous in their efforts to welcome Jenny into their busy lives. Being language teachers, they naturally had strong opinions about Jenny's French training.

"What I want," Jenny explained when they asked about her plans for French lessons, "is a methodical approach at an elementary level. That should allow me to recover some of my high school French and absorb new material at a steady but realistic pace."

"*Ah, non*," Michel said, shaking his head. "You are *très intelligente*, Jenny. You will become bored with an elementary course. You must jump in at a level that will challenge you!"

Jenny tried to explain that they were seriously over-estimating her linguistic self-confidence, but the DuPonts assumed she was simply being modest.

"You must not stay at home while David is at school. You must put yourself in situations where you can chat with salespeople, waiters and passengers on the bus," Michel counseled.

"And you must participate in conversations more actively!" Josette interrupted. "You are always too quiet. You only listen. You must speak up. You must become more aggressive. You have the beginner's shyness."

"They're right, you know," David commented after the DuPonts left. "The only way to learn a language is to speak it."

"I don't disagree with you, David, but Michel and Josette don't understand how much my upbringing, personality and chemistry militate against the steps they propose. I don't enjoy shopping, and I'm uncomfortable in crowds. If I have the option of mail order, I always take it, even in Boston, which I know like the back of my hand. I'm an introvert. I don't chat with strangers. I didn't in Boston where language was no impediment, and I can't imagine doing so in Geneva, in French. It's hard for you to understand because you're an easy conversationalist. It's a trait I envy enormously. You never get tongue-tied. You seem to be able to talk to anyone about anything. Except maybe regarding sensitive romantic topics," she amended.

David smiled, but remained silent, allowing her free rein to vent her feelings.

"I don't know how you do it. I run out of superficial chitchat after the first two minutes. It's one of the reasons I so dislike cocktail parties, regardless of the language. And as far as becoming more 'aggressive,' as Josette suggests, I was raised to consider it rude to barge in on a conversation. Have you ever noticed how frequently francophones interrupt each other, stepping on one another's sentences and speaking with their mouths full of food? I accept it as a cultural difference, but it goes seriously against the grain for me. Overriding five decades of social training is not a simple matter."

"Jennifer Longworth, I would *never* ask you to override your Bostonian social training." David's expression was deadpan, but Jenny easily detected the teasing note in his voice. "I do think, however, that you can find ways to learn French within the framework of your existing habits and interests. If you find something you enjoy doing, it might provide a setting to work on your French. The Garden Center offers courses on fruit trees and shrubbery pruning, for example. If you went, you'd be surrounded by people who share your interests."

"I'd be surrounded by people I don't know," Jenny argued. "David, we've talked about this, but you are so outgoing and so people-oriented that you can't fathom the enormity of it. I have no trouble going out and doing things with you. I feel safe with you." Her voice softened. "I always have," she added, touching a finger to his lips. "But you're talking about my getting on a bus by myself, sitting in a strange place with unfamiliar people, and trying to function in a language I can barely follow. I'm agoraphobic, and in my world, those are the ingredients that lead to panic attacks."

"But you went out in Boston all the time," he protested. "When we visited, you took Sandie and the kids all over the place and never batted an eye."

"Going out is not a problem when I'm with friends. Plus, I love Boston and know it inside out – every street, every store, every parking lot, every subway station. The agoraphobia was pretty much latent while I was there. I certainly wasn't immobilized by it. Here, though, there's a lot coming at me at once. All things are possible, but my adjustment to Geneva is likely to be at a snail's pace."

"*A un pas de tortue*," David offered.

Jenny frowned. She replayed David's sentence in her mind but couldn't decipher it.

"By a step of torture? With torturous steps?" she guessed.

He grimaced.

"I give up," she said.

"At a snail's pace," he translated.

"I thought the French word for snail was *escargot*."

"It is, but the expression in French is 'at the pace of a tortoise,' from Aesop's fable, The Tortoise and the Hare. So, repeat after me: *A un pas de tortue*."

Jenny gave him back the phrase. Her accent was perfect.

"*Et voilà*," he said. "You've just improved your French within the existing framework of your habits and interests."

Jenny was grateful for David's gentle support, but she could no longer avoid a difficult truth. The life she had built in Boston was hers to control. The agoraphobia she had endured since childhood rarely surfaced there because she found pathways around situations that were, for her, social landmines. Those pathways had become so much a part of her existence that she forgot how carefully constructed they were. With the move to Geneva, all her clever detours and dodges were lost. *I guess I just have to keep at it*, she sighed. *A un pas de tortue*.

Still, when David took a call from Dominique Charbonnet inviting them to come for dinner along with the DuPonts the following Saturday, Jenny's gut reaction was, *Oh, no. Not another French dinner party*.

Jenny didn't know Dominique, but she had met Dominique's husband Julien over a decade before, on her first visit to Geneva. At the time, Julien was the Principal at l'Académie Internationale and was embroiled in a political squabble with the school board. Jenny's memory of the occasion was reinforced by the fact that she had recently chanced upon an old newspaper clipping, filed with Sandie's school employment contract, featuring a picture of Julien and a description of the conflict. Julien ultimately left l'Académie Internationale to head a local business college.

As David wrote the dinner date onto their calendar, he chatted about the changes that followed Julien's departure from the school. Then, without warning, he dropped the bomb. "I've often thought Sandie had an affair with Julien," he said. "He was so upset about her death he couldn't come inside for the memorial ceremony. He sat out in his car during the whole three hours."

Jenny searched David's face for signs of a joke. She found none. *Did I hear him correctly?*

"You think Sandie had an affair with Julien?" she repeated, incredulously. "I have trouble believing Sandie would have an affair with anyone!"

"Julien is a charming man," David said in a level tone. "Sandie liked him very much."

"She may have liked him very much," Jenny replied, "but she loved you. I watched the two of you together over lord knows how many years. I watched the way you teased Sandie and the way she fussed at you, and what I saw was love. How can you even think that she would take up with Julien?"

"I know she loved me. At least, I certainly always felt that way," he concurred, "but that doesn't preclude her having an affair. And if she did, I don't have a problem with it. I've settled it all out in my head. The only thing that bothers me is not knowing for sure."

Jenny was stunned. *How can he not have a problem with it?*

"Did you ever ask her? Or even just talk about it around the edges? What makes you so sure she had an affair?"

"It's a sense of how she was around him – more animated, more playful, more …." He hesitated. "More vibrant. And then, before she went into the hospital for the last time, she said something about how our marriage worked 'because you gave me my freedom.' I think that was her way of telling me."

"Have you talked about this with anyone else?"

"No, you're the only person I trust to be discreet about it."

"But you said it bothers you not to know for sure. Have you considered asking Sandie's closest friends? If she was having an affair, wouldn't she have confided in at least *some* of them?"

"Possibly, but I doubt they'd ever tell me. If they knew Sandie was having an affair and covered for her then, the chances are that they'll continue to protect her reputation even now that she's dead – or maybe keep silent to 'spare' me. And if they have no knowledge of any affair, my raising the issue could generate a round of gossip that would be all over the school before day's end. It's a no-win situation. So in all probability, I'll never know the truth. But when we have dinner with the Charbonnets next weekend, I'll be curious to hear what you think of Julien," David commented before blithely moving on to other topics.

Jenny didn't push any further. She needed time to digest his words. David made no mention of the subject in the days that followed, and Jenny felt uncomfortable bringing it up. She was tempted to call Bibi, but David had implied that he wanted the issue kept under wraps. "You're the only person I trust to be discreet," he had said.

She busied herself with domestic projects, but all the while her mind kept spinning. *Sandie? Having an affair? Sandie, the beloved wife? Sandie, the perfect mother? Sandie, the adulteress?* It didn't seem possible, but David wasn't given to flights of fancy.

Should I assume he was right? Should I assume he was wrong? And of what use are assumptions anyway? Sandie is innocent until proven guilty, but now I feel like David; I wish I knew for sure. Because if it's true, my perception of David and Sandie's marriage is way off base.

Midweek, David had an open schedule in the afternoon. He came home at 12:45, bringing his schoolwork with him. It was warm enough that Jenny puttered in the garden after lunch, while David sat on the terrace grading papers. He looked tired and seemed unable to concentrate. He eventually gave up and said he was going to take a short nap. Within minutes, Jenny heard Bach's cello suites coming from the CD player in the living room. She went on full alert. These were the suites whose somber notes filled the mortuary during Sandie's cremation service. David opened the French doors. The music filled the yard. He came back out and started working on the school papers again but was soon staring into space.

Jenny went and hugged him. "Can I help?" she asked gently.

"No," was the reply. He added nothing more.

Jenny went back to weeding, but after an hour with no change, she returned and sat down beside him.

"Tell me what's wrong," she insisted.

"Nothing special. Nothing spectacular."

She had been warned that grief could blindside people – bring them to their knees when they least expected a blow. This seemed to be such an instance. David was down, and she saw no way to help him back up.

David took a second stab at a nap. Close to five, he reappeared with a glass of wine. He was sufficiently preoccupied that he didn't think to offer one to Jenny. She pulled up a chair beside him.

"David, something is really weighing on you. Please talk to me about it. Even if it doesn't help you, it will help me. I worry that I've done something wrong or let you down somehow."

"You haven't done anything wrong," he said, shaking his head. "And you haven't let me down," he added, making an unsuccessful attempt at a smile.

Is it grief? Is it distress about the possibility of Sandie having an affair? Is it the prospect of seeing Julien Charbonnet on Saturday? Jenny was at sea.

In a lighter tone, she attempted to broaden the conversation. "We could play Twenty Questions, and I'll try to guess what's bothering you."

"No, Jenny," was his response. "Let it go." He definitely didn't want to talk.

At the end of the week, David got home late, worn out after a faculty meeting and fighting a cold. He tossed and turned during the night. At dawn on Saturday, he got up without a word and descended to the kitchen. Jenny heard the ping of the microwave as he heated up some coffee, followed by the sad tones of the Bach cello suites. *Sandie's funeral music again. That's a bad sign*, she thought.

Jenny roused herself and went down the stairs. There were no lights on, and the windows allowed only the dull illumination of the heavy gray cloud cover. She went to give David a good morning kiss. "Is your cold any better?" she asked. Her voice quavered mid-sentence, and David caught the tremor.

"What's wrong, Jenny?"

She couldn't hide her distress. "I'm really worried about you! You seem so sad and depressed, and you keep playing the Bach cello suites."

David softened immediately, took her in his arms, and rocked her to calm her down. "You may only associate the Bach with Sandie's death," he explained, "but I love the cello pieces. It doesn't necessarily mean that I'm thinking of Sandie. It's just a bad time in general," he said, trying to reassure her. "The rain always gets to me. My cold is debilitating. School politics are dragging me down. But spring is here. It will all be okay," he promised.

"I told you the other day that I feel safe with you. I want you to feel safe with me," Jenny insisted. "I want you to know it's okay to unload whatever's bothering you."

"I *do* feel safe with you, Ducks. If I could put my finger on the exact source of my malaise, I'd serve it up to you with truffles and cream. Unfortunately, there are places in my head that are sometimes awash with fog. Visibility is zero, and analysis is not possible. Maybe the fact that I don't try to make up excuses is proof of how safe I feel," he concluded, summoning a weak smile.

That helped, but Jenny couldn't rule out the thought that their evening plans were weighing on David's mind. There were two events on the schedule, the second one being dinner with Julien and Dominique Charbonnet.

The first social call was a party for one of David's former students. They went with the DuPonts, and for Jenny, Michel and Josette were the only familiar faces among the mixture of young people and teachers. David and Michel soon went outside to smoke. Josette spotted a friend and settled into a two-person corner, deep in conversation. Jenny found herself stranded.

Where is he? When she realized David was nowhere in sight, panic struck. Jenny went to a window and pretended to admire the view, trying desperately to get her breathing under control. No good. Then, suddenly, three pre-teen boys barged into the room, clustered around the computer screen, and started up a noisy video game. Jenny tucked herself in beside them and arranged her face to look as if their playing fascinated her. David reappeared a few minutes later. By then she had regained control, and she downplayed her reaction. David was understanding about her panic attacks, but since he had his own issues to deal with, Jenny didn't want to burden him every time they hit.

"You doin' okay, Ducks?"

"I'm fine. Ready to leave, but fine."

David, Jenny and the DuPonts went directly from the first party to the Charbonnets' apartment. Jenny fixed a smile on her face, but it was patently false. *I am not looking forward to this*, she thought as she greeted their hosts. She was sufficiently preoccupied by David's suspicions about Julien and Sandie that she didn't even attempt to follow the French conversation. She tried to see Julien through Sandie's eyes. He was pleasant-looking, of average height, with a full head of graying hair and a closely trimmed beard, but there was nothing arresting about his appearance.

Julien certainly wouldn't stand out in a crowd, but I have to admit that love alters one's vision. When Jenny looked at David, she still saw, beneath the layers of age, the handsome college student with tousled hair, soft dark eyes and mischievous grin. The hair had thinned, surrendering to a bald spot at the back of his head. Baggy folds and deep crows' feet now outlined those eyes. The grin, however, was still there, and whenever David flashed it, it was like the sun coming out after a rainstorm.

They didn't leave the dinner party until nearly midnight. There was no discussion on the way home because they were sharing a ride with the DuPonts, but the minute they walked in their front door, David asked for Jenny's assessment. "So, tell me about Julien Charbonnet," he said as they headed for the kitchen. He flicked on the fan and immediately lit a cigarette.

"Well," she began, "when we arrived, I told Julien that I remembered meeting him at a barbecue you and Sandie gave the first time I visited Geneva. 'Ah, yes,' he reminisced. 'That was when I was young and handsome.' And this was in English, so I'm quoting verbatim. It was said in an almost sly tone. I found it frankly suggestive.

"Before dinner, when he served hors d'oeuvres to Josette, he played with her hand. Later, when he walked around the table with the wine, he touched her shoulder as he poured. He did the same thing with his wife. He is extremely physical – very touchy-feely. I would definitely say a womanizer. At the end of the evening, he managed an unnecessary and overly familiar stroke down my back as he helped me with my coat. It was a very seductive gesture. Personally, I found it offensive, especially given the circumstances, but he probably sends out signals without much thought, just to see what will happen. He may have a sixth sense in spotting women who yearn for attention and recognition. It also seems to me, given his habit of coy asides and confidences, that he loves the game. I'm guessing that pursuit provides major entertainment value."

David brought out two brandy snifters, pouring a dollop for Jenny and a double dose for himself. "Go on," he nodded.

"Certainly Julien would go after someone as attractive and friendly as Sandie. But would she respond to him? She and I both fell in love with you, so in theory we have similar taste, but I felt no attraction to Julien at all. I asked myself what there might be to draw her. I came up with two possible factors."

David listened in silence. He leaned back casually against the counter, but he was fully alert.

"The first is obvious. I remember Sandie as being very physical. She was always touching people, taking Dellie's hand, hugging Marc, or walking arm in arm with friends. She also worked to heighten her attractiveness with nice clothes, cosmetics, perfume, etc. I infer that she enjoyed physical affection."

"Yes," David confirmed.

"Whereas you rarely caress or snuggle. Casual physical contact is not your strong suit. You're not even ticklish! You don't seek to be touched, and often you neither notice it nor respond to it, unless it's directly connected with sex. I've known you for a long time, David Perry. I know you are an incredibly deep-feeling and thoughtful man, but you come up way short as far as cuddles go. You have some serious lacunae in the romance department. You're sort of an absent-minded professor when it comes to Valentine sentiments."

"Ducks, love isn't about romantic verbiage," he opined. "It's about sharing a glass of wine on a Sunday afternoon."

"Women like Sandie and me may accept – or at least respect – your view intellectually, but we still want gestures of affection. Julien came to l'Académie Internationale when? The mid '80's? You and Sandie had been married around ten years at that point. She may have felt hungry for that kind of attention. They worked closely together, yes? He would have had lots of time to win her confidence."

"And the second factor?" David asked.

"The second factor I can only speculate about. If there was an environmental pressure, like turning forty, stress at home or at work, you being distracted by some project, or perhaps even the threat of another women, it could have pushed her to seek affirmation that she was attractive, interesting and valued. I guess I should ask the obvious. Were you, in fact, having an affair with someone at that point? Or had there been an earlier affair Sandie might have found out about?"

David shook his head. "There were a couple of flings, but I never had an affair," he said firmly.

"What do you mean by a couple of flings?"

"Nothing serious."

"As in, flirtations?"

"As in one-night stands."

Jenny looked at David askance. "One-night stands sound pretty serious to me," she declared. "You were a promiscuous rogue in our student days, but you were always honest about it, it was the sixties, and everyone involved was single. The rules change when you're married, even if your libido doesn't."

"One-night stands are just sex. An affair involves emotional as well as physical attraction, and a degree of commitment."

"David Perry, I can't believe you are sitting there telling me that despite being married, it was okay for you to bed women with whom you felt no emotional connection."

"Look," he said, "it was a long time ago. When Sandie and I lived in Paris, I did a lot of seminars for the English-language training program I worked with. We'd go off to some country resort and do weekend workshops for a group of maybe thirty adults from companies all over the country. When the Saturday evening sessions ended, we'd all go down to the bar and party. Married or not, everyone was at the seminar on his or her own. Hopping into bed with someone was part of the entertainment. Nobody expected to encounter anyone else again in the outside world. There wasn't an ounce of emotional investment. It didn't mean anything."

"Right," she said grimly.

"Truly, it didn't. Jenny, this happened in France, not in Boston. We're not Puritans over here."

"I understand that the French aren't Puritans. Neither were you and I, back in the sixties. But this is less about sex than it is about trust, and promises, and honesty. If two people agree to an open marriage, that's different, but to me, when you make a promise to someone that you will 'cleave to them only, forsaking all others,' it's not something you treat lightly. If you haven't agreed in advance to a non-exclusive relationship, the impact of infidelity can be pretty devastating. It can seriously undermine your confidence in your spouse, yourself, and your marriage."

Jenny's mind suddenly tripped over old and unpleasant memories. "I think that's what finally killed my first marriage – what really forced a break with Seth. If he'd been truly contrite and wanted to mend his ways, I might have forgiven all those trysts. But he dodged and covered and lied to the point where I couldn't believe a word he said about anything."

"I never lied to Sandie," David asserted.

"But you think maybe *she* lied to you," Jenny replied.

David narrowed his eyes, but said nothing.

"So, when was the last time you participated in a 'fling?'" Jenny asked, closing a mental door on her first husband.

"They pretty much ended after Marc was born. Fatherhood changes your priorities. And your outlook. At least, it did mine. Plus, we left Paris then. No more weekend seminars," he added with a grin.

"David, this isn't funny."

"I didn't say it was funny," he countered. "Though I'll admit it was fun," he added.

"Oh, god, you are incorrigible!"

"Jenny, it just wasn't a big deal. Sandie was aware of my attitude about fidelity from the start. She and I were together for three years before we got married, and during that time, I saw other women. She was aware of that fact, and it can hardly be a surprise to you." David paused and gave Jenny a meaningful look. Jenny had been one of those "other women" when David arranged a side trip to Boston while visiting family in the States.

"But as you said, that was before you got married. Wedding vows change things. Did Sandie know about the weekend shenanigans at the seminars?"

"I don't think she knew the specifics, but I can't imagine it would have shocked her. I seriously doubt she expected me to settle down cold turkey. 'What's important is that she knew I took my commitment to her seriously."

"But you did 'settle down' eventually? By the time you and Sandie moved to Geneva, you were behaving yourself?"

"At that point, all my energy went into learning how to teach middle-school kids. I won't say I never looked at another woman after we moved here, but I kept my thoughts, and my hands, to myself."

"Maybe Sandie could read your thoughts," Jenny pointed out. "Women have special radar for that kind of thing."

"And Julien's radar?"

"Well, whatever the reason or the timing, if Sandie was depressed or unhappy, Julien would surely have picked up on it, and been in a position to offer sympathy. It's possible one thing led to another. The trouble is, I think I would have sensed it if Sandie had given up on you. This is a primal thing. I used to watch the two of you with envy. What I saw was love."

"I don't feel that our mutual love or our marriage was diminished by this," David stated firmly. "I think Sandie would have assumed I would understand, or at least forgive, her trying to fulfill a need I didn't address. I'm not particularly physical and, unlike Julien, I'm definitely not touchy-feely."

Jenny considered this. "You think this happened while Julien was at l'Académie Internationale? Presumably it ended when he left? I can't imagine Sandie risking exposure or any incident that would harm her family."

"I think it started while Julien was at the school, but my guess is that it lasted until the year Sandie died. It doesn't really matter, but still, I wish I knew for sure."

Me too, Jenny thought. *If Sandie had a prolonged affair, it casts a very different light on my perception of her life with David.*

To Jenny, David and Sandie had always seemed like the perfect couple – the perfect fit. They had their disagreements, but the few Jenny had witnessed were ended by David's teasing charm. He tended to treat arguments as a game, not a personal affront, and Sandie always seemed very confident about the solidity of their relationship.

During Jenny's first visit to Geneva, over a decade before, Jenny and David had lunch at a celebrated restaurant in memory of their friend Ramon, who had died of AIDS the previous year. Sandie had to work that day and couldn't go with them. When they arrived, David introduced Jenny to the master chef, André, who was an old friend.

Oddly, Jenny experienced a moment of discomfort during the introduction. *Might Sandie's absence suggest that David and I are up to something?* When they returned home that night, Jenny raised the subject directly with Sandie. "I love being with David," Jenny told her, "but I do sometimes worry that my obvious affection for him might give people the wrong idea about our relationship. We had a really great time at lunch. I hope I didn't inspire a round of salacious gossip!"

Sandie had dismissed Jenny's concern. "Do not worry," she said. "At Chez André, people pay attention only to the food, not to the others who are dining."

David had found the exchange amusing. "Fear not, Ms. Boston Proper. It's not that I mind having a wee tumble with a lovely lady, but I made sure there were no vibrations about you and me and the haystack at the restaurant. That's why I mentioned to André that Sandie had to work today, but promised she would come at the very next opportunity. Sandie's ideas about fidelity differ singularly from my own: she's for it, and I don't give a shit, as long as everybody involved knows, including Sandie."

Sandie was within hearing range, but made no comment. "Clandestine affairs aren't worth the trouble," David continued. "When I go back to Chez André, or anyplace else, I want to spend all my energy on food, drink and company and not waste one quantum worrying about who knows what, or thinks what, about who I'm with and why."

At the time David spoke those words, the affair with Julien – if indeed it had happened – would presumably have been launched.

Yet David believed Sandie was strongly "for" fidelity. Jenny couldn't reconcile the two. *Of course,* she reminded herself, *the affair may never have taken place.*

Jenny was about to add something further as she climbed into bed, but David began to snore the minute his head hit the pillow. *Back burner for now,* she decided, *but this subject is far from closed.*

The following evening, David called Marc after dinner to check in. Valerie answered. "Marc is not here," she reported. "He went this morning to see a photographic exhibit in Lausanne. I expected him back hours ago." There had been heavy rain all day, and Valerie was worried. David immediately became worried as well.

"Marc may simply have gotten involved in something and not thought to call home," Jenny suggested. "He isn't exactly known for his punctuality or his communication skills," she added, trying to diffuse David's mounting agitation.

David wasn't open to reassurance. At 9:00 p.m., there was still no word from Marc. "You go ahead and go to bed," he told Jenny. "I'll stay down here and stretch out on the couch. That way, if Marc or Valerie rings, I can take the call without waking you."

The wall phone will ring in our bedroom regardless, Jenny thought, but she bit back the words. David was tense, and clearly in no mood for debate. At ten o'clock, he called Valerie again, to find that Marc had just walked in. It was as Jenny suspected. Marc ran into someone he knew at the exhibit. It hadn't occurred to him to call and tell Valerie he had changed his plans. Jenny could hear anger in David's voice, but it gradually downshifted to relief.

Is this normal? Jenny wondered. *I know parents are programmed to worry about their children, but Marc is often late and rarely forthcoming about his plans and activities. Is David reacting like an ordinary father, or is Marc a release valve for other concerns? Maybe David's still processing our evening with Julien. I wish there were some way to settle this question of an affair, but I don't see how.*

Jenny was in the back yard picking the last of the season's daffodils when a vaguely familiar face peered around the corner of the house.

Jenny's mind raced to put the face in context and find a name. *Think, Jenny, think! She was at Sandie's funeral. She's a former colleague of David's. Her name is … um ….*

"Hello, Jenny. Do you remember me? Adelaide Swanton," the woman said, holding out her hand. "I am so sorry to have missed the wedding," she apologized. "I've been in Argentina, visiting my sisters ever since Christmas, and I've only just returned."

Adelaide had grown up in a trilingual household in Buenos Aires. Her father was British, her mother German, and she spoke an English so perfect it was hard to believe it wasn't her maternal tongue. Every consonant was clear and precise, and every vowel had beautiful depth and tone. She was a handsome woman, with perfect posture, and, like Jenny, Adelaide made no attempt to hide the gray in her hair, which she wore cropped short in a halo of natural curls.

"Your husband said you would be home this morning, and I wanted to drop this off." Adelaide handed Jenny a small package. "It's a belated wedding gift," she explained. Jenny unwrapped it to reveal a polished wooden box. Inside the box were two napkin rings featuring exotic-looking wood and carved with the initials "D" and "J." Jenny was deeply touched. The house was full of things with Sandie's monogram. Prior to Adelaide's gift, the only item linking David's name with Jenny's was the set of initials engraved inside Jenny's wedding band.

"These are beautiful, Adelaide! And it makes me feel more at home to have my very own napkin ring!"

"I'm glad you like them," she smiled. "The Wichi Indians in Northern Argentina do wonderful things with local woods, and I've always admired their handiwork."

"Please do stay for a cup of tea," Jenny urged. "I'd love to hear about your time in Argentina."

Adelaide agreed to the tea but posed her own question before Jenny could ask about her travels. "Tell me," she said, "when did you and David decide to get married?"

Something about Adelaide inspired instant trust. Jenny's answer popped out with a candor that surprised her. "In some ways, I decided thirty-some-odd years back," she laughed. "David apparently decided soon after Sandie died, but we didn't raise the subject with each other until last April. Sometimes I think it's all serendipity; other times I think my whole life was preparation for this marriage."

Adelaide was intrigued. "I remember, from what David once said, that you've known each other a long time. When and how did you meet?" she asked.

Jenny described their student days in Harvard Square, their communal life at the off-campus apartment on Ware Street, and their youthful affair. "I followed David to Europe after our graduation. For a year we commuted back and forth between my bed-sit in London and David's closet-sized apartment Paris, but in the end, I missed Boston, and I wanted to go home. David was totally enchanted by life in Europe and wanted to stay. Finally, we went our separate ways. We were looking for very different lives at that point," she concluded.

"But you kept in touch?"

"Oh, yes. It wasn't an angry parting. The love was still there, but what he wanted and what I wanted just didn't fit. Initially, the friendship was kept alive primarily through letters. Then, in 1989, I lost a very dear classmate, Ramon Delgado. He was a good friend of David's as well and was actually responsible for our meeting one another."

"Was there an accident?" Adelaide asked.

"He died of AIDS," Jenny answered. "He didn't tell any of his old friends that he was ill. I didn't find out until after he died. Ironically, I had been trying to track him down. I had recently divorced. My life was at a crossroads, and I had some major issues to sort through. Ramon and I had a very special relationship, and he was the one I most wanted to talk to.

"I was very upset by his death. David's invitation to come to Geneva to celebrate his forty-fifth birthday coincided perfectly with my need to touch base with friends from our student days. Plus I was still looking for someone to talk to about where my life was or wasn't going. I knew David would be a good sounding board."

"Had you been here before?"

"No. I met Sandie for the first time when they came to Boston, way back when she was pregnant with Dellie. After that, I saw David and Sandie every few years during their periodic travels to the States, but I had never spent time with them in Geneva. When I finally made the trip and saw Sandie in her home environment, I got to know her a lot better, and having ten whole days with David was healing and wonderful. Actually, it was too wonderful. Maybe Ramon's death unearthed a lot of feelings long buried. Whatever the reason, I had to confront the reality that the old passion was still there."

Adelaide's eyes widened. She lifted the teacup to her lips and raised her brows, but made no comment. Jenny hadn't planned to be so candid, but it felt safe, and it was a relief to let some of it out.

"It's okay," Jenny laughed. "Nothing happened. David was obviously content with his life, so I marshaled all my self-discipline and conducted myself as the old friend I was supposed to be. One of the things that made this easier was that I liked Sandie, and respected her. I know that Sandie was uneasy about me at first, but she chose to trust me with David. During that visit, Sandie went off with a friend who was on a buying trip for her decorating business. She left David and me unchaperoned for three days. I appreciated her trust, and I wanted to be worthy of it."

"And was David aware of your feelings at the time?"

"No. Sandie could read beneath the surface, but David was oblivious, as I wanted him to be. Would you like some more tea?"

Jenny looked at the kitchen clock. They – she – had been talking for over an hour.

"That would be lovely," Adelaide nodded. Jenny brewed fresh cups for both of them, then continued with the saga.

"During that first visit to Geneva, I also got to know David's children. Marc was about eight, I think, and Dellie was five or six. In the years that followed, we started sharing holidays, both stateside and in Europe. And apart from the enjoyable linkages, Sandie and I also shared a common bond as cancer patients."

Adelaide seemed taken aback. "I wasn't aware that you had breast cancer."

"No, not breast cancer. Mine was thyroid." Reading dismay in Adelaide's face, Jenny moved quickly to reassure her that David had not signed up for another deathwatch. "My endocrinologist was initially pessimistic, but two years of radioactive iodine treatment did the trick. It damaged my saliva glands, but it worked, and here I am. All my recent scans have come out clean.

"Sandie and I had similar reactions to being a survivor. You recognize how great a gift each day is. We sometimes talked about our cancer experiences, but most of our communications centered on our daily lives and the usual things women share. Sandie knew I loved David. She also knew I respected her position. I was grateful to her for giving him a happy life, and had long since made my peace with the way things were. I like to think that's why she felt comfortable handing him over to me."

"Handing him over to you?"

"You know Olga Gerasimova, don't you?" Jenny asked.

"Of course," Adelaide answered. "Olga is the Director of Human Resources at l'Académie Internationale. We've all worked together for years. She and Sandie were quite close."

"Well, Olga told me a story about one of her last visits with Sandie at the hospital. According to Olga, Sandie knew she was dying. She speculated that once she was gone, David would not do well on his own. 'But,' Sandie reassured Olga, 'I don't worry for him, because I know that Jenny will come, and she will take care of him.'"

Despite the many times Jenny had repeated this tale, she had to get up for a box of tissues at the end. "Olga's story made the transition a lot easier for me. I think of Sandie and me as a tag-team. David echoes this notion, accusing me of conspiring with Sandie to keep his clothes in good repair, his cigarette butts out of the lawn, his voice down to a dull roar, and his behavior within the limits of everyone's tolerance."

Adelaide smiled. It was widely known that David could sometimes be obstreperous.

"He's lucky to have you. We're all very fond of him, but I suspect he might be challenging to live with at times," she commented diplomatically.

"I don't disagree," Jenny laughed, "but remember, I've known this man since our college days. The reason he's challenging is because he's so complex. David is three or four people rolled into one. He's traditional in his manners but unconventional in his behavior. Has he ever told you much about his background?"

"No, not really," Adelaide replied. "I knew Sandie far better than David. I've never heard him talk about himself."

"That's par for the course. He's very modest. If you ask him where he went to college, he'll answer 'in Boston.' You have to push to get him to admit he went to Harvard. He's very bright, but he doesn't use his intellect to intimidate people."

"That is certainly true," Adelaide agreed. "I've worked with him on some of the school theatre productions. He's very respectful of his colleagues, and he is superb at transmitting knowledge while still giving the students room to discover their own talents and passions. He's rather more self-effacing than many of his compatriots."

Jenny smiled at Adelaide's polite way of suggesting that the Americans on the faculty were often outspoken about their views and opinions.

"I think some of that modesty comes from his mother, who raised him as an 'old school' Southern Gentleman. He grew up with 'Yes, Ma'am,' and 'No, Sir,' and was taught to remaining standing until all the ladies were seated. I was raised with stern Victorian manners, but David honors customs that exceed even my mother's strict rules. Despite that decorous training, his Southern Gentleman persona can shape-shift in seconds into a down-home country boy, straight out of the hills of Tennessee, with an 'Aw, shucks' aura, and earthy language that would have made his mother faint. The gregarious side comes from his father. I met Mr. Perry at our college graduation. He ran a small lumber and building supply business in Chattanooga and worked with people from all walks of life. He was a natural salesman, energetic in his communication, full of stories and jokes – a real pump-your-hand, look-you-in-the-eye kind of person. David definitely inherited his gregarious nature from his dad. That's where he got the grin too."

"And you are from Boston, yes? It has a more European flavor than the American south, does it not?"

"An English flavor, I think, more than continental European. It's certainly different from David's part of the US. David lived with the south's racial prejudices as a boy. Fortunately, that aspect of his upbringing didn't survive. He rejected it as a teen, and protested against it as a college student. He has a strong commitment to social justice, and that's the one arena where's he most likely to stir things up.

"Take all these elements, polish them with three decades of living in Europe, sprinkle with a love of teaching and a passion for cooking, and that's David. Suddenly all the pieces fit. Or at least they do for me," Jenny concluded.

"I can see that," Adelaide commented with a smile. "Your love for him shines through."

"I only hope my joy is not a source of pain and conflict for you and Sandie's other close friends."

Adelaide reached a hand forward in a gesture of reassurance. "Don't worry," she said. "We are all very pleased that David has someone like you to be with. Sandie would be pleased as well."

Another hour had passed. *This kind soul has given up her entire morning to listen to me babble on about David!* Jenny was conscious of how hungry she was for English conversation and a *tête-à-tête* with a sympathetic female. It was frustrating, however, that there was one subject she couldn't broach: the possible affair between Sandie and Julien. *I see no way to explore the issue with Sandie's friends. To even raise the possibility is to impugn Sandie's reputation.*

But the question bothered her like the sound of a buzzing fly, trapped between a window and a screen, bumping about trying to find a way out.

Breakfast Guest

The blue balloon blew in for breakfast,
Tumbling unexpectedly out of the
Sunlit green and dappled shadows
Pushed and twirled by gentle gusts
In the early Shawmut morning.
It rolled unhurriedly over laurel branches,
Bounced softly on Jenny's flower beds
And settled slowly on the lawn.

A closer look suggested it had spent
The night free, abandoned to wander
As the night breeze pleased,
Floating its way among the pine-needles
And thorny branches lying in ambush,
Heedless that they might prick it –
That its aimless unsuspecting path
Might lead it to a tragic end.

D.P. – July, 1996

Chapter 3

For l'Académie Internationale's spring break, David planned a drive to Florence with Michel and Josette, with a stopover en route to visit friends who lived near Pisa.

"There's a box of maps in Sandie's office," he told Jenny over breakfast. "When you have a minute, could you look through it and pull out whatever we have on Italy? I want to figure out our route."

After David left for school, Jenny got the map box off the shelf and started through the contents. There were Metro maps for Paris and Berlin, road maps for most of Europe, and some magazine clippings touting travel suggestions. And then she spotted it – something totally incongruous: a newspaper article announcing the appointment of Julien Charbonnet as the new President of the Salève Business School. There was a photograph of him at the top center of the story.

The discovery gave Jenny goose bumps. *This is the second time I've found a clipping featuring Julien.* There had been a story about him attached to some Académie Internationale documents in one of Sandie's desk drawers. Jenny had thought nothing of it at the time, but that was before David shared his suspicions. David had speculated that "in all probability" they would "never know the truth." The article in the map box convinced Jenny otherwise.

Jenny had recently unearthed a receipt for the bail Sandie paid when Marc was arrested, at age sixteen, for selling marijuana. When Jenny showed it to David, he was astonished. "Sandie never told me about this," he protested. "Never said a word about Marc's arrest. She must have concealed it to shield Marc from my likely reaction, which I can tell you, wouldn't have been a happy one."

But why, then, would she keep the receipt? Jenny had puzzled.

Now, remembering the bail receipt and looking at the clipping in her hand, it dawned on Jenny that Sandie saved everything, even things she didn't want anyone else to see. *If Sandie had an affair with Julien – an affair stretching over years as David suspects – there must have been discreet tokens. Whatever they were,* Jenny concluded, *Sandie would have kept them, probably "hiding" them in a way that made their presence seem entirely plausible. David's eyes might miss them, but I'm pretty sure mine won't.* An out-of-place newspaper article didn't qualify as a smoking gun, but it put Jenny on full alert. *Time will tell,* she thought.

The day before Jenny and David's departure for Italy, Marc and Valerie came by for lunch. Marc and David had afternoon appointments and left together shortly afterwards, but Valerie stayed to do laundry. Once she had shifted a load into the dryer, she and Jenny went outside to bask in the spring sunshine.

They sat and talked. Or rather, Valerie talked and Jenny listened. "I am becoming to feel myself *découragé* about Marc," Valerie said, spilling out her frustrations. "He hates to come here. He only comes so we can wash our clothes and get free food. He hates to be with the DuPonts and the other friends of his father because they always will ask him questions about his future. He lies and makes up plans so they will get off his back. All he wants to do is to make graffiti and take the drugs with his friends."

"Valerie, when you say drugs, do you know exactly what he's using?"

"There is lots of hashish, but also he is, how do you say, popping pills?"

"Do you know what kind of pills?"

"No, but they are surely not the vitamins. Marc says there is no problem to use the drugs because his father has used them. He does not need a college diploma, he declares, because his father says it is *sans sens* – without meaning."

"If Marc says that, he doesn't understand his father," Jenny corrected. "David certainly smoked his share of marijuana when we were students in the sixties, but he was never a serious user. This I know for certain, because we used to live together. And I can well imagine David saying that a diploma is meaningless, in the same way that he considers a marriage certificate meaningless. But Marc misinterprets his father's words. David's point is that it's the learning *behind* the diploma that matters, as it's the commitment *behind* the marriage certificate that counts, not the piece of paper."

That evening, Jenny approached David about her afternoon with Valerie. "I had a troubling conversation with Valerie about Marc," she began. "She painted a disturbing picture. I think you need to hear what she said, but you'll have to be judicious in how you handle it. I don't want to create problems for Valerie. If you cite her chapter and verse, Marc will know were you got the information, and it could destroy the relationship."

"I'll do my best," David said candidly, "but if I lose control, I lose control. The shit's just gonna have to hit the fan."

"I'm caught between a rock and a hard place," Jenny admitted. "I feel an obligation to support you in your decisions about Marc. I feel an obligation to confront Marc because it seems he's heading down a bad path. I feel an obligation to protect Valerie's privacy and give her room to work this relationship out. Given that I have zero experience as a parent, I don't know which way to jump."

"Mixed metaphor," he said. "You can't jump any way at all if you're caught between a rock and a hard place."

"David, don't joke about it. This is serious."

"Of course it's serious. I don't know which way to jump either. Being a parent doesn't give you any magical insight. Sandie herself was at a loss when Marc got into one of his angry moods and was rude to her. But you can't control what happens in life. You just have to do the best you can. Still, for me, it would help if you and I jump in the same direction."

Jenny absorbed with interest the information that Marc had been difficult with Sandie. *I remember there were times when Sandie was worried about Marc. She once told me how angry he could be and how critical, but I assumed it was a classic father-son conflict. I didn't know Marc pointed some of that behavior in Sandie's direction too.*

David watched Jenny in silence for a minute as she struggled to sort out her concerns. Then he refilled their wine glasses and leaned back in his chair. "So what did Valerie say?" he asked.

Jenny sidetracked. "I *do* want to jump in the same direction as you do. I don't want a house divided. But if I disagree with you about the children, I need to speak my mind. I will only do so in private, like now, never in front of them. But I owe it to Sandie and the kids to tell you exactly how I feel."

"Fine," he said evenly. "So what did Valerie say?"

Jenny summarized Valerie's complaints. "Even if only half of Valerie's assessment was accurate, Marc is living a depressing and self-destructive existence," she concluded. "The drug issue is worrisome enough on its own, but I was equally disturbed by her comments about Marc's hating to come to the house and his lying about his plans. I know it's been painful for him to lose his mother, but as Valerie once said, if he wants to honor Sandie's memory, he should pull himself together and finish his education. It may sound harsh, but from what I see, he spends a lot of time feeling sorry for himself and being angry at the world."

David shook his head sadly. "I can't live Marc's life for him. He's got to find his own path in his own way."

Despite David's words, it was obviously hard for him to watch Marc flounder. It was the eve of their planned holiday in Florence. They should have been eager with anticipation, but Marc weighed heavily on their minds. "I'll talk with him when we get back," David promised wearily as he turned out the bedside lamp.

"You're a good father," Jenny said, wrapping her arms around him.

The next morning, they collected the DuPonts and left for Italy as scheduled, passing through the Mont Blanc tunnel, skirting Genoa, and stopping for lunch in Portofino. As they ate their *bruschetta* beside the picturesque Mediterranean harbor, the tensions of Geneva – the worries about Marc, the questions about Julien – slowly evaporated in the warm Italian sunshine.

Their initial destination was a small hilltop village in Tuscany, where Carlo and Eleanor Genazzini had restored an old farmhouse and were busy nursing a grove of young olive trees. Eleanor, a native of Georgia with a ready smile and a warm open manner, had met and married Carlo when he was working in Atlanta for an international technology firm. They were an exceptionally handsome couple, Eleanor with her wide-set blue eyes and wholesome American farm-girl looks, and Carlo with his chiseled Italian profile and ramrod bearing, reminiscent of a Renaissance nobleman.

The farmhouse was near the top of a hill, surrounded by two hundred and seventy degrees of olive groves and sloping pastures with grazing sheep and goats. Far afield, you could see the azure blue of the Mediterranean and the island of Elba.

"Wow!" Jenny exclaimed. It was her first trip to Tuscany. "This is gorgeous!"

"Yup," said David, smiling at her enthusiasm.

Carlo spoke excellent French, making the visit easier for the DuPonts, who had no Italian and for whom prolonged English was a strain. They sat on the terrace, sipping wine and enjoying the spectacular view. After a few minutes, Eleanor excused herself and disappeared. Jenny recognized the sounds of dinner preparation. Since the others were chatting in French, she left the group and headed for the kitchen.

"Can you use an extra pair of hands?" she volunteered.

"How are you at grating cheese?" Eleanor asked, holding up a block of aged Parmesan.

While they worked, Jenny answered Eleanor's questions about how David was doing and how she was adjusting to her new life.

"I don't think I could have taken on a marriage like that, where the grief is still so raw," Eleanor commented as they carried plates to the table.

"You make me sound almost saintly," Jenny laughed. "I assure you I'm not! Certain aspects of my marriage may have elements of a rescue mission, but it doesn't bother me. The way I saw it, the man I loved was in danger of drowning. I wasn't about to wait for the waters to calm before diving in and trying to keep him afloat. And it's not just a one-way street. There are moments of pure joy. David opens doors for me figuratively as well as literally. I'm a retiring introvert. He's an indefatigable extrovert. If it weren't for David, I would never have sat on your terrace, enjoying your beautiful view. And I wouldn't be standing here in this lovely setting, talking with a new friend, and smelling whatever that delicious smell is that's coming out of your oven!"

In short order, Eleanor presented her guests with a feast of artichoke frittatas and local specialties. It was a nice change from the French cuisine that was their normal fare in Geneva. During the meal, Eleanor and Carlo told stories of past visits they had exchanged with David and Sandie – visits filled with fun and adventure. As Jenny listened, she found it difficult to reconcile suspicions about Sandie and Julian with the Genazzinis' tales of the Perry family's cheerful home and pleasant social life.

In the morning, Carlo drove them across a dirt track to the neighboring farm to buy olive oil. As they stepped out of the car, a homely little mongrel greeted them with a modest wag of his tail, then wandered off, nose to the ground. Though it was barely ten o'clock, the farmer immediately offered strong coffee laced with stronger grappa. When they finally got around to sampling oil, Michel and David were in an exceptionally cheerful mood. By the time they departed, they had jointly purchased ten kilos of extra-fine virgin oil.

The two couples left the Genazzinis after lunch, making their way to Florence with frequent detours through picturesque towns and villages. The next day began with a visit to the Uffizi Gallery. *Uh oh*, Jenny thought as they walked through the increasingly crowded rooms. David loved the Uffizi, but Jenny felt claustrophobic and edgy. "Dearheart, I'm going to find a quiet corner somewhere," she whispered.

"You okay?" David asked. "If you're getting panicky, we can leave."

"No, I'll be fine. I just need to get out of the crush. Meet you at the main entrance at noon?"

David nodded agreement, and Jenny retreated to a relatively empty corridor where she waited for the others to finish their tour.

Afterwards, they went to the central market, housed in a great covered hall. Jenny derived far more enjoyment from looking at real fruit than she did from looking at paintings of it, no matter how celebrated the artist. She kept this heresy to herself, but she had no hesitation showing her enthusiasm. "What a wonderful market!" she exclaimed. "The stalls are so incredibly colorful! And what are those?" she asked, pointing to a grouping of pear-shaped vegetables with purple and white stripes.

"I think they're some kind of eggplant," David guessed. "We can try them for dinner," he said, pulling out his wallet.

They had lunch in a street café, then wandered around, visiting an ancient pharmacy, viewing Michelangelo's David and treating themselves to gellato. But while the idea of strolling around Florence had seemed inviting, the cobbled streets and uneven sidewalks created problems for Jenny's sometimes troublesome hip. Any misstep caused a jolt. By the time they crossed the Pontevecchio, Jenny scarcely dared to divert her eyes from the bumpy roadway to peruse the boutiques that lined the ancient bridge.

Two days later, when they traveled to Siena, she ran into a similar problem. With its medieval warren of twisted alleyways and winding steps, Siena was a nightmare of steep stony streets. "You gonna make it, Ducks?" David asked with concern as Jenny repeatedly scanned the street surface for obstacles. "We can always stop for coffee and sit for a while."

"No thanks, Love. No stopping. I just need to operate at tortoise speed."

"*En français*," he said firmly.

"What? Oh," she said, as the light dawned. "*A un pas de tortue.*"

"Good," he nodded. "Tortoise speed works for me too. Gives me time to heat the atmosphere," he grinned as he fished a lighter and a pack of Gauloises out of his pocket.

They toured the massive Siena cathedral, which afforded the brief respite of level ground. Walking into the ornate high-ceilinged library, David directed Jenny's attention to the paintings that covered the walls. "The concept of perspective wasn't discovered until the fifteenth century," he explained. "Before that, paintings weren't to scale. Artists didn't know how to capture depth and distance accurately. These frescoes by Pinturicchio were done just as perspective was coming into its own. Artists were falling all over each other to show off this new skill."

"It's fun traveling with a history teacher," Jenny said, smiling. Her more heretical thought she kept to herself: *This cathedral is a longtime favorite of David's because of these paintings. It's an instant favorite of mine because of this nice even floor!*

After lunch on the Piazza del Campo, David took Jenny's arm as they threaded their way back to the car through the labyrinth of cobbled streets. "This is probably why the Italian immigrants were so comfortable with the North End in Boston," he commented, pointing to the narrow alleyways between the buildings. Jenny had always viewed Boston's "Little Italy" as congested and sadly barren of trees. It had never before occurred to her that the very aspect that disturbed her might provide a warm sense of the familiar to immigrants from these ancient Italian cities. David's shared insight and his knack for knitting together past and present offset her frustration with the terrain.

At the end of the week, they began their homeward trek, heading north through the Tuscan countryside. "Ready for a little greenery, Kid?" David teased.

Jenny had to shake her head at the irony of it. *Most people would be thrilled with a personalized tour of the great cities, great museums and great cathedrals of Europe. But these mean nothing to me compared with a drive down a country lane where I can catch a glimpse of the local flora and fauna. I much prefer a humble cart track to a fabled urban boulevard. I am emphatically not a city girl!* Jenny had warned David about this, but she wasn't sure he understood how extreme a case she was.

Not long into the drive, David detoured through a small town in search of a vacation rental where he and Sandie had long ago spent two weeks with children and friends. After one or two wrong turns, he found it – an old hunting lodge, beautifully landscaped. It was clear there were strong memories attached. David was withdrawn for the next hour. *Who were the friends?* Jenny wondered. *Did they ever vacation with Julien and Dominique Charbonnet?* She didn't feel comfortable asking, but she couldn't help but speculate. *If their stay was a happy one, perhaps he's seeking to recapture some piece of it. But maybe his agenda is darker. Maybe he's wondering whether he was just too blind to notice that there was an affair was going on right in front of him.*

Once back in Geneva, they had the weekend to recover from their journey. David called Marc on Saturday and invited him for Sunday luncheon, along with Valerie. "I asked him to allow some extra time afterwards so we can talk about where his life stands at the moment and where it's going," he told Jenny.

"I'm glad you're doing this, David. I know you think everything will settle out in time, but I really sense that Marc needs some hands-on guidance and support."

David spent Sunday morning preparing a minor feast, but the appointed hour came and went with no sign of Marc and Valerie. "Marc's not answering his phone," he reported, after calling twice without success.

Remembering David's recent worry over Marc's tardy return from his rainy trip to Lausanne, Jenny thought David might become overly anxious. Instead, he shrugged off Marc's lapse. *Given Valerie's comments about Marc being increasingly erratic regarding his responsibilities, maybe David's not surprised by Marc's "oversight,"* Jenny realized.

David finally got hold of Marc in the early evening. "They're going to come for supper instead," he announced.

"What happened with lunch?" Jenny asked.

"Marc said he and Valerie were doing something with friends, and he forgot about the lunch invitation."

"He also forgot to answer his phone," Jenny observed with a touch of acidity.

"Jenny, Marc is not the most responsible of people, but neither was I at that age. Let's just focus on the positive."

Jenny refrained from further comment, but in light of Valerie's warning that Marc did his best to "keep the adults at bay," her mind kept going.

Marc's explanation doesn't compute. Did Valerie forget the lunch also? Or did Marc never bother to mention it to her? If that was the case, he may have planned to "forget" from the outset.

During dinner that evening, the conversation was relaxed. As dessert was served, however, Marc looked at his watch and mentioned that he and Valerie wanted to go to a film in downtown Geneva.

"We still have a conversation ahead of us, Marc, and I don't want to put it off," said David, shaking his head. "We're overdue for a thoughtful discussion about your future, including the college applications you've been talking about."

"Tonight's the last night the film is playing," Marc protested, "and Valerie's really up for it." The reference to Valerie was delivered in swift American slang. Jenny couldn't tell from Valerie's puzzled look whether the statement was less than accurate, or if Valerie simply didn't understand Marc's English. David insisted that they still needed to have a serious talk, but he was too chivalrous to risk making Valerie miss a film she was "really up for."

"Go see your movie," he allowed, "but come by tomorrow afternoon. I should be home from school by four." Marc reluctantly agreed. The next day, Jenny half expected another evasive tactic, but

Marc arrived, somewhat subdued, shortly after five, and the two Perry males closeted themselves in Jenny's office.

"Marc is serious about going to San Francisco," David reported once Marc left. "I think this time he may get it together."

"Did you ask him about drug use?"

"I did, but he swears he only smokes marijuana."

"What about the pills Valerie mentioned?"

"He said he's been bothered by allergies all spring, and he's been taking some kind of antihistamine tablets. It's a simple over-the-counter medication."

"Why would Valerie think it was something else?"

"Apparently she asked him about it once, and Marc made some smart-assed remark to make the pills seem mysterious and exotic."

"Not a great way to strengthen his relationship with Valerie," Jenny observed.

"No, but she's weathered it enough that she's apparently debating about whether she should try to follow him to the States after her graduation."

Jenny remembered her own decision, at a similar age, to follow David when he left the US for France. She didn't discount the problems, but it seemed like encouraging news. "I hope she does," Jenny commented. "I think Valerie is good for Marc. She's positive and focused. She clearly cares about him, but she doesn't put up with much foolishness."

"Sounds a bit like you and me," David teased.

"Except that I put up with a *lot* of foolishness," Jenny countered.

A grin played on David's face. "Hmpff," was his only response.

Just as Jenny thought things might be settling down on the stepchildren front, a panicked call came in from Paris. Delphine needed an advance payment to reserve a place in her Art History class's field trip to Spain. Jenny had given Delphine lessons on how to wire money from the education trust that covered her college expenses, but Delphine was late in requesting the transfer. She was convinced she would be bumped from the trip, and she was spinning out worst-case scenarios – missing the Spanish museums, failing the follow-up exam and even failing the class.

"Dellie, the simplest solution is to alert your professor and stop by the bursar's office at school," Jenny counseled. "Explain the situation and find out if a short delay is going to pose any serious problems. The next step depends on the answers you get."

But when Delphine talked with her father, he reacted to her distress as if she were in a grave crisis. He was ready to race off to Paris. "If the wire transfer isn't there by Wednesday," he fumed, "I'll damn well get on a train and deliver the reservation fee myself!"

Jenny's attempts to calm David met with an angry reaction. She was used to his temper, but it was so rarely directed at her personally that she was taken aback. She immediately retreated, tackled the dinner dishes, then busied herself doing laundry until bedtime. They said nothing further to each other except, "Good night."

Tuesday morning, there was still tension in the air until David broke the ice. "Look," he said, "I'm the first to admit that I don't know about handling finances. That's something Sandie always took care of. But I have to figure out a way to get money to Delphine on a timely basis. This business of transferring funds from her education trust isn't working. I want to set up a different system."

Jenny took a deep breath. "Dearheart, the issue isn't the system. The transfer was delayed only because Dellie misjudged how long it takes to shift money from the US to France. Where we run into trouble, you and I, is that I feel we should help Dellie take responsibility and build confidence in managing her budget, rather than immediately bailing her out. She's not a child. She's a bright and competent young woman. This is a minor glitch. She can handle this."

"Well, I know you think she can," David replied, "and maybe she isn't a child, but she's not really an adult yet either. And I'm not sure she has her mother's financial acumen. I think Delphine's a lot closer to me in temperament. When she's on the phone, I listen to more than her words. I listen to the tone of her voice. When she called, I could hear the distress and fear."

"I don't contest that. I'm just saying that the distress is normal, and the fear is groundless. Rather than let those feelings govern, we should help Dellie discover how to handle situations like this so that next time it happens, which it will, she'll be less distressed and less fearful. I promised I would bow to your final judgment concerning Marc and Dellie, and I will, but it's not in Dellie's best interest for you to go haring off to Paris waving a fistful of Euros. Besides," Jenny teased in an effort to reduce the tension, "there are many more efficient ways to deliver money to Paris, starting with Fedex or whatever the European equivalent is."

That brought David up short. He hadn't thought of an overnight delivery service.

"Why don't you call Dellie back," Jenny suggested, "and tell her to check with the bank before close of business today. If the funds haven't cleared, and she absolutely has to have the trip money in hand, we'll get it to her by tomorrow afternoon."

Jenny's suggestion was accepted, and she carefully avoided any hint of "I told you so" when Delphine called that evening to report that the crisis was over. The US wire had cleared Delphine's French account.

With that problem solved, Jenny started preparations for the trip to Boston and her high school reunion. After gathering the papers she would need during her visit, she withdrew three manila file folders from a stack Sandie had kept in one of the office bookshelves. Carefully sandwiched between the second and third folder, she found a commencement program for the Salève Business School, with a congratulatory letter to the graduates, and a photograph of President Julien Charbonnet standing with a group of students.

This time the red flag flew high. *Sandie was so meticulous, so organized. Nothing in her office was ever out of place. Why put a commencement program in the middle of a stack of manila folders?* Jenny's instincts said this was not innocuous. This was the kind of deceptive tactic a woman would use if she wanted a picture whose presence could be explained away with the simplest of white lies: "Oh, thanks!

I was looking for that. I saved it for Dominique, then I misplaced it and couldn't think what I had done with it!"

That's two clippings and a program. Do I tell David? Jenny considered for a long moment. *It doesn't bring him any closer to resolution, and it's a painful subject. Case continued without a finding,* she finally decided. *It's still just circumstantial evidence. But circumstantial or no, I'd really like to talk this out with someone. Yet how can I do that without violating David's privacy? Or Sandie's?*

Then suddenly it clicked: "case continued" – "circumstantial evidence." *If there's anyone I can trust with confidential information, it's Ross. Sort of like attorney-client privilege.* Jenny's trip to Boston was just days away. *I'll share this with Ross while I'm there. He'll be able to give me some objective advice.*

She took the program and stuck it back among the remaining manila folders. She had a sudden urge to go and wash her hands. *This could get really messy,* she cautioned the face in the bathroom mirror. *Pandora opened her box against Zeus's orders, but with innocent curiosity. David hasn't forbidden me to open this one, but my motivation goes beyond curiosity, and I'm not feeling particularly innocent about it.* She dried her hands, shifted her mind back to her check-off list for Boston, and returned to her office.

The weekend of Jenny's departure, David spent Saturday morning attempting to download the self-portraits his class had drawn for the yearbook. He was clearly having trouble.

"Would you like me to give it a try?" Jenny offered, but David warned her away with a curt "no."

Uh oh. Somebody's not happy, she realized.

David finally slammed his hand down on the surface of the desk and went up to the kitchen. Jenny had learned enough about David's moods to know he needed time to cool down, so she let him be. She heard him open the liquor cabinet and pour something into a glass. Given the duration of the gurgle, it sounded like a triple dose. David's drinking had moderated significantly since Jenny's move to Geneva, but moments of heavy stress could still push him to excess.

"I'm in no mood to cook," David declared grimly an hour later. "We'll go to L'Entrecôte for dinner. They don't take reservations, so we should leave now, before it gets too crowded."

Jenny went upstairs to change. She had barely shed her bluejeans when David called up to ask if she was ready to go. There was impatience in his voice. Something was bothering him, and it had nothing to do with the few minutes it took her to change clothes and grab her pocketbook. David was standing in the living room when she came down the stairs. She put her arms around him, and tried to give him a hug. "I love you even when you're in a bad mood," she said, teasing him gently.

He pulled away, muttered something in French, then went abruptly out the front door. Jenny stood rooted to the spot. She felt defeated and angry. In all the years she had known David, he had never been this negative, this unreachable. *Is there a side to him that's been hidden from my view? Were there moments like this for Sandie? Did they happen often enough that Sandie sought an outside support system – Julien?* Jenny grabbed a handful of tissues, struggled to compose her face, and forced herself to go out to the car. She turned her face to the side window, and they drove to downtown Geneva in icy silence. Her throat was so tight it was hard to swallow. They parked, walked to the restaurant and joined the end of a line that snaked through the door. Jenny searched her bag in vain for a pair of sunglasses. She knew her eyes must be red and puffy. David broke the impasse with a casual remark. He was waving a white flag and attempting normal conversation, but Jenny's voice was not yet under control. She just nodded and said, "Mmm."

David walked downwind to the street corner to smoke a cigarette. When he came back, the line had moved enough that they were through the door and into the foyer. Knowing Jenny's aversion to crowds, David made an effort to protect her as people pushed past them to get out. She pressed into him, wanting comfort desperately, and he put an arm around her. "Don't know why these assholes don't take reservations," he said. "Drives me crazy to have to wait like this." He didn't apologize in the words she wanted to hear, but he acknowledged his bad mood and said ruefully, "Don't take it personally, Ducks." It helped. She was still rocky, but it helped.

"My taking it personally isn't the issue," she countered. "I love you, David, and I want to be a good wife and a good friend. To do that, I need to understand what's going on in your head. This started out as a tussle with your computer. Your temper often flares when inanimate objects don't behave as you wish, but there had to be more going on than a battle with your PC. You were drinking whiskey in the middle of the afternoon and spoiling for a fight. What did I miss? Is there a problem with Marc that you're not telling me about? Is this the old grief hitting you from a new angle? Is Sandie and Julien's possible affair a factor in all this?"

"It's probably a little bit of everything," he conceded. "I worry about Marc, but as for his problems, you know everything I know – which isn't a whole lot. As for grief, it's already hit me from every conceivable angle, and there's not much I can do about it. Some of the kids whose yearbook photos I was working on spoke at Sandie's memorial service." He lapsed into silence.

"And Sandie and Julien?" Jenny probed cautiously. "You haven't said a word about them since the night we had dinner at Julien's apartment."

"What is there to say?" he shrugged.

"It's certainly occupies *my* mind," Jenny replied. "If I have questions whirling around in my head, surely you do too."

"Questions like what?"

"Well, over the years, I developed an image of Sandie. I thought I knew her – her values, her priorities. Now I have to consider that I was way off base."

"Nobody knows anybody completely. We all keep something of ourselves back."

"This is more than *something*. Now she's a mystery to me."

"Jenny, everything you saw in Sandie, everything you knew about her, is still true. The Julien issue raises the possibility of pieces you and I didn't see, but that doesn't invalidate the ones we did. Sandie isn't a mystery. Aha! We finally have a table!" he announced, following the waiter who beckoned from across the room.

Maybe I should tell him about the commencement program, Jenny debated after they were seated. She toyed with her cutlery. "How did Sandie react when you got into a grumpy mood?" she asked.

"She would either ignore me, scold me, or duck, depending on its severity."

"Did you talk things out afterwards?"

"I'm not much of an analyst, Jenny. 'Mine not to reason why.'"

"Did Sandie want to talk things out afterwards?"

He shrugged.

"Now that could be as good an excuse as any to consider an affair with someone chatty and attentive!" she said in a joking tone, hoping to elicit a smile.

No smile was forthcoming.

"Talking is important," she insisted, becoming serious again. "I'd like to talk about Sandie's affair – alleged affair – for example. You say you'd really like to know what happened, yet you don't seem comfortable discussing it."

"It's not a question of comfort. If talking would reveal anything new, okay, but it won't. There's a whole raft of possibilities, none of which may be legitimate. Why spend time spinning theories?"

"To some degree, it's just how my mind works. I'm a detail person. I like everything to fit together logically. I like to understand all the pieces."

David regarded her in silence. *Conversation to be continued,* she thought, *but obviously not right now.*

"Would you mind if I explored this with someone else?"

David seemed startled by the idea. "Like who?" he responded, frowning. "Frankly, Jenny, I don't think it's anyone else's business. And the last thing I want is to trip a wire which will start rumor and speculation bouncing around Geneva."

"It would be far away from Geneva. I was thinking of someone discreet and objective, like Ross."

"I'm not going to tell you that you can't talk to your friends, Jenny, but I don't see what a conversation with Ross can possibly contribute to our understanding of what happened – or didn't."

"I think, in Ross's case, the contribution could be to my understanding of why I'm so unsettled by the whole thing."

"Suit yourself," he said, draining the last of his espresso from its cup. Then, in a gentler tone, he added, "Do what you have to do."

That night in bed, as she lay in his arms, David thanked Jenny for attempting to help with his computer project, trying to soften the impact of a difficult day.

"Sorry I got ticked off this afternoon," he said ruefully. "I get frustrated sometimes. It's not the first time it's happened, and it won't be the last."

"I'm glad you're back in a good space," she observed. "I'm sorry that my teasing upset you."

"You shouldn't worry about it," he allowed. "It wasn't about you, and I always get over it."

"Yes, you always get over it. But you miss the point of my concern. I know I can't always help you. But I never want to add to your pain – or your anger."

"Listen, Mother Teresa, I'm the only one who can add to my pain and anger. The way I process things is the way I process things. It's my own goddamn responsibility and my own goddamn fault. If I do something to piss you off, feel free to throw it right back in my face. I deserve it. And what's more, I'll eventually appreciate it. Anything you do to maintain your own sanity while you put up with me is something I can only be grateful for. And if you *really* want to score brownie points, why don't you stay here next week instead of abandoning me and going off to Boston?"

Jenny smiled in the dark. *David has the oddest ways of saying, "I love you." He's admitting he's really going to miss me.*

"Sorry, Angel. It's a non-refundable ticket."

"Hmpff," he replied.

Sunday morning, Jenny finished packing her suitcase and put an "I love you" note in David's shaving dish for him to find on Monday. He drove her to the airport and walked with her to Passport Control.

"We have plenty of time," he commented as they approached the entry point, "and there are no lines. You don't have to go through yet."

"No, but I have my book, and you hate hanging around airports. There's no point in just standing here."

"We could go get a coffee," he countered.

"I thought you didn't like long goodbyes," she teased.

"When I say goodbye, it'll be short, but we're not there yet."

As they sat in the little airport café, it was clear to Jenny that the angst of the previous day was completely gone. When they returned to Passport Control, David held her in a long wordless hug, uttered a quick *bon voyage*, and then watched her progress until she disappeared beyond security screening. Jenny started missing him minutes after takeoff. When she finally walked into her condo on the other side of the Atlantic, the first thing she did was head up to the loft to check her e-mail. David's message was waiting for her.

De: David
A: Jenny
Envoyé: 12 mai, 2002
Objet: Sunday afternoon

Washed the car, filled it with gas, forgot to get milk. See, I'm already forgetting things, and I just noticed it wasn't even on your reminder list, so a hell of a lot of good your goddamn list is if it doesn't remind me to buy milk.

I've decided to go to Paris to see Delphine next weekend. Maybe that'll keep me out of trouble.

Now I'm listening to Vivaldi, watching it rain, and thinking about you. Welcome back to Beantown.

Love, David

From: JWLongworth
To: DavidP
Date: May 13, 2002
Subject: Monday Morning

Hiya. I'm settling in and organizing my calendar. I'm going to have dinner with Ross some night this week so I can meet his new companion, Kevin. I'll see everyone else after the reunion events.

Hope the sun is shining in Geneva. Remember that tomorrow is trash day, and that Marikit will be there at 10:00 to clean. Miss you.

Love, me

Mid-afternoon Jenny called Bibi in California. One of the things Jenny most appreciated in Bibi was her reliably blunt and outspoken character, but it was precisely this trait that prompted Jenny to decide, before she dialed the number, that she would make no reference to Sandie's possible infidelity. *This has to remain classified, especially since it may not to be true. I need serious discretion, and that's not Bibi's strong suit. At this stage of the game, Ross is the only one I trust to provide it.*

Bibi picked up on the second ring. "Hey there, Swiss Miss!" she chimed. "You in Boston?"

"Yup. I got in last night."

"Loved your travelogue on the Tuscany trip. You should start a blog or something! But what's happening on the home front? How's it going with the stepchildren?"

"It's your basic roller coaster. I'm working on developing a thicker skin, but just when I think I'm doing okay, I manage to step in it. I forget that there's still a lot of adolescent behavior lurking behind those adult exteriors, and I'm sometimes caught off guard. The last time Dellie visited, I took a wash she had just done and popped it in the dryer so I could run a load of my own. That evening, David took me aside. 'Dellie doesn't like the dryer,' he cautioned. 'Sandie used to hang the laundry on the clothesline out back, and Dellie wants to do the same.' I had no problem with that until David added that Dellie was really upset about the whole thing. 'She'd rather you didn't touch her clothes,' he said. Ouch! I asked if I should talk with her about it, but he said no. 'Let it go. It's not really about the laundry. She'll get over it.'"

"And did she?" Bibi asked.

"Pretty much. At least I think so. Dellie's not one to hold a grudge. By in large, she seems to be doing really well. She still misses her mother a lot, but she likes college life and loves being in Paris. She's struggling with managing on a budget, but I'm trusting that her mother's genes will win out over her father's. She just went through a minor crisis because she misjudged the timing of a money transfer. Her father got more panicky about it than Dellie did, and we had some minor fireworks. She's a capable young woman, but he still thinks of her as a five year old, off to kindergarten for the first time."

"And David's son? How is that going?"

"Marc is the one who worries me. He's pleasant one minute and hostile the next. Valerie, his girlfriend, says he's using drugs. It's hard for us to know what's really going on; he's very close-mouthed."

"What about his friends?" Bibi asked. "Can you get any clues from them?"

"We don't know any of his friends. He never brings anyone by the house except Valerie. David says this is the way it was all during high school. Marc was distant from his classmates. His friends were kids from other schools and other neighborhoods."

"That doesn't sound good. Back when my Daniel was arrested for stealing spray paint from a hardware store, it turned out that he was in cahoots with two buddies he met hanging out at the park. They were all sneaking out at night to decorate the cars on the street with profanities and their initials. Pretty dumb, huh? Signing your own vandalism? Anyway, I had never even heard of his cohorts, much less met them. If Marc has friends he won't bring home, believe me, it's a bad sign."

"How old was Daniel at the time?"

"Fourteen. Almost fifteen."

"Marc is well out of his teens. Hopefully he's past the stage where it's considered cool to spray-paint cars, but if Valerie is right, he's still doing political graffiti on the city's walls. Still, there's some positive news. He's thinking about going to San Francisco to study photojournalism. It would be good for him to have a fresh start. If he pulls it off, it will increase our chances of spending some time in your corner of the world!"

"Three cheers for that! And how's the *ménage-à-trois*?"

"The *ménage-à-trois* is as expected," Jenny replied. "Sandie remains very 'present,' but I'm exerting myself slowly but surely."

"Is Sandie's memorial rose still on the mantel?"

"Yes."

"You still polishing the silver?"

"Only when it gets tarnished. Bibi, that's a very odd question."

"So it's still Sandie's house," Bibi said.

"In some ways it will always be Sandie's house. Sandie is part of David's history, part of who he is," Jenny asserted, not for the first time.

"But how long are you going to put up with being a guest in Sandie's house? You should at least pack away the silver. You don't use silver. You don't *like* silver! From where I sit, you might as well be living in Manderley with the ghost of Rebecca."

"No parallel, Bibi. Rebecca was a baddie, remember? Whereas Sandie was everybody's favorite person," she countered.

A powerful urge to reveal David's suspicions hovered ominously in Jenny's mind, but she fought back the temptation.

"It's not all sweet and harmonious," she continued after taking a deep breath, "but that's not Sandie's fault, or David's. It's just life. What I have the most trouble with are my own insecurities. It's hard for me to avoid comparing myself with Sandie. Take our recent Italian trip, for example, and my aversion to cities. Sandie grew up in Paris. She was at home in cities. She loved the bustle, the noise, the street scene, and the constant activity. There's no way I can measure up to that."

"But why should you have to measure up? Enough is enough, already. Sure there are some things she liked more than you do, and maybe did better than you do. But so what? There are tons of things you like more than she did, and do better than she did. I mean, how many rivers did Sandie ever clean up?"

Jenny had to laugh. She and Bibi had met while volunteering on a long-ago Charles River clean-up project in the days when Bibi still lived in Boston.

"I don't think I can take credit for cleaning up the Charles River, Bibi. A few river banks here and there, but hardly the whole river."

By the time they finished chatting, they had used up Bibi's entire lunch hour.

> *From: JWLongworth*
> *To: DavidP*
> *Date: May 14, 2002*
> *Subject: Tuesday*
>
> Had a long phone conversation with Bibi yesterday. She thinks I should gather up my e-mail reports and write a book. Given all the places we've visited, the meals I've described, and the challenges of living with you, she can't decide whether it should be a travelog, a cookbook or a gothic novel.
>
> Having dinner tomorrow night with Ross. I'm looking forward to meeting Kevin.
>
> Love, J.

> *De: David*
> *A: Jenny*
> *Envoyé: 15 mai, 2002*
> *Objet: Re: Tuesday*
>
> You write the gothic novel. I'll do the cookbook. Miss you.
> *Bises*, David

Jenny had arranged to meet Ross at a popular Mexican restaurant in Quincy. Within minutes after her arrival, she spotted him walking across the parking lot with Kevin at his side. They were a study in contrasts. Ross, tall, slender, with chocolate skin and a head of short-cropped white hair, was still in his three-piece lawyer suit. Kevin, several inches shorter with a sturdy build, was casually dressed in khakis, a crew neck sweater and a tweed sports coat. He was Black Irish, with the traditional pale Celtic skin and blue eyes, but very dark hair. It was a descriptive term in common usage, but it seemed an odd designation when Jenny saw him juxtaposed against someone of African heritage.

Ross and Jenny exchanged an enthusiastic hug, then Ross performed the introductions. "Jewel, Kevin McGarry. Kevin, Jennifer Longworth." Kevin started to hold out his hand, but Jenny bypassed it and hugged him too.

"And should I be calling you Jewel or Jennifer?" Kevin asked.

"Jewel's a nickname from college days," Jenny told him. She looked at Ross. "Kevin knows the history?" she asked.

"Yes," Ross answered simply.

"It was our friend Ramon who first coined the name. It's just my initials, JWL. Actually, most people call me Jenny. But call me whichever you like – Jewel, Jennifer, Jenny. I answer to all of them."

They placed their orders and for the next half hour, Jenny listened to their tales. Kevin had the Irish gift for storytelling and did most of the talking. Ross watched him the way she sometimes watched David.

"Do you like living in Europe, or are you missing Boston?" Kevin asked.

"I love living with David, but that said, I definitely miss Boston. Here I'm empowered. I feel capable, competent and independent. In Geneva, I don't. I'm having more than a few adjustment issues," she admitted. "Still, I think it's good for me. My life in Boston was so comfortable that I rarely ventured outside of it. Living in Geneva forces me to try new things. David lifts me out of my cozy habits and carries me along new paths."

"You don't miss working? Ross said you used to have your own firm here."

"Not really my own. I was a senior partner but there were several other CPAs involved. For which, thank heavens! It made it easier to withdraw without feeling I was abandoning my clients. Anyway, no, I don't miss working. So much was let go when Sandie became ill that I have plenty to keep me busy, and David appreciates the house being brought back to life. He's my job now. Pretty sappy, huh?"

Ross and Kevin looked at Jenny, looked at one another, and smiled without comment. They all passed on dessert, but Ross ordered another round of margaritas, then posed his own question. "What about your Shawmut condo, Jewel? Will you keep it?"

"That's one of the things I need to decide. I thought we'd come back for Thanksgiving or Christmas, but there is a lot of competition for David's time during the academic year. We'll definitely do a trip here in July or August. I'm going to sell the car after that. The condo, though, I'm not sure about. I'll have a better idea of how to proceed after I see how David likes summers in New England."

Ross excused himself to use the men's room.

Kevin took a sip of his margarita. "Ross said you and Ramon were very close."

"Yes," she replied. "Ramon was special. Back in our student days, there was a shortage of campus housing junior year, so a small group of us ended up in an old apartment building on Ware Street. Ramon was our pathfinder, a cross between the Pied Piper and Peter Pan. He was always introducing us to new experiences – classical Oud music, exotic teas, Spanish recipes, foreign films. He was my confidant and most trusted male friend – a wonderful person."

Kevin remained silent.

"Kevin, David calls me a busybody, but I'll say this anyway. You needn't ever feel jealous of Ramon. He's part of what makes Ross who he is. Ramon would have wanted Ross to be happy just as Sandie would have wanted David to be happy. Ross helped me get through some dark times. He's one of the world's nicest human beings, and he … is on his way back to the table this very minute. You both have my absolute best wishes for the future, whatever it may bring."

They said their goodbyes in the parking lot. "You have the address?" Ross asked. Jenny nodded. "Come up to the third floor," he added. "I'm the first office on the right."

Kevin looked at Ross quizzically. "Jenny's coming over to see our new offices tomorrow," Ross told him. "I'm going to give her a tour."

When Jenny arrived the next morning, Ross got himself a fresh cup of coffee, made a mug of tea for Jenny, and then ushered her into his office.

"This is a great building, Ross. You have a nice view," Jenny commented as she took a seat opposite his desk.

"I do," he agreed. "Now, before we start, is this a professional consultation?"

"Yes and no. I don't really need an attorney. I need an objective listener, far from Geneva, who will treat what I say with total confidentiality."

"You have a secret," Ross said levelly.

"Right."

"Jewel, the best way to keep a secret is not to tell anybody."

"Yes, but if I don't talk about this with someone, I'll go crazy."

He nodded and sat back in his chair. "Proceed," he said.

"David thinks Sandie was involved in a longstanding affair with the former Principal of the school."

"And?"

"I've found some things that support his suspicions."

"And?"

Jenny hesitated. "I'm not sure what to do. I don't know how to handle it."

"What do you *want* to do? How do you *want* to handle it?"

"Ross, you sound like a shrink."

He smiled. "The witness will please answer the question," he said.

"David says he really wants to know for sure. I'd like to help him lay the issue to rest. But the things I've stumbled on aren't proof. They're just red flags." Jenny described the items cached in Sandie's files and among her office supplies.

"Suspicious, agreed," Ross commented, "but also purely circumstantial."

"And because they're circumstantial, I don't think I should wave them in front of David's face."

Ross frowned. "That's an odd turn of phrase, Jewel."

"What is?"

"When you wave something in front of someone's face, you're either demanding their attention or thrusting evidence upon them which they have heretofore resisted accepting or acknowledging. You said David 'really wants to know.' Are you sure about that?"

"That's what he says, although he claims it won't make any difference. He says it won't diminish the relationship they had. But I think it's really complex. Grieving can involve revisiting and regretting past arguments or neglect – anything the mourner wishes he could take back, only now it's too late. I think David wants to know so he can ascertain his level of responsibility."

"The witness is speculating," Ross observed.

"Well, what else can I do but speculate?"

"You can shift your focus away from David and onto you. Let David deal with David's issues. You deal with yours."

Jenny gave Ross a puzzled look.

"Think back, Jewel. In your opening statement, you said, 'I don't know how to handle it.' So work on 'I,' not on David. You're a consummate problem-solver when you set your mind to it. What's the advantage *to you* of telling David now? What's the advantage *to you* of waiting until you have more 'facts?' What's the advantage *to you* of doing anything at all? Why do you feel this is your problem? And while you're at it, consider these questions: Are you an impartial observer? Are you sitting in the Jury Box? Are you sitting at the defense table? Or are you with the prosecution?"

Jenny was momentarily silenced.

"I'm going to pop across the hall and give this folder to my paralegal," Ross said. "Want another tea?"

"No, thanks," she answered quietly.

"I'll be right back," he said, allowing Jenny a moment to gather her thoughts.

Within minutes, Ross returned and reclaimed his chair. He looked at Jenny, but said nothing.

"Okay," Jenny began. "I'd like to think I'm an impartial observer, but if that were so, I wouldn't be sitting here. I'm upset by the idea of Sandie's infidelity because, if it's true, I believe it will hurt David, no matter what he says."

"And do we have confidence that David has been a paragon of marital virtue throughout?"

"No, but his indiscretions were minor and very early on, while they still lived in Paris," she replied, giving a brief summary of David's weekend conference "flings."

"Do David's past infidelities upset you?"

"When he first told me, yes, but David cut a wide swath before he got married. I guess I was a little naïve assuming that he would change his habits overnight. And anyway, it was a long time ago."

"Hence a very qualified 'yes,' that rings 'no' in my ears. Yet Sandie's infidelity, purely speculative and unproven, distresses you to such a degree that you've arranged this consultation to discuss it. I think we can definitely rule out impartial observer," he concluded wryly.

"My instincts say Sandie's guilty. It's just a matter of time before the proof emerges."

"And are you actively involved in seeking that proof? Do you feel a need to play detective, hunting down clues rather than just leaving it alone?"

Jenny considered. "I don't feel I'm hunting down clues, but neither am I ignoring them when they present themselves. When David's hurting, it brings out the Mother Bear in me. So getting at the truth is a way of helping him heal. Whatever pain he's feeling about this has a better chance of dissipating if there's closure."

"You're focusing on David again. What about you?"

"I can't separate the two things. My reactions are inextricably tied up with his."

Ross gave her a skeptical look. "When a Mother Bear's cubs are threatened, does she seek the truth?" he asked. "Or does she go after the source of the threat with intent to kill?"

"I'm hardly going after Sandie with murderous intent," Jenny protested. "I just want to know what happened and why, so David can put all this behind him."

"Be careful, Jewel. Examine your motives. Beware a rush to judgment. Even if the affair took place, there could be mitigating factors. It could be David who bears the primary responsibility."

"Actually, I think that's the way he sees it – that if Sandie had an affair, it's because she needed a level of romance and affection that he failed to provide."

"Jewel, you are a very human woman trying hard to be an angel for David's sake, and it's confusing and distressing you no end. I think you have formed a conclusion without waiting to hear all the evidence. Are you familiar with the phrase, *nihil nisi bonum?*"

"Of the dead, speak nothing but good."

"Right. I want you to think about that, because it's good advice. You may be trying to solve this case with the best of intentions, but it could blow up in your face. If the truth is unpleasant, and you are the bearer of bad tidings, someone may want to shoot the messenger. So tread gently."

Ross glanced at his watch, and Jenny understood that their discussion was at an end. "I'll do my best," she promised in a subdued voice.

"Now off you go, Princess. I've got a real client on his way. Let all this percolate for a while. I'm here if you need me. When you decide about your next step, let me know."

"Thank you, Ross," she said, giving him a hug in the doorway.

"Careful, careful, Jewel! Not here! People might suspect we're having an affair!"

May, 2002

Across your garden

In late afternoon, the sun beneath the rain
Casts long shadows, long plains of light
Across your garden, become our garden,
Since you have left to garden elsewhere
Where I have yet to plant a spade,
Where I long to plant our garden once again
Even though I'm happy here, as happy as
One can be having lost his gardener.
Despite the sun, a soft rain continues.
"The Devil is beating his wife," they say.
I never beat you, but made you suffer no doubt,
And didn't know how much I loved you
Until you had gone away.

Chapter 4

De: David
A: Jenny
Envoyé: 16 mai, 2002
Objet: Re: Wednesday

Got to run, Honey Chile, got to go draw nekked ladies for my art class, then go to the theater with the Académie Internationale crowd, cook dinner, then go to bed. Off to Paris this weekend. I'll be staying with Delphine. Sleep tight.

Kisses and love, David

From: JWLongworth
To: DavidP
Date: May 16, 2002
Subject: Thursday

Naked ladies, theatre, haute cuisine? I'd best come home soon, or I will lose you to the wild and wily nightlife of Geneva. Did you see the dermatologist about that mole on your back, and if yes, what did she say?

Had a good dinner yesterday with Ross and Kevin. Kevin is cute, and very Irish. I'll fill you in when I get back. Reunion events start tomorrow evening and run through the weekend.

Have a safe trip to Paris. Big hug to Dellie when you get there.

Love you, J.

De: David
A: Jenny
Envoyé: 17 mai, 2002
Objet: Friday

The dermatologist said I was suffering from a terminal case of silliphilia and henpecking. The biopsy confirmed that my Bull Shit level is off the charts. She prescribed increased nicotine and caffeine and suggested that if they didn't produce the desired effects, I might have to consider intravenous MaryJane and Jack Daniels.

The play was good. Gotta go brush my teeth. Have fun with your high school buddies! David

Jenny was vexed by David's evasiveness about his dermatology visit, but she mimicked David's teasing tone.

From: JWLongworth
To: DavidP
Date: May 19, 2002
Subject: Sunday

I'm sorry to hear that your BS level is so high, but I still want to know what the dermatologist actually said.

It was a good weekend and a good reunion. I got to repeat the story behind my invitation to Geneva a dozen times over. I never get tired of it.

How was the Paris trip? How was Dellie? Did you see anyone else? Where did you eat? What did you eat?

Love you truly, madly, deeply. J.

De: David
A: Jenny
Envoyé: 20 mai, 2002
Objet: Re: Sunday

Paris was fun. Saw the usual suspects. Had lunch at La Tartine and wandered around the Left Bank. Later went for a movie and a Chinese-Thai meal.

Did the Egyptian exhibit at the Louvre. I met Delphine afterwards, saw Mme Lamont, and *after that it was back*

to Heidiland. I don't know why this goddamn machine has
suddenly shifted into italics!
Better get off before I explode! David

From: JWLongworth
To: DavidP
Date: May 21, 2002
Subject: Tuesday
The g-d machine produces italics when the operator
– that's you – clicks on the slanted *I* (for italic) symbol
that sits in your tool bar. My guess is that you let your
cursor wander and then clicked your mouse.
You still haven't given me an accurate report on your
back wart. Italics are no excuse.
Love, me

Jenny devoted the next day's lunch to Rachel Aronson, whose husband Josh died just three months before Sandie. More than anyone except David himself, Rachel had helped Jenny understand what David was going through by sharing so forthrightly her own experience of loss and grief.

Rachel spoke candidly about the ups and downs of widowhood and then turned the questions back to Jenny.

"Our marriage is something of a roller coaster ride," Jenny observed. "Being with David is wonderful, but there are moments when he still misses Sandie. The grief surfaces in odd ways and at odd times. Neither he nor I can tell when it's going to hit. I worry that I'm not doing enough to keep him on the positive side of the emotional spectrum."

"Jenny, the hard truth is that sometimes there is no 'enough,'" Rachel counseled. "Sometimes, in fact a lot of times, he's going to slip over to the negative side because that's what grief is all about. Marriage is a challenge under the best of circumstances. You took on a very complicated emotional situation. Just remember that Sandie wasn't perfect, despite how much David loved her. You don't need to be perfect. You just need to be loving."

"I do understand that Sandie wasn't perfect." *Tread carefully,* Jenny reminded herself. "David acknowledges Sandie's imperfections, but he tends to blame himself, as if he didn't pay enough attention to her or didn't appreciate her enough. It's irrational, but sometimes guilt just settles like a cloud, and he withdraws. I've had people tell me I should demand more attention from David – ask for less emphasis on Sandie, cessation of the rituals, removal of her collections and her photographs. 'This is your time,' they say, 'not hers.' But my time or not, David's grief is still real. If he doesn't express it, it's just going to fester inside him."

"I agree," said Rachel. "I'm sure anyone who tells you 'This is your time' means well, but they're wrong to expect David to deny his feelings. Josh is with me every minute. I couldn't remove him from my thoughts if I tried. I need my friends to accept and welcome him as part of my present, not just part of my past."

It was advice that Jenny would draw on time and again in the months ahead.

De: David
A: Jenny
Envoyé: 22 mai, 2002
Objet: Re: Tuesday

What back wart? I don't have a back wart. I have a mole. You must be thinking of somebody else. See you Saturday.

Kisses and good night. David

From: JWLongworth
To: DavidP
Date: May 22, 2002
Subject: Wednesday

David Perry, if you keep dancing around it, you only exacerbate my concern. PLEASE clarify the situation NOW. Not Saturday.

I had a nice lunch with Rachel Aronson. She thinks I'm amazingly wonderful to put up with you. I might have replied that you were worth the effort, but since mushy stuff makes you uncomfortable, I decline to confess to any such thing. Herewith a light kiss on your bald spot instead.

Love you. J.

Jenny's virtual kiss elicited some concrete information at last.

De: David
A: Jenny
Envoyé: 22 mai, 2002
Objet: Re: Wednesday
The doctor didn't say boo to a ghost. She just cut the damn thing out. I saw her this morning for a change of dressing. I specified vinaigrette. I see Dr. Payot in two weeks. I've booked the mortician for the week after that. I don't give a damn what they found, and they haven't said.

Kisses, David

Jenny enjoyed the playfulness of their exchange, but she was aware that David had little confidence in modern medicine. For nine years, Sandie had endured radiation, surgery, drugs and chemotherapy. The treatments had prolonged her life, but in the end, they hadn't saved her. David had a considerable intellect, but it was his emotional response that governed.

From: JWLongworth
To: DavidP
Date: May 22, 2002
Subject: Answers, please
You may not give a damn, but I do. Tell them you have a nosy wife. Tell them I want to be the one who chooses the mortician, and I need to know how much lead-time I have.

Love, me

De: David
A: Jenny
Envoyé: 23 mai, 2002
Objet: Thursday

Yeah, yeah, I told her I had a nosy wife – told her I had *two* nosy wives.

She said I was fortunate to have removed the "beauty spot" on my back because it was in a position to go whacko. That's not really what she said, but since I didn't understand what she said, I have chosen whacko. The official lab report should arrive in a few days, and she will forward it to Dr. Payot, whom I will see if I survive that long.

Meanwhile, I have reserved an ambulance and iron lung so I can meet you at the airport. You are planning to come back, aren't you? 'Cause there are thousands of people trying to rent the iron lung, and I promised to confirm my reservation.

Bye, David

Jenny pursed her lips at David's remark about having two wives. Rachel had stressed how important it was to her that her late spouse be recognized "as part of my present, not just part of my past." That seemed to be where David's mind was as well. *I can accept that he wants two wives in the present,* Jenny concluded. *It helps him deal with the pain of Sandie's absence. But I'm looking for a future in which the first wife is in the past. Sweetly remembered. Fully appreciated. Still loved. But in the past.*

She issued a sigh. *Where is my magic wand when I need it?* she pouted.

Giving the e-mail a second read, Jenny also noted the discreet anxiety in David's inquiry about her return. *He knows I'm more comfortable in Boston than in Geneva. But surely he doesn't think I would give up on him so easily!*

From: JWLongworth
To: DavidP
Date: May 23, 2002
Subject: Re: Thursday

Yes, I am planning to come back. I look forward to hearing from Dr. Payot and getting a responsible account of all this.

I'm still on for the Saturday arrival. The itinerary is on your dresser, but I'm attaching the flight info just in case.

Much Love, J.

David was waiting for Jenny at the Geneva airport. Her delight at seeing him was off the scale. When they reached the house, he took her bag upstairs. She went up to unpack and found a beautiful apricot rose on her bedside table. It was a lovely surprise. David rarely gave her flowers. There was always a rose in the living room, but it was dedicated to Sandie. Jenny noted fleetingly, on arrival, that Sandie's vase on the mantel, usually graced with a red rose, held a soft yellow blossom for a change. *David is taking good care of both his ladies.*

She went back downstairs and found David on the couch in the living room, reading the paper. "Thank you for my rose, Love. It's really beautiful." She bent down and gave him a kiss. He tossed the paper aside, slid his hands up her arms, and pulled her down onto his lap.

"Missed you," he said, as his hands began to roam.

They kissed again, this time deeply. Jenny could feel the tingling warmth of desire spread through her.

"Shall we go upstairs?" she murmured.

"Too far," he answered.

"David, all the shutters are wide open, and so is the door to the garden," she protested.

"Too bad," he said, shrugging out of his clothes. Jenny struggled playfully to escape until her body overrode any worries about propriety and the neighbors. The outside world disappeared and for a long time afterward, they lay glued to one another in warmth and contentment.

David ultimately recovered himself, and nuzzled her breasts. "Welcome home, Ducks," he grinned. He rose, gathered his clothes, and headed into the kitchen to prepare lunch. Jenny stayed where she was, absolutely helpless, for several more minutes. Throughout the afternoon, little frissons of joy kept bubbling through her, and she marveled — not for the first time — at what this man could do to her equilibrium.

Sunday they went to market and stocked up. David had a five-day school trip starting Monday morning. "Wanna be sure you won't starve while I'm away," he told her. Later, as David checked his e-mail, Jenny sorted through the bills he had piled up in the center of the dining room table, and glanced at the junk mail and odds and ends stacked beside it. Among the debris was a sheet of lined paper covered with David's handwriting. It was a poem: *Across Your Garden*. Jenny picked it up and felt the happiness drain out of her as she read it. David spoke of his longing to be with Sandie. "[I] didn't know how much I loved you until you had gone away," he agonized at the end.

Oh, I do not need this. I do not need this. We had such a wonderful weekend, and this just wipes it all out. This is proof that David sometimes looks at me and wishes he were seeing Sandie instead. Images flashed in Jenny's mind of the many times David's eyes had grown cloudy and his thoughts had wandered off. *He was looking for Sandie, thinking of Sandie. He said it himself in the wedding poem he gave me: "The time has passed for me, when love lay soft and light...."*

David's grief and sense of loss were hard for Jenny to deal with, but until recently, she believed Sandie had earned this devotion, and deserved it. She had viewed Sandie as a paradigm of wifely virtue. Now there was a shadow: Julien Charbonnet. And now there was an element of anger in her reaction. *Were we deceived?*

Jenny recalled a conversation in which Sandie had described one of her favorite summer pastimes. "I love to take rest days just alone sometimes," Sandie had said. "I say *adieu* to David and the children, and I go by myself with a book and a picnic lunch for the ferryboat ride around Lake Leman. It is ten hours to make the full circle of all the ports, so when it is finished I am *très relaxe!*"

It sounded delightful at the time, but now Jenny wondered. *Was Sandie's story legitimate, or was it a cover? Was she alone? Was she even on the boat?* David had recently mentioned that Julien had property in France, somewhere near the Atlantic coast. *Is that why Sandie suggested Brittany for the last joint vacation we planned – the one we had to cancel because of Sandie's chemotherapy?*

"Beware a rush to judgment," Ross had warned.

I will beware, Jenny cautioned herself, *but I'm not at all happy about any of this.*

David telephoned from school Monday afternoon just before leaving on the field trip. "Got the lab results. The mole was a basal cell carcinoma," he reported dryly.

"Thank god they got it in time!" Jenny exclaimed.

"Gotta die of something," was his response.

Jenny made no attempt at a comeback. After they hung up, she tackled domestic chores in an effort to distract herself from dark thoughts. "Just please don't let me come across any more poems for Sandie," she mumbled as she gathered up old newspapers.

At nine o'clock, she got into bed with her book, but her mind kept going back to the poem. After half an hour, she gave up trying to read.

Nine hours difference means it's lunchtime in California, she calculated. She got out of bed, went to the phone and dialed Bibi's number. Bibi's cheery answering machine advised that she was out, and that the caller should leave a message at the sound of the beep.

"Just me," Jenny advised the recorder, "and it's bedtime over here. Call me tomorrow?"

The next morning, Jenny wandered around the empty house in a fog of depression, berating herself for her mood swings and her inconsistency. *Is there anything new in this? Is there any startling concept I haven't encountered before?* No. Yet it hurt, that poem, those words of anguish. Jenny wanted David to be glad he was still alive rather than wishing he were dead so he could be with Sandie to "plant our garden once again."

She went to her computer and e-mailed Bibi the text of the poem. "This is the agenda for our phone conversation," she wrote.

The phone rang at five. "Is he home? Are you free to talk?" Bibi asked, bypassing any greeting.

"He's away for the week with a bunch of eighth-graders. They're off exploring ancient caves and life-styles of the pre-historic."

"Okay, first a question. What does 'The Devil is beating his wife' mean?"

"I don't know if it's French or just one of David's southernisms, but when the sun shines and it's raining at the same time, people say, 'The Devil is beating his wife.'"

"And he thinks he made her suffer? How? Why?"

"Well, based on what he wrote, I think he feels he didn't appreciate her as much as he should have."

"Is that what's bothering you? 'Cause that one, I can't help with."

"I guess, more than anything, I just need to vent. I keep thinking I've settled out my insecurities vis-à-vis my relationship with David, and then something like this comes along and knocks me for a loop."

"What did David say about the poem?"

"I haven't asked him about it. I found it mixed in with a pile of papers on the dining room table."

"When was it written? Is it recent or an old one?"

"I'm pretty sure he wrote it the day I left for Boston. There was an e-mail waiting for me in Shawmut that said he was 'listening to Vivaldi, watching it rain….' In the poem, he describes watching the late afternoon sun appear beneath the rain. I know he wasn't happy about my going home. Faced with being alone for two weeks, he may have felt depressed and uneasy. When I'm upset, I tend to write in my journal until I've gotten past it. David does the same thing, only with him, it's poetry."

"So, which is it? Are you angry with David, worried about him, or feeling sorry for him?"

"Mostly, I'm feeling sorry for me. It's hard to be angry with David. There are times he misses Sandie terribly and feels all sorts of pain and sadness. Rachel keeps assuring me that while it's part of the grieving process, it's part of the healing process as well. What gets me is that I haven't eradicated my worry that what David needs now and what he'll want in the future might be very different. I still function as a life raft sometimes. When David writes poetry about longing to be with Sandie 'even though I'm happy here,' I feel pretty discouraged. I'm not Sandie, and I never will be."

"Have you talked with David about feeling so insecure?"

"A couple of times. But he dismisses it as foolishness. Since I'm excessively logical in most other areas of my life, he is baffled by this recurrent anxiety, which, I'll admit, seems irrational when I trot it out."

"Do your friends over there have any take on it?"

"My Geneva friends are David's friends, which means Sandie's friends. What can I say to them? That I'm upset by a poem that implies David wants to be with Sandie more than with me? They all loved Sandie. They too would rather be with Sandie than with me. I may be nice, fill in the blanks, whatever, but I will never measure up to Sandie in their eyes. I'm the proverbial square peg in a round hole."

"You *are* down! So, either you throw in the towel, or you get yourself back to a happier frame of mind. Mucking about in middle ground is a waste of time. Have you got any chocolate in the house? Chocolate cures almost every problem."

"I thought it's supposed to be chicken soup."

"Chicken soup cures the body. Chocolate cures the soul."

"You seriously think a bar of *Crémant* will transport me to a mindset of unconditional love for my husband and total serenity living in this *ménage-à-trois?*"

"Longworth, unconditional love exists only in dogs. With humans, there are always conditions. But the chocolate will taste really good, and you'll feel totally justified in eating it. Beyond that, I don't know what advice to give. Maybe talk to David about the poem when he gets back?"

"I expect he'll say pretty much what I said to you – that it was a gray day, he was feeling lonely, he missed me, he missed Sandie, and he dealt with it by writing a lament."

"So already you've forgiven him and solved your problem. Maybe you only need *half* a bar of that chocolate."

Their conversation continued for several minutes, but moved to lighter subjects. By the time she hung up the phone, Jenny was in a more positive frame of mind.

I just have to keep my eyes on the prize, she told herself. *I'm here because I love this man, and because he needs me.*

For the remainder of David's trip, Jenny was back on an even keel, but the nights alone were hard. The house felt empty. It was not a scary emptiness, just a vacuum. David's absence underscored the reality that he was Jenny's point of connection with everything in Geneva.

Friday afternoon, her eyes kept straying to the clock. She treated herself to a bath and polished her nails. When David walked in, he was tired, but to Jenny, he looked absolutely great. "I'm so glad you're home," she said, standing on tiptoe for a kiss. He poured them each a glass of wine, and they sat at the kitchen counter.

"Terrific field trip," he reported. "Tautavel was great. We were studying the lives of the cave dwellers who once lived there, and, except for the museum, it was all hands-on. I had the kids pulverizing ochre for cave drawings and chipping silex to make flint stones." After relating his stories, David asked Jenny about her week. She said nothing about her earlier depression, offering up instead a wifely summary of domestic doings. They had a cozy evening and a sweetly erotic night in celebration of his return.

Sunday evening, Delphine called from Paris. She chatted with her father, then asked for Jenny's help locating a document she needed for school. The next morning, Jenny searched through Sandie's files. She found three binders marked DELPHINE, filled with medical records, high school certificates and other items. She went through each one page by page. She didn't find the material Delphine wanted, but she came across a document titled *Testament*, in Sandie's handwriting. "If David and I die before Marc and Delphine come of age, and it becomes necessary to name a guardian, it is my request that Julien Charbonnet be appointed. He is a longtime family friend in whom we have total confidence."

As far as Jenny could see, Julien had never evidenced the slightest interest in either Marc or Delphine since Sandie's death. Stories about Julien's past political battles included veiled references to financial impropriety. *Yet Sandie was prepared to entrust him with her children, whom she cherished above all else, despite questions about the way he handled money and his now-apparent indifference to her offspring?* Jenny sat back, shaking her head. It wasn't the kind of evidence that would hang Sandie in court, but it settled Jenny's mind to a moral certainty. *Sandie most certainly had an affair with Julien Charbonnet!*

She wanted to call Ross, but it was only 10:00 a.m., which meant 4:00 a.m. in Boston. *God I hate this time difference!* She put the binders away and moved about the house watering the plants, all the while trying to imagine Sandie with Julien. The rose in Sandie's vase had wilted. Jenny had always replaced it in the past with respect. For the first time, she balked, her anger bubbling to the surface. *How could you, Sandie?* Jenny scolded. *David loved you. How could you cheat on him? How could you lie to him?*

Jenny was so upset that she left the wilted flower as it was and descended to her computer.

From: *JWLongworth*
To: *Ross*
Date: *June 3, 2002*
Subject: *Smoking Gun*

It's too early to call you, but I have to tell you that I just found a smoking gun in Sandie's files. She signed a *Testament* naming Julien as her guardian of choice for the children if she and David died before the kids reached 21. He's a seriously inappropriate candidate for all sorts of reasons. No objective parent would ever choose him. The only possible explanation is that her feelings for him blinded her. J.

Jenny was back at her computer after lunch when she received a reply from Ross. It contained just one word: "And?"

She was brought up short. Ross had simply lobbed the ball back into her court.

"And," she started to reply, then acknowledged that she had some thinking to do. *And… I'm going to tell David about it? No, I'm not. Why? Because it isn't proof, which leaves me back where I started.*

She returned her attention to the computer screen.

From: JW Longworth
To: Ross
Date: June 3, 2002
Subject: Re: Re: Smoking gun
And … I'm feeling frustrated and angry and stymied. Are you free for a phone call? I'd like to talk before David comes home, which will be around 4:30 p.m. (10:30 a.m. your time). J.

From: Ross
To: Jewel
Date: June 3, 2002
Subject: Re: Re: Re: Smoking gun
Can't. Leaving for the office in five minutes. In court all morning. If your "what is the loving thing to do?" mantra isn't working, repeat the Serenity Prayer. (Google!) And since you seem to be moving for conviction, I suggest you take the day to consider possible mitigating circumstances.
Stay Sweet, Ross

Stay sweet. There's a challenge! Jenny struggled unsuccessfully to realign her thinking within a framework of logic. She opened her journal file and began to type.

Credit column: David loved Sandie and enjoyed his life with her. She deserves to be honored as a good helpmeet and a good mother. Her trust in me was a major influence in David's decision to marry me and in the children's acceptance of me (sort of) as part of the family.

Debit column: If Sandie had an affair, the potential hurt to David is huge. And I'm feeling hurt too. I invested in Sandie emotionally because I believed she loved David as much as I did. I spent a lot of years keeping my feelings for him in check, playing by the rules, respecting David's marriage and respecting Sandie. If Sandie was cheating on him, she was cheating on me too.

This is getting me nowhere, she finally decided. *When all else fails, go do some gardening.* She shut down her computer, gathered her tools, and set to work pulling weeds. It was an activity she could count on to calm her down. By late afternoon she had worked her way around to the garage. The lattice screening supported four climbing rose bushes, heavy with buds. Half way up, she spotted a freshly opened yellow rose with red-tipped petals, Sandie's favorite color combination.

Ross had repeatedly counseled her not to rush to judgment. *I suppose, if you go to a professional for advice, you should accord some respect to what he says.* She took a deep breath and let it out very slowly. She cut the rose and carried it into the house.

It's important to David that Sandie always have a fresh rose. Grant me the serenity to accept the things I cannot change.

She looked at the rose for a long time. Serenity was not forthcoming. *David has forgiven Sandie without even being sure of the deed. So why should it bother me? It's almost as if it's more about my relationship with Sandie than David's.*

"Stay sweet," Ross had urged.

But how? Jenny wondered. *What is the loving thing to do?* She had to run her mantra several times before an idea gradually took shape.

She went up to Delphine's room and pulled out the binder where Delphine had stored the sympathy cards and letters of condolence the family received when Sandie died. *Remind me,* she thought as she opened it. *Reassure me of how much Sandie was worthy of David's love, whatever transpired with Julien.* And so she sat, going through it page by page, revisiting the anguish and pain, the love and loss:

> All I can do to feel somewhat better is to accept that she is no longer in pain. I want you to know that every time she spoke about you, she lit up, even when we saw her in the hospital. You were adored. I am so glad that you had the time to talk, and that she did not suffer too long. I know she will be looking out for you, knowing the kind of person she was and how much she loved you! Adelaide

> Dear David,
> There is a candle lit in a church, but more important, in my heart. This shouldn't be happening. I remember her years ago; she loved you from the start, though you continued screwing your way through the female population of the world! But she played her cards well, was patient, and you married and have raised a wonderful family. I am sure that you, Marc and Delphine mean everything to her. Claudine

> My dear Perry: It is a crushing blow to read what Sandie and you and the kids are going through. That dark, spiraling disintegration of the senses, and the almost mean-spirited (because they are false) momentary recoveries, are surely about as unfair a thing as a body and a family ever endures. You should know in how many cities and on how many continents the tears flow. I wish I were nearby so I could weep alongside you, my dear old friend.
> Much love to you all. Jeff

> Oh, God, David, we are so very, very sorry. Sandie was such a great mother and wife. She truly adored her family. Eleanor & Carlo

We pray that Sandie is quietly released into your heart forever so you can keep her safe. We love you, David, and it has been a joy to have known and loved such a beautiful person as your Sandie.

Peace be with you, Edie & Jeremy

It is just beginning to dawn on me what a loss we have all suffered. Images of dear Sandie keep coming into my mind, wonderful images of a woman who was always full of *joie de vivre* and had that girl's spirit of which you wrote, even while being your lover, mother, tutor, tamer and regulator. As do you all, I really miss her. Jack

Jenny paid particular attention to the letter from Julien Charbonnet:

I have just learned that Sandrine left us this evening. I too have tried to prepare myself, but the sadness is nonetheless terrible. You know the affection that we carried for her, which she returned to us as well.

I am thinking of the great hole she is going to leave in your lives. I believe she held on as long as she was able, to see Marc and Delphine become young adults. She knew for several years that she was in remission but she never gave up.

She will remain forever an example of life and love, beautiful and smiling in our hearts. Julien

Jenny wasn't sure enough of her French to determine if the reference to the affection "which she returned" might have a double meaning, but the words were obviously sincere.

Jenny closed the binder and put it back. Sandie may have made some mistakes, but her shortcomings didn't negate the characteristics extolled in the condolences. Jenny ranked Julien as a predator, but there had to be something redeeming about the man if the affair lasted as long as David thought it did. *Alice in Wonderland was right. Curiouser and curiouser.*

David was in a good mood when he arrived home. "I picked up some *magrets de canard* – duck breasts. Summer's practically here. Time to crank up the grill!"

David wheeled the grill out of the garage and into the back yard. As he filled it with charcoal, Jenny got out the broom to clear the terrace of the accumulated debris from the garden.

"Call out the army! She's found a goddamn leaf on the terrace!" David teased, waving his cigarette in the air for emphasis.

"It's not just the leaves," Jenny retorted primly. "I need to sweep the terrace because of the cigarette ash you drop everywhere."

David burst out laughing. "You and Sandie! Jeezus! She was forever complaining about the ashes I dropped all over her terrace, yelling '*Attention aux cendres!*'" He shook his head and returned his attention to the grill.

Jenny stood stock still. She had a sudden image of a cartoon character with a light bulb appearing in a balloon over its head.

"You're just like Sandie," David was always saying.

But if X equals Y, doesn't Y also equal X? If I'm just like Sandie, isn't Sandie just like me? If I have uncertainties in my relationship with David, she must have had some too.

When dinner was over, Jenny retreated to her computer.

> *From: JWLongworth*
> *To: Ross*
> *Date: June 3, 2002*
> *Subject: Mitigation*
>
> Doing my best to stay sweet and explore mitigating factors. I've been trying to understand this from Sandie's perspective. David unwittingly unlocked the door for me this evening with another of his constant references to how Sandie and I are so much alike. I've always been focused on our differences, so I missed the obvious: If X = Y, Y = X.
>
> David is a very loving human being – caring and affirming. The downside is, he's seriously undemonstrative – not inclined to hold hands or give

casual caresses. Even his verbal expression of affection is indirect and subtle. We've talked about this more than once. I understand his foibles, and I feel I know him inside out, but despite this, his inconsistent attentions can still bother me. Would Sandie's reaction have been any different?

David always seemed happy with their marriage. I assumed Sandie was also. I could see David's affection for her, but he's not the kind of husband who comes up behind his wife, puts his arms around her and nuzzles the back of her neck. There are lots of little ways in which he demonstrates his love, but perhaps Sandie didn't recognize them as such.

I always thought of her as so attractive and so socially confident that I couldn't imagine anything was missing from her life. Yet I remember conversations in which Sandie expressed frustration at David's lack of romanticism. At the time I assumed her reference was to superficial things, like David's failure to notice a new hairstyle or a new outfit. But maybe her frustrations went a lot deeper. Sandie wouldn't have had an affair, certainly not one running nearly a decade, unless she had problems with David.

Are you in court again tomorrow morning? I could write volumes about this, but I need your piercing cross-examination to keep me within bounds. Is there a time I can call?

Super thanks and much love, J.

From: Ross
To: Jewel
Date: June 3, 2002
Subject: Court calendar
Heavy court calendar. Weekend call?

From: JW Longworth
To: Ross
Date: June 4, 2002
Subject: Re: Court calendar
Can't do a weekend call. We're off after David's Friday classes to meet up with California friends of his

who are over here touring Provence. Probably do me good to take a break and get out of Geneva. When your next week's calendar is settled, let me know, and we'll pick a time to talk.

Love, J.

David and Jenny reached the Provençal village of Arpaillargues early Friday evening. They easily found the hotel where David's friend Jeff had booked rooms for both couples. While Jenny freshened up, David placed a call to Jeff. "Come meet us in the courtyard," Jeff told him.

Tall and trim, with a clean-shaven head and a California tan, Jeff rose to greet them as they stepped into the terraced dining area, and the two men exchanged a warm hug.

"Jenny, meet Jeff Stone, journalist, wine connoisseur and occasional author. Jeff, this is my bride, Jenny Longworth."

"Congratulations and best wishes," Jeff said, giving Jenny a kiss on the cheek. The *maître d'* presented them with a complimentary Kir just as Jeff's girlfriend Kelly appeared, prompting another round of introductions.

They gave a few minutes attention to the menu, placed their orders, then caught up on each other's lives. Jeff's father had recently died of cancer. The disease quickly took center stage in the conversation.

"My dad refused heavy sedation so he could remain lucid, but the decision didn't serve him well," Jeff lamented. "He was in such pain, so puzzled and distracted by it, that I was never able to have the last talks with him I hoped to have. Looking back, I would have preferred to see him ease away in a drug-induced blur."

"Sandie needed heavy sedation in the end," David commented, "but at least we had the whole summer to talk. We discovered the problem in June, when Sandie went in for tests because of chronic fatigue. When we discussed the scan results with the children, I told them candidly that I was scared, and it was pretty obvious that Sandie was too, though she was trying to keep up a brave front. It was hard for the kids to deal with," he continued. "Especially Marc. I think

Marc's decision to go backpacking in Eastern Europe was both a flight from the family's anguish and a denial of the inevitable conclusion of Sandie's illness. He was away all of her last summer. By the time he returned, she was so ill that she was barely aware of his presence. He's still angry with himself for that," David concluded.

The conversation veered into a discussion of the challenges of parenthood, and they talked late into the evening.

They were awakened in the morning by the pealing of bells from the nearby church. Jenny opened the shutters and leaned out the hotel window. Across the street, barn swallows were dipping and swooping into their nests under the eaves of the buildings.

Kelly slept in, but Jeff joined them for breakfast. After his second cup of coffee, David excused himself to go in search of a *Tabac* where he could buy a fresh pack of cigarettes.

"You're doing a great job in a very sensitive situation," Jeff told Jenny when David was out of sight. "David's grief is very present in everything he does. It can't be easy for you when so much of his conversation is about Sandie," Jeff observed.

Jenny appreciated the strokes. "I'm used to it," she answered frankly. "But you're right. It's a constant."

"And that doesn't bother you?"

"Not in the way people might think," she ventured. "I want the day to come when memories of Sandie bring a smile rather than tears, and I want that day to come yesterday. But it won't. I have a good friend who lost her husband a few months before David lost Sandie. We're in touch regularly, and she keeps me grounded in the reality of what David is feeling. It's going to take a very long time for the pain to diminish.

"And here's the thing," she continued. "If David is thinking about Sandie, it would be awful if he had to watch his words around me. If I insisted that her name disappear from our conversations, David would have to hold a part of himself remote from me. And what would be the point? He might be able to hide his memories, but that wouldn't erase them. Sandie was central to his life for three decades.

It's natural that she remains so strong a reference point." She lowered her voice as she spotted David returning. "I just have to focus on being as important to him in the future as she was to him in the past."

Jeff had come armed with a list of tourist sites he wanted to see, so their first day was spent checking them off. The second day, they set out for Uzes. On their way into the town, David noticed a *brocante* – an antique shop – and stopped to see if they had a small sunburst mirror. "Sandie really wanted one for her mirror collection," he explained to Jeff. "She spent years searching, without success."

When David spoke to the proprietress, he described something with a roughly three-inch radius. "No," she said, "I haven't seen one like that."

As they chatted, Jenny perused the aisles of bric-a-brac and suddenly, there it was, a sunburst mirror. Two of the "rays" were bent, and it was twice the size David was looking for, but Jenny urged him to buy it anyway. "We can always have the spokes straightened, and we can easily reorganize the mirror wall so everything will fit." *And we can have closure – at least regarding the mirror collection!*

He agreed to the purchase. "At last Sandie's mirror collection is complete," he beamed as it was being wrapped.

"Adding a final piece to each of Sandie's collections holds great importance for David," Jenny whispered to Kelly. "It's a ritual of sorts: you honor the subject, and then you move on. David is moving on at a very cautious pace, *à un pas de tortue* as he would say, but slow and steady wins the race."

With promises of a someday visit to California, they parted company with Jeff and Kelly and headed back to Geneva that afternoon. The phone rang shortly after their arrival. David switched to English and an enthusiastic greeting as he answered it. "It's for you, Jenny," he said after a minute.

That must be Ross! she thought. "I'll take it in my office," she told David, and quickly trotted down the stairs.

"Hello?"

"Hey, Kiddo. Haven't heard from you since you got back to Geneva."

"Bibi!" Jenny had expected Ross's voice on the other end of the line, but she deftly changed gears. "Hi! We just walked in. We've been in Provence all weekend."

"Longworth, you are getting so spoiled! How's David doing? Any more sad poems?"

"No, he's been cheerful and chipper ever since his return from the school trip."

"And you? Did you try the chocolate cure?"

"No, but I'm better anyway. We really did have fun this weekend. My big news is that tomorrow I will finally bite the bullet. I'm going in town to sign up for the fall French class series at the International Women's Center."

"Are you nervous about it?"

"Not about registering. Everyone at the Center speaks English."

"Are you still reading newspapers and working on vocabulary in the meantime?"

"Yes, but I don't feel I'm making much progress. We have a crew here that's started some repair work in the basement. David thinks my interaction with the workmen will help my French, but anything beyond *Bonjour, Merci,* and *Au revoir* requires David's intervention, because I keep getting even the simplest messages wrong. The other day, I told David that the plumber was coming at 7:00 a.m., but of course, I misunderstood. It was the heating technician, and he showed up at 17:00, which is 5:00 p.m."

"I can see where that might pose a *serieuse problème,*" Bibi concurred.

"*Une problème serieuse,*" Jenny corrected. "The French usually put their adjectives after their nouns. And actually, I could be wrong about the gender. I think it may be *un problème serieux.*"

"See, you *are* making progress!"

Jenny didn't share Bibi's confidence, but the next day, she successfully negotiated the bus and tram connections and signed up for the Center's French program. She had rehearsed the run earlier with David, so she understood the fares and the ticket machines. It was only on the return trip that she noticed with dismay that two different trams ran on the same track. She wasn't sure which was the correct one. *Don't panic. Don't panic.* She took a deep breath. *Logic and reason. You can walk it, Jenny. Just stay on Route de Chêne. Eventually you'll get to the cross street for the bus.* In roughly thirty minutes, she reached the bus stop, only to discover that, except during rush hour, the bus ran just once an hour. She faced a forty-five minute wait. *I can do it on foot in less than that.*

She was pleased with herself by the time she reached home. *Good weather – good walk – good exercise!* She fixed a quick lunch, then retreated to her office. She filed the instructions regarding her French course, and considered her next project. One of the bookshelves housed a stack of songbooks and sheet music from school programs in which Sandie had participated. *This is a good time to tackle those,* Jenny decided. *I'm sure the school's music department would appreciate having them.* She pulled the relevant binders off the bookshelf and started to sort them. Halfway through a pile of opera scores, she found a Salève College catalog.

Jenny knew before she opened the cover exactly what she would find. The first page featured "A Message from the College President," complete with a smiling photo of Julien Charbonnet. "Oh, Sandie," she sighed. It was yet another piece of evidence to add to a mounting pile, but Jenny felt no satisfaction in its discovery. She took the catalog out to the garage and stuck it deep into the paper-recycling bin.

From: JWLongworth
To: Ross
Date: June 10, 2002
Subject: Stepping back
  I just found another article-cum-photograph, hidden in Sandie's music collection. I'm convinced the affair happened, but I'm struggling to understand the "why" of it. My mind just keeps spinning out new questions.

I think I've viewed Sandie through a distorted lens. I always assumed that she was happy and self-confident. Yet Sandie once confided to her friend Olga that, regarding David's proposal of marriage, "I caught the train between stations. Purely by chance," she told Olga, "I was in the right place at the right moment."

That could be me, talking about David's decision to marry me because *I* was in the right place at the right moment. So if *I* sometimes worry that the passage of time might change his perspective and interest, might the same have been true for Sandie?

Maybe she didn't feel as secure as I once thought. And if David seemed less attentive as their marriage progressed, might it have heightened Sandie's insecurities and made her fear she was no longer attractive to him?

Spin, spin, spin. The wheels are whirring away, but we're off to Paris soon to help Dellie move, and after that we go into heavy countdown for the end of the school term. Unless something cataclysmic happens between now and then, I won't pester you further with my speculations until we get to Boston in July. Meanwhile, I'm going to try to step back from this issue and see if I can come back to it later with a fresh perspective.

With thanks for your patience and forbearance, much love, Jenny

PS – Hugs to Kevin

From: Ross
To: Jewel
Date: June 10, 2002
Subject: Re: Stepping back

You're not pestering me, Jewel, but I do agree that you should step back from the issue. And when you're ready to tackle it again, I suggest you start by cluing David in on everything you've come across – and thought about – thus far. He's not a child to be shielded from the truth. Don't treat him like one.

Good luck with the fresh perspective!

Love, Ross

Grace

While sipping wine, I watch the progress
Of the night across the village.
In the east, a deep December blue;
No early winter moon is yet in view
Above the jagged, snow-capped Alps,
Already pearl gray against the darkening sky.
The south still holds a sweep of light,
Washed-out aqua, muslin-white.
To the west, gold bleeds to crimson, my sight
Of nearby trees now silhouettes.
I pause to fill my glass again,
Then check the evolution of the light.
The eastern darkness drowns
The afternoon's late blue. Low clouds,
Once white, now cloak the mountain ridges
In somber shades of splotchy gray.
Fading azure columns stream westward down
Bands of setting sunlight towards the red
And yellow glow, gathering to make
A final fight against the dark. Sunshine
glinting on a distant airplane wing
Commands my eye.
Contrails mark the quiet battlefield
Below the stars.
How much grace can blueness buy?

D.P. – December, 1997

Chapter 5

Delphine had spent her freshman year in an apartment on Rue Capron, near Place Clichy, but the apartment owners wanted it back for the summer. "I'm going to have to move just as we're starting exams," she lamented.

"Don't worry," her father counseled. "We'll come to Paris and help you."

After a brief hunt, Delphine found a sublet on Rue Coquillière, in the first *arrondissement*, near Place des Victoires. When the time came for the transition, David and Jenny took a Friday evening train to Paris. Saturday morning, they headed to the department stores to help furnish Delphine's new quarters.

"Let's check out the neighborhood," David suggested after they dropped off their purchases. As they explored the area, David nodded his head in approval. Rue Coquillière was full of life, with little shops, three produce vendors, a *charcuterie*, a bakery, cafés, a laundry, and a wine bar, where they stopped for lunch. A cheery waitress in her late forties handed them a one-page summary of the lunch choices, followed by eight or nine pages of wine possibilities.

"Only in France are the wine lists longer than the menus," Jenny observed with amusement.

Toward the end of the meal, David mentioned to the waitress that Delphine had just moved to the *quartier*. "I hope I can count on you," he joked, "to see that my daughter behaves and eats right."

The waitress understood the fatherly concern that underlay the banter and asked where the apartment was. "You must stop here often," she told Delphine, "and you must tell me if you have any problems. My name is Sandrine, and you can ask for me anytime."

Father and daughter exchanged a wide-eyed glance. *David must be delighted to find a nearby mother-substitute to keep an eye on Dellie the way Madame Lamont used to do at Rue Capron,* Jenny assumed.

"That's absolutely incredible," David declared after the waitress left their table.

"What's incredible?" Jenny asked.

"Her name," he replied.

"Sorry? Her French was too fast for me, and with the surrounding chatter, I didn't catch her name."

"It's Sandrine," David said softly. "It's Sandie."

Only then did Jenny understand the enormity of what had transpired. *He must see it as a sign that Sandie is somehow watching over Dellie.*

They transferred Delphine's clothes and books from her old apartment on Sunday morning. "Do you want help unpacking?" her father asked.

"No thanks, Dad. I'd rather do it at my own pace."

Leaving Delphine surrounded by boxes, David and Jenny went for a stroll in the direction of the Seine. They stopped at a café along the embankment, then started over the Pont des Arts – the wide footbridge at the head of the Ile St. Louis. Halfway across, they paused to observe the progress of the barges heading downstream.

"This is where we scattered some of Sandie's ashes," said David, matter-of-factly.

Jenny watched the water swirl around the abutments. "The Pont des Arts was a good choice," she said gently. "This is a beautiful spot. I remember your story that you and the children had to hold off while a barge passed, lest Sandie's ashes go onto the boat instead of into the river."

She drew a slow breath. *This is as good a time as any,* she told herself. "You know," she began, "that reminds me. Just before we came here to help Dellie move, she asked if I could track down some documentation for a course credit from l'Académie Internationale. I went looking for it in the binders Sandie kept, and I came across a *Testament* Sandie wrote. It expressed her wish that Julien Charbonnet assume the role of guardian if something happened to you and Sandie before Marc and Dellie turned twenty-one."

David looked at Jenny with keen interest, but made no comment.

"The issue is half moot, because Marc's now a legal adult, but Dellie still has a bit to go. Having a valid directive about a guardian is important. There could be financial issues relating to the house. Given your concerns about Julien, however, it might be a good idea to revise the document."

David pursed his lips, but said nothing.

"If you want, I'd certainly be willing to take on a guardianship. You could also turn to Michel and Josette, or maybe Mehrak and Manuela."

"Do it," he said crisply.

"Do which?" she replied.

"Redo the *Testament* with your name as guardian. You can copy the French, or write it in English. It doesn't matter. I'll sign it, and when I have a chance, I'll ask Michel and Mehrak to serve as back-up."

Jenny nodded silently, leaving David room to take the subject further. Instead, he shifted focus entirely.

"Let's pick up some *madeleines*. I'd like to check out that bakery near Delphine's apartment."

"Is it okay if I go backpacking in Spain this summer?" Delphine asked as the three of them consumed the pastries. "Two girls from my History of Art class want to do a trek. We'll probably start in Barcelona and head up to Catalonia and the Pyrenees. We're thinking sort of mid-July to mid-August."

David had been looking forward to having Delphine back home, but he was supportive of the plan. "Actually, that's good timing," Jenny said. "Your father and I have been talking about a trip to Boston," she noted, reminding David of a recent conversation, "and we can fit it into the same time frame, so we'll see you on both ends."

They said their goodbyes and caught a cab to the Gare de Lyon. The train was crowded with passengers who, like them, had spent the weekend in Paris and were now homeward bound. As the journey progressed, the train began to empty. When enough seats opened up, David moved across the aisle. "This will give you more room," he said.

That's an odd comment, Jenny thought. *I'd rather stay snuggled against him than have all the room in the world.* She was about to protest, then thought better of it. *Maybe David is the one who needs more room — more space to process the emotions evoked by the mention of Julien, the memories from the Pont des Arts, and a helpful waitress named Sandrine.* David stared out the window for the rest of the journey, silent and still.

The following day, when Jenny presented David with the revised *Testament,* he signed it, dated it, and handed it back to her. "That should do it. Thanks," he said, but nothing more.

What is he thinking? Should I push? Jenny wondered as she filed the *Testament* in her legal folder. Uncertain as to her next step, she checked her in-box. From Bibi, there was a forwarded collection of cute dog and cat photos with captions. Beneath a soulful golden retriever's face it read: "One reason a dog can be such a comfort when you're feeling blue is that he doesn't try to find out why." *Maybe I need to practice a more canine-like approach to David's reticence,* Jenny considered, *and just give him space.*

The final week of school was packed with end-of-year activities, among them a special concert in honor of Josette's retirement. As they took their seats in the school auditorium, Jenny sensed that it was a bittersweet moment for David. "The original group of teachers whose work and team concept drew me to Geneva is all but gone now," he remarked. "I'm the last of the dinosaurs."

The program began with a performance of Josette's favorite opera duets and arias. The first offering was a sprightly piece from the Marriage of Figaro, but the next series was from Cosi fan Tutte, romantic and emotional. Jenny could see David struggling to control tears. It was a struggle he lost. Not only were these Josette's favorite pieces; they had been Sandie's as well. David got worse as the program continued, and Jenny got worse right along with him, holding his hand tightly in hers. The final piece was Offenbach's *Belle nuit, o nuit d'amour*. David dissolved. The instant the lights went up, he fled the room on the pretext of needing a cigarette. Jenny sat for a moment thinking he would return. When he didn't, she went in search and found him just outside on the stair ramp, smoking with Olga's husband Jacques. Though they were talking, David's gaze avoided Jacques' eyes, wandering instead through the trees and squinting at the parking lot lights. Jenny stood by silently, waiting for their conversation to end.

Adelaide Swanton appeared, brightly clad in an embroidered Argentinean summer frock. "Could I leave my car here and ride with you and David to Josette's retirement dinner?"

"Of course," Jenny answered, trying to summon a smile.

"Do you have an allergy?" Adelaide inquired, studying Jenny's face. "Or is this emotion?"

"Emotion," Jenny admitted. She and Adelaide walked down the ramp a ways. "That music must have included Sandie's favorite pieces, because David choked up early in the program and hasn't recovered yet. It hurts to realize there's nothing I can do to help him."

"Some things we just have to go through alone," Adelaide commiserated. "Would you prefer that I go in my own car?"

"No," Jenny answered. "Actually, it might be better if you're with us. When David gets sad, he doesn't like to talk about it until the emotion has passed. Your presence will give him a chance to regain control. And maybe me too."

And indeed, David's equilibrium was quickly restored. When they reached the restaurant, he swiftly joined the throng, cracking jokes and chatting with colleagues.

Dinner was served in a courtyard entirely taken over by the retirement party. David and Jenny sat with Michel and several DuPont family members. The minute Jenny was settled, Josette's brother, sitting next to her, lit up a cigarette, as did his wife across from her.

Even though they were outdoors, the smoke drifted sideways, not up. Jenny looked at David helplessly, and he traded seats with her. Then behind her, at a table not three feet away, several other people lit up. David was protective, but there wasn't much that he could do. *Look happy, Jenny,* she kept thinking. *Don't embarrass David in front of his friends.*

She struggled to nod and clap at all the right moments, but she couldn't follow the speeches. The group started singing songs she didn't know. *I am so obviously an outsider that everyone in the restaurant must see it.* The street noises startled her. She jumped at an unexpected horn blast. She couldn't stop her hand from trembling as she clutched her wine glass, fighting against panic. Finally, finally, they left and dropped Adelaide back at school to collect her car. Only then did Jenny's breathing return to normal. To conquer her own malaise, she turned her attention to David.

"You hit some rough spots during the concert this evening," she ventured.

"That's life," was his comment.

"It helps me when you can talk about it," she prodded gently.

For a moment there was silence. Then, "Music tends to get to me," he said. "I'm not sure why. I really did have a good time," he reassured her. "Yes, there were some holes I fell into, but there were lots of good things happening alongside the sad reminders. I was just as aware of those good things as I was of the pain. For me, the joy in the occasion isn't lost just because there is also some sorrow involved."

He's in better shape than I give him credit for, Jenny admitted. She considered telling him how she had fared during the evening, but decided against it. *I'll be able to talk about it more objectively after a good night's sleep.*

As she had hoped, she felt better in the morning and related the previous night's travails over breakfast. "It's nothing new and surprising, but still, I'm sorry I wasn't a cheerful participant in Josette's celebration."

"Why apologize?" he asked. "I was down part of the time too."

Delphine called from Paris in the late afternoon. "Is Dad home yet?" she asked when Jenny answered.

"No, he's still at school. They're getting things ready for this evening's student theatre production."

"Um…."

Jenny sensed Delphine's hesitation.

"Is there anything I can help with?"

"Not really. He sounded kind of distant when I called last night," Delphine said. "I just wanted to apologize in case I woke him up."

"You didn't wake him up. It was a hard night for him." Jenny described the concert, the arias and David's tearful reaction.

"Well, if last night was hard, tonight will be hard too," said Delphine matter-of-factly. "Mom participated in most of the plays at school, and they'll probably say something about her. So better not wear any makeup," she cautioned.

It was close to six when David came home. He and Jenny ate a quick supper, then drove back to the school for the performance. During the intermission, a teacher Jenny didn't know came over to greet David. Dropping her voice, the teacher said, "This is the week that was, David. I'm so sorry. I do remember."

"Thank you," he said. "So do I."

At first Jenny didn't understand the reference. "What was she talking about?" Jenny asked David in a whisper.

"Sandie's scan results came during the last week of school," he answered. "Sandie insisted on postponing the start of her chemo until after Delphine's graduation."

She must have understood that it was the beginning of the end, Jenny assumed.

At the close of the play, the faculty director thanked the performers and helpers. As Delphine had predicted, the director made reference to Sandrine Perry, but Jenny couldn't understand the remarks. She looked at David, but he made no move to translate, and he remained silent on the drive home.

I'm not going to push on this, Jenny decided. *If he wants to talk about it, he'll talk about it, on his own timetable.*

David capped the end of the school term with a backyard barbecue for the French language program staff. The party lasted late. Most of the guests departed by nine, but the hard core gathered on the terrace, contentedly smoking and sipping brandy. Jenny had to retreat because of the smoke, so she busied herself cleaning up in the kitchen. Finally, lest her absence seem rude, she rejoined the group, settling at the far end of the table to distance herself from the fumes. David was telling the gathering about the weekend with Delphine in Paris, highlighting his exchange with the waitress who was Sandie's namesake. Not surprisingly, at the end of the story, several members of the assembled group stole discreet glances in Jenny's direction to assess her reaction.

Is it always going to be like this when David has friends over? Jenny wondered. *Me hanging about at the edge of the circle, trying to keep up with the language but away from the smoke?*

After a few minutes, Olga left her seat and came over to sit beside Jenny. She had spots of color on her cheeks in witness to an evening of wine and camaraderie, but there was always something grave about Olga's face. With her Slavic features and her intense eyes, Olga reminded Jenny of a gypsy fortuneteller gazing into her crystal ball. Fortuneteller or not, Olga was uncanny in her ability to read people.

Pitching her voice below the general chatter, Olga frowned, placed a hand on Jenny's arm and said, "I know you are strong. But you are carrying too much. I am here for you. For *you.* Not for Sandie. You are the one who is alive." Jenny was startled by Olga's words. She felt her throat go tight and her eyes begin to sting. Olga had definitely struck a nerve.

"It would be nice to have lunch or something," Jenny admitted.

"School is over for David and the teachers, but we in administration must keep working. Let us not put this off. Come tomorrow? At noon perhaps?"

"That should be okay," Jenny answered. "I'll check with David."

"David!" Olga called out, preempting her. "I steal your bride for lunch at my office tomorrow. This is possible, yes?"

David raised his glass in confirmation, and the date was made.

Jenny packed a picnic lunch for two, and David dropped her at the school at noon. She sat in the small lobby at the entrance to the administration building and waited. When it got to be 12:20, she worried that she might be in the wrong place, but Olga rushed in a few minutes later.

"I am so sorry!" Olga exclaimed. "I had to work off campus this morning. Then there was an accident near the Mont Blanc Bridge, and I was stuck in traffic," Olga complained, as Jenny laid out slices of David's Cajun meatloaf, a half loaf of *semi-complet* bread, and a wedge of soft cheese. "Because of my delay, I will not have as long as I wish for us to talk."

"Then we should start right away," said Jenny. "It's been almost two years since we first met, and I still don't know how you ended up in Geneva. David said you grew up in Romania and spent several years in the States. There must be a good story behind all that!"

"Good, I don't know, but it has been an interesting life!" Olga briefly described her journey from childhood behind the Iron Curtain, through teenage years with relatives in America, then to France with her first husband. "When he died, I was there in Paris with a small son. It was a miracle to meet Jacques. It is how I know what David feels since you have come to Geneva. Jacques has family in the Haute Savoie, so we moved here. My languages helped me find work at l'Académie Internationale, and since Jacques is a writer, it was easy for him to work at home and take care of my son when he was little."

"How did Jacques feel about being the stay-at-home parent?"

"There I was lucky! Jacques doesn't feel he must only live the traditional role of a man. He has been an excellent mother as well as a father!" she laughed. "And you?" she asked. "What is it like for you to be the stepparent?"

"A challenge," Jenny answered candidly. "I have to be careful with parental issues. My advice and viewpoint are just as likely to add fuel to the fire as they are to calm whatever storm is brewing."

"Have there been problems with the children?"

"It's more that David and I have philosophical differences when it comes to the kids. I think Dellie could benefit from some *laissez faire*, while Marc really needs structure and accountability. I'm really sorry Sandie isn't here to help Marc find the confidence to go forward, because I see no simple way to help him. He seems like a really unhappy young man. I can sense his distance. It's almost as if he's wary of me. Dellie is usually friendly and open, but even with her, there have been some incidents that make it clear that she's not ready to fully accept me into the family.

"Negotiating issues relating to the children is further complicated because I have to factor David into the mix. I promised him I would bow to his final judgment concerning Marc and Dellie, but he's incredibly protective and often reacts emotionally rather than logically when something is amiss. Josette once commented that David is trying to shoulder the role of mother as well as father, making him doubly concerned when things go awry. He's like a lioness guarding a pair of cubs."

"And you are very different in how you see things?"

"Very. I'll give you an example. Dellie's college expenses are being paid out of a small education trust I set up when Sandie was still alive. This past semester, Dellie had a class field trip to Spain that required an extra fee."

"I know of this trust," Olga interjected. "I had several conversations with Sandie about it. But I interrupt. Go on."

"Dellie was late asking for a wire transfer of money for the field trip, and she called home in a state of panic, fearing she had blown her chances of going. David reacted as if the world were about to end. He was ready to race off to Paris. 'I'll damn well get on a train and deliver the fee myself!'

"I argued that we should help Dellie consider ways to solve the problem on her own."

"How did David react?" Olga queried.

"He didn't want to hear it."

"And how did it end?" Olga asked.

"David was so agitated that he overlooked one of the rational options – sending money via an overnight delivery service to Paris. When I pointed this out, it bought us some time. The problem was mooted when Dellie called back to report that despite the tight timing, the wire transfer had cleared her bank, and the crisis was over."

"So perhaps you are a better stepmother than you think," Olga suggested.

"No, just a better financial manager. And though I believe David is too protective of his children, I have to admit that when it's *me* he's protecting, I love it. I had to take care of myself for a long time. It's wonderful to have someone else really look out for you. So my complaints in that area may be a little hypocritical.

"At least with Dellie," Jenny continued, "the problems are mostly external. She may struggle with bank procedures and school timetables, but her outlook on life is positive. She bounces back quickly from setbacks. Unfortunately, Marc's still floundering, trying to find his place. As I said, I think he could benefit from a lot more discipline, but David leans toward letting him find his own path."

"I don't know Marc well," Olga confessed, "but I do remember that at school, he was a difficult student. There were sometimes problems that were covered over, for Sandie's sake. Her friends had no wish to worry her when Marc upset a class or broke rules."

"That's too bad," Jenny rejoined. "It doesn't serve a child to ignore bad behavior, and in the long run, it doesn't serve the parents either. In any event, both Marc and Dellie are young adults now, and certainly don't look to me for mothering. I think they prefer to see me solely as an old family friend, not as their stepmother. In truth, I see myself that way too. The bakery gave out roses to its customers for Mother's Day, and David brought one back to the house. I didn't feel right claiming it for myself, so I put it into one of Sandie's window pitchers. Sandie is still the real mother in that family."

"Yes, Sandie adored her children," Olga agreed thoughtfully. "During the difficult times, that is what held the marriage together."

Jenny looked at Olga in surprise. *What did I just hear?*

"Perhaps Sandie did not speak of this with you," Olga said, considering the expression on Jenny's face, "but it was not always an easy marriage – at least, not for Sandie. When they first came to Geneva, David was completely occupied in learning how to teach middle-school children. Sandie was home by herself with Marc and Delphine. She was hurt that David seemed to care more about his job than about her."

"David told me that he practically lived at the school for their first few years here," Jenny acknowledged cautiously. "He sat in on other teachers' classes, attended seminars and workshops, and did everything he could to find his sea-legs and hone his skills."

"This is true," Olga confirmed. "David wanted to be excellent as a teacher, but there was a great cost for his family life. He was so often absent that Sandie felt abandoned. She began to fear that David saw her primarily as a helpmeet. But her maternal commitment was absolute. There was only once when she seriously thought about divorce."

"Divorce!"

"You are shocked," Olga observed. "But see it from Sandie's point of view. As the children grew, she took a job to give more opportunities for them. David is not a man to be selfish with money. He does not wear an expensive watch, or want the newest computer. But he is not careful. He doesn't make budget plans."

Jenny couldn't help but smile. *Olga's right about that*, she thought. *David is hopeless at balancing the family checkbook, much less at projecting a realistic budget.*

"It was Sandie's dream to have a house, not to live always in an apartment. To buy that house, she pledged her entire pension fund as – what is the word?"

"A down payment? Loan collateral?"

"Yes, those things the bank needs to give a mortgage. She planned for every payment, every expense. Then, the week they moved into their new home, David called a man to plant the front of the house with azalea bushes. He did not ask Sandie. The cost was over five thousand Swiss francs. There was no money to pay for this."

"I've heard this story from his friends and from David himself," Jenny interjected. "He said Sandie was so angry that she couldn't decide whether to divorce him or just murder him on the spot. He sort of laughed about it when he told me."

"Well, be assured, it was not a joke. You have the expression, the straw that breaks the camel's back? Sandie was worried by the finances of the new house. She felt she carried the whole emotional and strategic burden. David had a higher salary, but always it was Sandie who held the budget within bounds. With the new house especially, every *centime* was critical. Now suddenly David did something to put her life dream in danger. For Sandie it was the end. She came to me with her despair. 'He is the father of my children, and I love him for that, but he is always off in his own world. I get nothing from him but worries!'"

Jenny listened, struggling to realign her image of Sandie's marriage with Olga's tale.

"Sandie was crying – and furious. 'He doesn't care about the house, and he doesn't care about me! It's over! I can't do this any more!' I could not help her about the azaleas, but by the end of the afternoon, I was able to convince her that David *did* care very much about her – that his love was real and present, even if it didn't take the form she wanted."

"How did you manage that?"

"I made her listen to a story," Olga answered. "I was at the hospital when Sandie had her mastectomy. This was the summer before they bought the house. David was there too, of course, and we waited for Sandie to wake up from the anesthesia. There was an unexpected problem. Sandie suddenly was in a coma. When the doctor told David, he collapsed into a chair, bent over, and hid his face with his hands. It was so clear to me then that David was very frightened that he might lose Sandie. It was so clear that he really loved her. That is the story I told her – the story of what I saw in the hospital. David is not romantic. He doesn't say sweet things. But Sandie finally believed that David's love for her was sincere."

Jenny shook her head. "I've heard several references to the azalea crisis, but I never dreamed that the marriage came so close to foundering. Sandie's choice of you as a confidante may well have saved it," Jenny commented.

Olga looked as if she were about to say something, but instead checked her watch. "I am so sorry," she said. "The clock ticks. I must return to work." But as she rose to leave, she paused. "What I told you at the party last night, I meant it. You worry too much about honoring Sandie and taking care of David. You cannot forget to honor and take care of *yourself*. David is a good man. A very kind man. But he does not always recognize that a husband must work hard to keep the love of a wife. His new wife. His present wife. He should not always say Sandie's name every few minutes. You should not have to put up with that," she added.

"Olga, I *am* taking care of myself. I'm not 'putting up' with David's feelings. My strategy is to make sure that he knows he can trust me with them. A ban on references to Sandie would force David to keep a part of himself hidden. I'd rather show him that our relationship is strong enough to weather all this."

"He's lucky you see it that way," she said.

Jenny considered this. "I appreciate what you're saying. If this were an early courtship – a new relationship – I'd probably keep a safe distance until he got past all this emotional upheaval. But I've known David through thick and thin. We're like brother and sister, except for the obvious sexual attraction. I accept him – and love him – the way he is."

Olga gave a neutral nod and closed the discussion. "I know you leave soon for America, but we must do this again when you are back from your summer travels. There is so much to talk about," she added as they exchanged a goodbye cheek kiss.

As she sat on the bus, homeward bound, Jenny replayed the conversation with Olga in her mind. *This is huge!* she thought. *David couldn't see Sandie's insecurities. Sandie couldn't see his love. And I couldn't see any of it. I thought their marriage was close to perfect. It's one of the reasons I always made it a point to show my respect for her, both when she was alive and after she died. "You worry too much about honoring Sandie," Olga thinks. But she views it as a selfless act. It's far more complicated. If I didn't honor Sandie, it would be difficult for David, impossible for the kids, and an invitation to sabotage by Sandie's friends.*

"How was your lunch?" David asked when Jenny walked in.

"Interesting," Jenny replied. "I really like Olga. She ...." Jenny paused when she spotted Marc's jacket thrown over the back of the couch. "Marc is here?" she asked.

"He's downstairs using your printer," David advised. "He has to make copies of something for the photojournalism program in San Francisco. I think he may actually see it through this time."

"Maybe Dellie's positive experience at American University is motivating Marc to give academia another chance," Jenny suggested.

"At least he seems to be on track for the move to the States," David noted. "I think it will help Marc enormously to get out of Geneva. Moving to Paris opened up new worlds for me when I was his age. I'm hoping Marc will experience a similar epiphany in San Francisco."

"A fresh start doesn't guarantee a change in outlook," Jenny cautioned, "but I agree with you that at least it enhances the possibility."

Marc emerged a few minutes later, papers in hand.

119

"Is there anything else you need?" David asked him. "Anything we can assist with in terms of logistics or other paperwork?"

The question was innocent, but Marc's reply was defensive. "I can take care of these things myself," he declared archly. He was out the door in less than a minute. He managed a "goodbye," but "thank you" was noticeably absent.

"I hope he *does* take care of things," David commented, shaking his head, "for his sake and his mother's. Education was enormously important to Sandie. Her own mother died while Sandie was still in high school. She had to go to work before she could graduate. She always felt insecure intellectually because of that," David reported. "She was very smart and very capable. She took enormous pride in her role in l'Académie Internationale's administration, but the lack of a diploma really bothered her. That's why she fought so hard to live long enough to see Delphine get her baccalaureate. When the ceremony was over, she looked at me and said, 'Now I can die.'"

Was Sandie intimidated by David's Harvard education? Did the admiration of the school principal help shore up her sense of her intellectual worth? Jenny wondered. *I'll have to ask Olga about that.*

Out loud, she shifted her focus back to the children. "How proud Sandie would be," Jenny remarked, "if she could see Dellie now, going to college in Paris and doing well in her studies. But by the same token, how anxious she would be for Marc, worrying about when – or whether – he's going to take hold of his life and move forward. Still, it's you, not Sandie, who's front and center. You're the one carrying the parenting burden, and I'm not much help. I'm afraid I'll say or do the wrong thing, and it will all backfire, torpedoing the San Francisco plans. Do you have any counsel about the best way to interact with Marc?"

"I haven't been sure of the best way to interact with Marc since he turned thirteen," David replied. "We had fun together when he was little, but the hormones hit with a vengeance, and after that it was rough sailing. For a long time we disagreed about almost everything. The only point of connection was art. I signed up for an art class on the human form and invited Marc to join me. The first time we went, he was startled by the nude model, but he got past that in two minutes, and he loved the course. He was good at drawing and serious about it. It gave us an activity to do and talk about together. Of course, his drawing skills quickly morphed into what he calls 'urban art.' The year Sandie got sick, I found a knapsack in the garage with half a dozen cans of spray paint. When I asked Marc about it, he was evasive and insisted it belonged to a friend of his. Under the circumstances, I didn't pursue it."

"Valerie mentioned graffiti as a current and regular activity," Jenny pointed out. "Has Marc given any indication of taking his interest to a more adult level? Maybe he could get involved in graphic design of some sort. It's not a bad way to make a living."

"Marc doesn't take kindly to suggestions, but he may get there on his own. Meanwhile, there are worse things Marc could be doing than graffiti," David concluded.

The conversation moved to easier topics. "I'd like to do a Fourth of July barbecue before we take off for Boston," David said. "Delphine will be home, and we can invite the neighbors. We'll have to do it on the sixth, though," David noted, "because the fourth is a Thursday and a normal work day."

The day of the barbecue, Marc and Valerie came over early afternoon to do laundry and help set up. After loading the washing machine, Valerie joined Jenny and Delphine in the kitchen, but Marc disappeared into his basement room. As she picked up a knife to help with slicing salad vegetables, Valerie reported that she and Marc were in the middle of another fight. "We are not speaking to each other all day. I am over with his behavior and his attitude. All he does is stay out late with his dropout friends. They think they are so big, smoking hashish and painting political words on walls. If he cannot change from this, I have no wish to go to America with him, and I have told him this."

Delphine said something in rapid French and Valerie laughed. The conversation shifted to Delphine's Paris adventures and went back and forth in both French and English. "Where is he gone?" asked Valerie when the salads were finished. "Marc should help with the *préparations.*"

Valerie went down to the basement in search of him, and suddenly the house was filled with angry shouts. David came in from the terrace, raced down the stairs and braved the storm. Marc was screaming at Valerie. Jenny couldn't understand his French, but the tone was chilling.

"Stop it, Marc," David commanded, quietly but firmly. "Stop it *now.*"

Marc kept shrieking, his yells reverberating through the house.

"Calm down, Marc. I mean it." Keeping his voice level, David ordered Marc to leave. "You are not welcome to return until you can conduct yourself in a civil manner."

Marc stomped out, spewing curses as he went and slamming the front door behind him. Valerie was in tears. "Will you be okay?" David asked her, giving her a hug. She nodded and followed him back to the kitchen. "I'd appreciate it if you-all would just carry on," David told Jenny and Delphine. "Everything will settle down. I'm going to go out and find Marc."

Half an hour later, David appeared with a scowling Marc in tow. Marc mumbled an apology. Jenny caught the phrase "infantile behavior." Marc remained withdrawn for the rest of the afternoon. David achieved a superficial change of gears and concentrated on setting up for the barbecue, but Jenny could see that he was still processing the incident.

Around six, the guests began to arrive. Jenny remained tense from the blow-up, but she did her best to appear serene on the surface. Children ate picnic-style on towels spread out on the grass while their parents gathered around the patio table. Their neighbor Mehrak was suffering from a disc problem, so rather than sit, he walked slowly around the table, plate in hand. "I am being very careful," he said. "I hope I can treat this with only physical therapy. Back operations are very serious."

"I can sympathize with your concern," David commented. "Sandie was extremely fearful of back surgery. The issue came up front and center when a scan revealed a lesion on one of her vertebra, four years after her mastectomy."

David spoke French with clearer enunciation and stronger consonants than native speakers, which allowed Jenny to follow most of his words. Her comprehension was also made easier by the fact that she knew the story. She and Sandie had discussed the lesion on several occasions.

"Because I am still young," Sandie had told her, "and because there is just this one spot, my doctor thinks that surgery to remove the vertebra will be best. The problem is that it is a very heavy surgery." Anxious about the pain, the risk, and the lengthy physical therapy involved, Sandie sought opinions from other oncologists. "The *spécialiste* we have seen in Lyon worries that to remove the vertebra may make the cancer spread much faster," she explained. "He suggests to test often, but not to have the surgery until everything else is tried first."

"When Sandie found a doctor who shared her reluctance," David continued, "she refused the surgery. She put her faith in radiation and a revised hormone regimen instead. She was willing to try anything to avoid that operation."

Would a different choice have brought a different outcome? Does David still wonder about that? He must, thought Jenny.

As the evening wore on, Delphine left the gathering to meet friends in town. Marc and Valerie followed in short order, but not before David briefly took them aside. "Be gentle with each other," he cautioned. "Life is very short."

A few of the neighbors withdrew after dessert, but the remainder settled down for an evening of conversation. David carried some plates inside and then disappeared. Jenny went indoors to retrieve another bottle of wine and found him puttering happily in the kitchen, starting a stock with rib bones and leftover vegetables. "David, please!" she scolded, attempting to shoo him back outside.

"I need you out there. I can't do the French, and you're the host, for heavens sake! Come join your own party!"

"Just like Sandie!" he rejoined. "I attend my parties the way I attend my parties. This is what I do," he teased.

"That doesn't make it right," Jenny retorted. "If Sandie and I agree on something, you should listen to us."

"You and Sandie agree on almost everything anyway," David countered, "but that doesn't make you right." He waited another five minutes in a show of independence, then rejoined their guests.

"You were incredible with Marc today," Jenny told David when they finally climbed into bed. "For your sake as well as his, I hope you're right that there's a sweet kid hiding out beneath that spiky exterior."

"That spiky exterior, as far as I can see, is a thick coat of armor. He told me that he and Valerie had a major fight this morning. She made it clear that she doesn't want to go with him to the US. I think the prospect of going alone is frightening for him. He's certainly traveled on his own. He doesn't have your agoraphobic leanings. But this isn't travel so much as crossing the divide between adolescence and adulthood. He's avoided it for some time now, and I have the feeling that it scares the shit out of him, especially since he no longer has his mother around to make him feel loved and safe."

"He has *your* love."

"Yes, but I'm not sure how much he feels he can rely on it. Maybe my kind of love doesn't make him feel safe. I don't want to show him the path. I want him to find his own."

"Well, I think you do a good job as a father."

"Mmmpff," was his response.

"Your spare ribs were pretty good too," she added, proffering a good night kiss.

"I should hope so!" he replied.

The next morning, Jenny readied things for their trip to Boston and went in search of a plastic folder for their itinerary. Amid the office supplies she found yet another article about Julien Charbonnet, with another smiling photo front and center. Jenny shook her head. *This is wearing me down!* Like its predecessors, she put the article into the paper-recycling bin, sequestered in the junk mail.

Jenny and David took their evening wine on the terrace and surveyed the garden. Normally the view was a source of pleasure, but it had been suddenly marred by the arrival of a monstrous crane newly set up in a corner of the pasture behind their house, looming over the tall hedge which usually guaranteed their privacy.

"My god, David! That crane is enormous. I've never seen one that big."

"Swiss buildings are made with poured concrete," David explained. "That crane means they're finally going to build the new houses they've been talking about for so long. That thing's going to be there all summer and beyond."

"Yecch!" said Jenny, making a sour face. "It looks brooding and malevolent. Totally out of place. It reminds me of those hulking mechanical battle beasts in *Star Wars*."

"It reminds me of the summer Sandie was ill," David said quietly. "A small cluster of row houses was being built about three blocks away. The crane arrived when Sandie got sick. It stayed until she died."

To their dismay, the crane again proved to be a herald of grim news. The evening brought word that Graham Wells, David's college roommate and lifelong friend, had a cancerous tumor.

From: Graham
To: David; Jenny
Date: July 7, 2002
Subject: bit of a problem
Dear ones, Well, I went in for a hemorrhoid banding, but they found an abscess, and behind that, a tumor. So, not so good. However, CAT scan indicates no spread. Cell type also best possible, kind that is generally cured completely by radiation plus chemo, without surgery,

which means you get to keep your basic equipment and don't have to buy plastic and all.

I'm starting daily rads immediately. When you arrive in Boston, I'll be in the hospital, bored, and eager to see you.

Love you, Graham

This is the last thing David needs right now, Jenny thought as she read Graham's e-mail over David's shoulder.

Graham and David were like brothers, with a history that went back nearly forty years. This was devastating news. David went immediately to the telephone, but only got as far as Graham's answering service. Jenny went to her computer.

From: JWLongworth
To: Graham
cc: DavidP
Date: July 7, 2002
Subject: Re: bit of a problem

Hi, G. You're lucky they caught this early. I know the treatment won't be fun, having been there, but cancer can be life-changing in good ways. It helps, of course, to survive it, so you can be around to experience the changes it brings.

We'll be on your side of the Atlantic in less than a week. Hang in there.

Love, Jenny

July, 2002

In honor of Amber's cat

Seen sideways, cats, when walking,
Calmly move like
Slowly clenching and unclenching fists,
Muscles riding rhythmically up and down,
Rolling systematically around,
Ample proof of latent power,
Little left, it seems, to luck.

Viewed in front, their forepaws nimbly
Bending and unbending
On a bias like a bowing
Ballerina's wrists, they add
A primadonna's lithesome grace,
Willowy as waving flowers.

Beheld from behind,
And strange as it may seem,
They waddle like a duck.
Though I may one day change my view,
That's how I see it now, and you?

Chapter 6

David called Graham's number the minute they walked into Jenny's condo in Shawmut. "He's still at the hospital," Graham's wife Barbara told them. "He had another chemo treatment this afternoon. I spoke with him about half an hour ago."

"How's he doing?" David asked.

"He feels pretty queasy and doesn't want any visitors at the moment," Barbara replied. "He needs a few days. I promise I'll give you daily reports."

David accepted Barbara's advice with reluctance. He wasn't happy about having to put off a visit with Graham. He considered a supermarket run, but Ross had thoughtfully stocked Jenny's refrigerator, allowing them to fix a light supper and go straight to bed.

The phone rang at 7:00 a.m. "Sorry to call so early," said Ross, "but I figured since it's after noon Geneva-time, you *voyageurs* would be awake before the birds. Kevin and I are invited down to Amber's beach cottage for the weekend. I told her you just got in, and she said to bring you along. We could swing by and pick you up, or you could meet us there."

"I'd love to see Amber," Jenny replied. "When do you plan to leave?"

"We'd like to head down by eight. She's expecting us for lunch."

"David's in the shower. I'll ring you back as soon as he's out."

When David turned off the water, Jenny stepped into the steamy bathroom. "Ross just called," she said as David toweled himself dry.

"We're invited to spend the weekend in Provincetown. We can ride down with Ross and Kevin or take my car."

"Provincetown? I haven't been to Provincetown since our student days. We can't see Graham yet, so why not?" he decided.

Jenny called Ross back and told him they would come, but in their own car. Within an hour, they were on the road.

"Where are we staying?" David asked.

"At Amber's beach house," she replied. "Amber is an old friend of Ross's. They met back when Ramon was alive, and he and Ross used to come up from New York for weekends. Amber's an artist and a good one. I think you'll appreciate her paintings."

Amber's cottage, originally a large boat shed, sat on pilings right on the beach in Provincetown harbor. After introductions and greetings, they all strolled down Commercial Street to visit the gallery where Amber was showing her work, then examined the shops and watched the endlessly fascinating street scene before returning to the cottage for lunch.

"I'm putting together a blueberry-picking expedition," Amber announced after their meal. "Who wants to come?"

"Haven't had wild New England blueberries in a coon's age!" David declared, signing on immediately.

"Why don't you go too," Ross suggested to Kevin. "That way, Jenny and I can stay here and gossip about you and David."

Jenny shot Ross a grateful glance.

"I'll go so long as you follow my Mum's rule," Kevin replied. "'If you can't be saying something nice, don't be saying nothing at all.'"

"I'll do my best," Ross returned.

Ross and Jenny retreated to the beachside deck as the others set out.

"I infer from your e-mail silence that there have been no cataclysmic events since our last exchange."

"Cataclysmic, no, but I discovered more hidden pictures of Julien, I finally told David about the *Testament*, and I picked up some really interesting information from Sandie's good friend Olga."

"This is the *Testament* naming Julien as guardian for the children? What was David's reaction?"

"He didn't really say anything. He just agreed that the role of guardian should fall to me or someone like Michel instead of to Julien, and authorized me to replace the *Testament* with a new document."

"And that was it? No discussion?"

"No. My sense was that he either didn't know about the *Testament*, or had completely forgotten its existence. I left the conversational door wide open, but he didn't choose to walk through it."

"And the 'really interesting information' from Sandie's friend?"

"Remember my X=Y theory? That if I felt unsure of myself, maybe Sandie did too? Well, apparently, it's true and then some. Sandie wasn't as happy in that marriage as I once thought. There was even a huge blow-up, when they first moved into their house, that had Sandie seriously contemplating divorce."

"A blow-up? You've said David has a temper. Did it get out of hand?"

"No, no, no. David only gets angry at machines. It was Sandie who blew up. The problem was that David, without consulting Sandie, went out and spent five thousand Swiss francs – that's close to four thousand dollars – to have a bunch of azalea bushes installed along the front of the house. His intention was innocent. He just wanted lots of beautiful flowers. But five thousand francs was money they didn't begin to have, and Sandie was left to clean up the financial mess. She was furious – and devastated. She viewed the azalea episode as evidence that David didn't understand or respect or even care how hard she had worked to make the house happen."

Ross listened silently as Jenny described Olga's successful intervention.

"So, assuming Olga's tale is accurate," Ross summarized, "Sandie spent much of her marriage feeling that the original romance had been downgraded to a kind of pragmatic partnership. In light of this, is it fair to be upset with her over a possible affair?"

"Sandie wouldn't have risked an affair for spurious reasons. But from my perspective, it's still difficult to fathom. If she was unhappy, why couldn't she tell him so, and talk to him about it? Why sully the relationship with deceit and infidelity?"

"Jenny, you're not making sense. You yourself sometimes feel insecure vis-à-vis David's attentions. You've been carrying this affair business around in your head for months now, yet you're still reluctant to push David to talk about it. And when you *have* raised the subject – as per the *Testament* – you've seen how hard it is to draw him out. Despite all this, you continue to view Sandie's actions as a personal affront. You're having real trouble letting it go."

"I don't want to let it go, because I think it bothers David, despite his protests to the contrary."

"I think it really bothers *you*. And I think some of that's because you're still upset with Seth."

"With *Seth*? What on earth does my ex-husband have to do with any of this?"

Ross leaned back in his deck chair, hands steepled against his chin. He was in sandals, shorts and a Lacoste polo shirt, but suddenly the aura was not casual.

"*There's* a good question," he commented.

"I haven't seen Seth since we got divorced. It's been well over a decade! Why would I still be upset with Seth?"

"I repeat, good question."

"Ross, what are you saying?"

"I'm not saying. I'm asking."

Jenny frowned. She couldn't read his eyes behind his sunglasses, but Ross's tone was no-nonsense. She sat silent for a moment, then made an effort to comply with his request.

"I never think about Seth. Or almost never. I was certainly upset with him at the time, but that was long, long ago."

"Let me come at this a different way. Suppose you find out that a friend of yours – someone from your accounting firm, let's say – had a discreet and longstanding affair. The affair is over now, but it upsets you. Maybe you're upset because you're disappointed by your friend's behavior. Maybe you're upset because your friend's husband is someone you like and respect. But how long are you going to *stay* upset? When are you going to declare it a closed chapter and move on? How can you justify continuing to pick at it, analyze it, and obsess about it *ad infinitum*?

"You're a detail person, Jewel, but obsession isn't your norm, except maybe when you come across a bank statement that won't balance. Yet you're worrying this case like a dog with a bone. You and Seth got divorced because he was blatantly unfaithful. It was an extremely painful rupture. He hurt you. He lied to you. He humiliated you. He was the bad guy, but he came out the other end with a trophy wife, the dog, and half the proceeds from the sale of the house. Forgiveness doesn't come easily to us mortals. It would be perfectly human of you to harbor some residual anger, even if you're not conscious of it."

"But my concern here is for David, not me. It's a totally different scenario."

"Is it? David told you that he wasn't the perfect husband. According to him, it doesn't bother him that Sandie might have had an affair. Do you *want* it to bother him? This is where you need to be really careful, Jewel. Remember *nihil nisi bonum*? People who set out to tarnish someone else's reputation usually do so for purposes of either revenge or personal gain – or both."

Jenny recoiled. "Are you saying I'm pursuing this for selfish reasons?"

"I'm saying that Sandie's alleged affair is particularly disturbing for you because you have a lot of issues floating around that are muddying the waters. I think that infidelity is a serious hot button for you because of Seth, and that it's fueling your distress. I also think that you *do* have something to gain if Sandie is guilty. Not in an evil way. Not in a vengeful way. I believe you are truly concerned about David's happiness and genuinely disappointed by Sandie's behavior. At the same time, I think you're relieved that she's not a saint. You have to be. Her imperfections make you feel more normal, more acceptable.

"We're social creatures, Jewel, and we tend to judge our self-worth by comparing ourselves with our peers. I've always gotten the sense that you were a little awed by Sandie. She was elegant. She was French. She was the one David chose to marry, and the one he stayed committed to until death did them part. I got a whiff of wistful envy from you every so often. Even now, that must surely color your view regarding your own adequacy and desirability as David's second wife."

Jenny absorbed Ross's words in silence.

"I'm not judging you, Jewel. As a gay black man, I've spent a lifetime on the receiving end of other people's judgments. I just want you to break through the smoke screen and see this situation for what it is, no more, no less. Use your common sense, follow your conscience and your better nature, and you'll come out fine."

"This is a lot to process, Ross."

"Yes, but you can handle it. Now stop obsessing, and let's just enjoy this sunshine."

When the blueberry pickers returned, they proudly displayed sand-pails full of blueberries. "Have you-all solved the problems of the world?" David asked as he settled into one the weathered deck chairs with a glass of wine.

Jenny just smiled and turned to Kevin.

"You've got a real prince for a partner, Kevin."

"Oh, Jenny," Kevin rejoined with an absolutely straight face, "in Ireland, we call them queens."

David nearly choked on his wine.

"Don't you just love Provincetown?" Amber laughed.

The rest of the day was spent in relaxed conversation. Amber's aging cat, Desdemona, wandered about investigating the guests, stalking the gulls and occupying perches that offered strategic vantage points. Around five o'clock, a young artist who was taking lessons from Amber stopped by and set up his easel just off the deck, wanting to catch the bay in the late-afternoon light. David was intrigued and wistful. "I love to paint," he said, "but I haven't painted anything since Sandie died. I haven't been able to find my way back to it." He stepped down onto the beach and went over to look at the student's work and technique.

Amber had been contemplating dinner preparation, but she was tempted by the same light that attracted her student and decided to do a quick sketch. "Amber, do you have a second easel?" Jenny asked quietly. "And some extra paints and brushes? I think it would be a real step forward if David could pick up a paintbrush again."

Amber nodded and ducked inside. She returned with her own materials, plus a second easel, a small blank canvas, a palette, and several tubes of paint. When David climbed back up on the deck, Amber handed him a brush and a trowel-like implement. "Here you go, Rembrandt," she teased. "Give it a try."

David had never used a palette knife before, and he started to play with it. Amber and her student painted the bay, but David turned his attention in the opposite direction, filling his canvas with a lively rendering of the back of the cottage. He deftly captured its uneven boards, bright blue trim, and homebuilt kitchen window with the cat lolling indifferently on the ledge. When he finished, he presented the painting to Amber as a hostess gift.

"This is wonderful, David," Amber exclaimed. "This is really good!"

"I appreciate the compliment," David replied, "but most of all, I appreciate your giving me the opportunity to paint again."

Amber looked at Jenny with a question mark in her eyes. *Should I tell him it was you who suggested it?*

No, Jenny silently answered, shaking her head slightly. *Mission accomplished,* she signaled, discreetly giving a thumbs-up.

Amber acknowledged the message with a smile and excused herself to start making dinner. They stayed the night in her loft and feasted on blueberry muffins for breakfast. Mid-morning they retrieved their car, expressed their thanks and headed back north.

Throughout the drive, Jenny's mind kept turning back to her conversation with Ross. She wanted to believe her feelings and actions were altruistic, but Ross had deftly exposed her self-interest. *You've been outed, Longworth,* she admitted to herself. *Yes, I do want Sandie's infidelity to bother David, so he'll appreciate my total commitment more fully. But I'm sorry for whatever pain this is causing him. And yes, I'm relieved that Sandie wasn't a saint. It frees me from having to compete with Madame Perfect Predecessor. Yet I liked her, and I can identify with some of her insecurities. Who's to say I wouldn't have committed similar sins if I saw life through her eyes and felt what she felt? This is never going to be tidy,* she concluded as they pulled into the driveway. *Ross is right. I need to find ways to process it, and then move on.*

"We should do it now," Jenny said as they brought in their overnight bags. "I suspect she'd much rather be in the garden than where she is."

"Right," David replied.

Jenny went to the dining room sideboard and withdrew the small vial David had given her following Sandie's death. David poured two glasses of wine and handed one to Jenny. Together they crossed the lawn. They stopped just short of the woods, in front of a long curved garden that Jenny had created the summer before and dedicated to Sandie's memory. A flat rock, engraved with *Sandie's Garden,* marked the beginning of a stepping-stone pathway. Putting her wine glass in David's care, Jenny opened the vial. She gently shook some of Sandie's ashes into the garden, then held the vial out to David.

"Do you want to spread the remainder?"

"No, I've done more than my share of that already," David answered. "I'll just watch."

When Jenny finished, David handed her back her glass and raised his. "Here's to you, *Ma Belle,*" he said softly, gesturing to the flowers now dusted with the residue of Sandie's body. "Sandie always envied your green thumb," he said, turning back to Jenny "She would have loved this garden."

They drank their wine, then walked back to the house, arms about each other. *One more step toward closure,* Jenny mused, *but still a ways to go.*

When David checked his computer, he found an e-mail from Marc.

> *De: Marc*
> *A: Dad*
> *Envoyé: 14 juillet, 2002*
> *Objet: hi*
>> hi,,, happy bastille day. hope everything is fine over there.
>>
>> on my side, well, i work all day and then i come here give food to the cat, then i do a little laundry, pick up the mail like a big, BIG BOY which i am piling like i was told on the kitchen table, then i go back down to the *appartement* and by that time it is 7pm passed, i have to feed myself (and it is not easy by yourself, even worse under stress) and then clean the dishes, by that time it is more or less dark and i feel like i haven't done anything of my day, i'm not going to draw u a picture. how fun can life get?
>>
>> love and enjoy - marc

David showed it to Jenny. She read and looked at him in astonishment. "What on earth is going on?"

"I don't know. Did you say anything about putting the mail on the kitchen table?"

"No. He probably got that from the house-sitter blurb. I posted our itinerary on the fridge along with my generic house-sitter reference sheet, which lists things like the neighbors' phone numbers and plant-watering instructions. It says something about not bothering to sort the mail, as in 'Just pile it up on the kitchen table.' It sounds as if things must be really rocky with Valerie," Jenny guessed.

"It also sounds as if Marc isn't staying at the house as I requested," David said, "but only stopping by to feed the cats."

"I think we should confront him on that," Jenny counseled.

"I doubt it would change anything," David replied sadly. "Marc is his own worst enemy. He heaps so much anger on himself that he doesn't need anyone else to add to it. I just hope this negative phase ends soon, and that Marc survives it."

"You're a kind soul, David Perry. I just hope you and I survive it," Jenny sighed.

The next day, David and Jenny saw Graham at the hospital. They had hoped for a long visit, but Graham was too exhausted for more than a brief conversation. Illness had transformed the lean sharp features in his normally handsome face into something gaunt and sepulchral. His eyes were vague and cloudy. His skin was ashen, his dark hair lank and dull. "He looks like hell," David said tersely as they walked out of the hospital, just minutes after walking in.

Jenny tried to be reassuring. "That's not unusual, given the chemo."

"He could barely talk," David said, shaking his head. "It reminds me of Sandie's decline, when she became passive and, in essence, gave up hope of recovery." He lit a cigarette, taking a deep drag to try to calm himself. "And he's not eating," he went on. "The goddamn hospital food is shit!"

They had planned to combine their hospital visit with a nostalgic tour of Harvard Yard, but David was so upset after seeing Graham that he had no stomach for further exploits that day. After he crushed the cigarette into the parking lot pavement, they drove back to Shawmut in silence.

Four days later, they got word from Barbara that Graham was open to another hospital visit. David immediately made a trip to the grocery store, then devoted the remainder of the evening to cooking. "I'm creating a 'four-power' chicken soup," he announced. "It's a combination of my recipe, yours, Sandie's and one from Edie Duval's grandmother. It's high time Graham got some real food instead of that hospital crap."

While David chopped and sliced in the kitchen, Jenny made phone calls. "It's not as carefree a vacation as I had hoped," Jenny reported to Bibi. "David's college roommate, Graham Wells, is undergoing chemo for colon cancer. The situation reminds David of the end-stage of Sandie's illness. Nothing I say as a cancer survivor seems to provide any reassurance. David dismisses my optimism as Yankee stoicism."

"What's the scoop? How sick is Graham really?" Bibi asked.

"Graham says his doctors seem confident in the outcome, but who knows? In any event, Graham is dealing with the situation in a positive way, being calm on the surface and doing his best to put his affairs in order. To me, that's the only approach that makes sense. It's a serious waste of precious time to sit around gnashing your teeth."

"You *are* a Yankee stoic," Bibi commented. "I'd be gnashing non-stop if it were me."

"That's close to what David's doing, so I've focused on organizing distractions. We've been running around visiting friends and doing touristy things in Boston."

They spoke for several more minutes, and then signed off. David was straining broth into containers when Jenny reappeared to check on his culinary efforts. "Smells good!" she told him.

The next day they drove up to Cambridge with a thermos of hot soup. When they entered his hospital room, Graham was so weak he couldn't even lift his head in greeting. His speech was slurred, and he had trouble focusing. His color was somewhere between slate and pale green.

"Hey, man, brought you some decent food for a change," David said, taking out the thermos and trying to sound cheerful.

"Dearheart, you should check with the duty nurse first," Jenny advised quietly.

David bridled at the suggestion. "Bullshit protocol," he said. "You want some homemade chicken soup, Graham?"

"David, the hospital staff really needs to be alerted about the soup," Jenny repeated. "Some treatments carry restrictions. Eating the wrong thing might screw up the protocol."

"With chicken soup?" David asked incredulously.

"Yes," Jenny answered firmly, "even with chicken soup. It would certainly have botched the treatment I was given – radioactive iodine – simply because of the salt."

David was taken aback. "Jeezus Christ!" He hadn't considered the possibility that his impulsive intervention might have a negative impact. An evening phone conversation with Barbara only served to exacerbate his concern.

"The doctor said it's going well, but he thinks Graham shouldn't have any more visits for a while," Barbara told him. "I'll let you know right away when it's okay to see him again," she promised.

Jenny filled their calendar with activities balancing her own interests with David's need for distraction. "We have to take a ride on the Swan Boats," she insisted. "I haven't done that in a hundred years. And afterwards we can do lunch and eat Indian pudding at Durgin Park. And do you remember that little North End bakery where we used to buy rum-soaked pastries and ricotta cheese pies? Let's go see if it's still there!"

Despite the nostalgic outings, David was tense and edgy until he got the call he was waiting for. "Graham has finished his first round of chemo," Barbara reported, "and he's home now. He wants you two to come for supper."

Graham was lying on the sofa, propped up with pillows, when they walked in. While he didn't rise, he looked significantly better, with a touch of normal color. Within minutes, the two men were swapping stories and sharing jokes.

"It's nice to meet you at last," Barbara said as she and Jenny retreated to the kitchen. "Graham and I have been married for over two years now, and I've heard story after story about you and David and Ramon and all your student exploits. We talked about going to Geneva for your wedding, but Graham said David wanted to keep it very low key. We thought we'd have a chance to celebrate properly when you came back here to visit. Needless to say, we didn't anticipate this rather scary twist of fate."

"I wish we were going to be in Boston longer to lend support," Jenny said. "We have to head back to Europe at the end of next week, but we'll probably return to the States for Christmas. I have some wonderful old photos of Graham. I'll bring them along to show you."

The women rejoined the men, and the conversation focused on Graham's medical protocols until David excused himself to go outside for a cigarette. Graham immediately turned to Jenny. "Unless we count your two hospital visits – which I don't since I was barely *compos mentis* – the last time I saw David was the week of Sandie's funeral. Frankly, I wasn't sure he was going to make it through. Now the man seems genuinely happy," Graham commented. "You're obviously taking excellent care of him. You've worked a minor miracle in a very short time."

"At one level, taking care of him is easy," Jenny replied candidly. "I tease him, praise his cooking, kiss his bald spot, manage his finances, tolerate his pig-headedness, and pretty much adore him. But I've hardly accomplished a miracle, minor or otherwise. He still has a lot of gray days. There are times he's up before dawn, and I find him sitting in the dark, smoking. And other times, he'll stay up until close to midnight, again sitting in the dark, working on a glass of brandy as well as his cigarettes. He's the center of my world over there, and when he's in trouble emotionally, I'm in trouble too."

"Well, I'm not at my best at the moment," Graham noted, "but I hope you know that you can be in touch anytime you want – anytime you need help or even just to let off steam. You and I both love David, and we are old-enough and safe-enough friends to share this kind of thing."

David returned as Jenny nodded her thanks. Graham was alert during dinner but began to fade as dessert was served. Jenny glanced at Barbara and got a clear signal that they should bring the evening to an end.

"He's bounced back from the chemo amazingly fast," Jenny commented as they walked toward the car. "It's a good sign."

"I sure as hell hope so," was David's only response.

The remainder of their stay focused on visits to Jenny's circle of friends and included a drive north to Rachel's summer house in Gloucester. The map Rachel had e-mailed to them bore the heading, "To Rachel & Josh Aronson's."

I'll bet Rachel is as reluctant to remove Josh's name from the directions as David is to take Sandie's name off the household accounts, Jenny speculated. As they pulled into Rachel's driveway, she came out to welcome them. Though Rachel and David had communicated in the past, they had never met. They smiled broadly when introduced, and hugged each other with warm affection. Their parallel losses rendered them instant and caring friends. "It feels as if I've known Rachel forever," David mused as he and Jenny headed back to Shawmut. "In the course of one afternoon, I've added a new sister to my family."

Their last day was reserved for relaxing at home with a steak dinner on the patio. David lit the grill and brought out some wine. As they waited for the coals to catch, David turned his gaze to Sandie's Memorial Garden. "It feels right that part of Sandie is here, mixed in with the flowers. Boston was one of her favorite places in the States. She always looked forward to staying with you in Shawmut. So did the kids. You planned the agendas with just the right balance of leisure and adventure."

"When you live in a condo community with a swimming pool and twenty acres of woodland, entertaining children is pretty easy," Jenny commented.

"You're being modest," he countered. "But Boston certainly has a special draw for Europeans. It's a walkable city, with charm, history and a human scale. Psychologically, it's far more my American home base than Chattanooga," David continued, "even though I was here for only four years. When I drove into Cambridge this morning to say goodbye to Graham, I started feeling really nostalgic. The symphony playing on the car radio was the same one that turned me on to classical music freshman year. Then that furniture store on Mass Ave had a panel of Marimekko fabric in the window. Always loved that stuff. I gave Sandie a wall hanging for our apartment in Paris that was almost identical. And finally, I landed a parking space right in front of 2 Ware Street. A legal one! Can you believe it?"

"What were you doing over by Ware Street?"

"I just wanted to take a trip down memory lane. See if the apartment building was still standing. Check out the old neighborhood."

"A lot of things have changed. It's a good bit tidier than it used to be, with the Inn instead of the old gas station. The laundromat's long gone too. Remember how we all used to pool our laundry so we could get the biggest bang for the buck? You were always so chivalrous, making sure you carried the heaviest clothes bags."

"Maybe I had ulterior motives."

"True, I *was* the only one in the group with a TV set."

"You had some other things more attractive than a TV set," David replied with a chuckle.

"We *were* naughty, *n'est-ce pas?* But most of our all-nighters had to do with my typing your SocRel papers in the wee hours. It was always a cliffhanger as to whether you'd be able to turn them in on time."

"'A long time ago in a galaxy far away.' We had no idea back then what life had in store for us."

"We still don't," Jenny pointed out. "That's why we should live each day to the fullest."

"Yes, Ma'am," David nodded and raised his glass.

Jenny raised hers in response. "To us," she said.

"To us," he replied.

The drive up the Southeast Expressway to Logan Airport was less than scenic, but as their flight rose off the runway, Boston Harbor was gloriously laid out beneath them, its islands surrounded by sailboats, yachts and fishing vessels.

"I wish we could have stayed longer," Jenny said wistfully as the plane headed out over the Atlantic.

"We covered a lot of ground," David said. "It's been a good trip."

He's right about that, she decided as David started leafing through the flight magazine. *He started painting again, he seemed genuinely tranquil when we scattered Sandie's ashes, and he finally got to meet*

Rachel. On my side, Ross was an absolute godsend, and I was grateful for Graham's comments too, about letting off steam. It was good of him to offer his support, despite his medical situation.

"Yes, I agree," she said out loud. "I'm especially glad we were able to spend time with Graham. His mindset is really positive, and the prognosis seems good."

Beyond David's quiet *"Inshallah,"* Jenny's remarks were met with silence. *He doesn't want to jinx anything,* she realized.

Their flight included an early morning stopover in Zurich before delivering them to Geneva. When they cleared customs, David searched the waiting crowd at arrivals. *He's hoping Marc has come to the airport to meet us,* Jenny guessed.

After five minutes, David went out and hailed a taxi. Alighting from the cab, it was obvious that Marc hadn't watered the outdoor planters. Most of the potted flowers were dead.

Marc greeted them at the door. "Sorry not to be at the airport," he apologized. "My car isn't working, and your car has got a kind of gas leak. I took it to a garage," he said, "but the mechanic said he had no time to look at it before your plane landed."

"That's okay," David told Marc. "We weren't expecting to be met."

Jenny wrinkled her nose as they walked inside. It was immediately evident that the cat box had been seriously neglected.

While Jenny unpacked, David took the car in for an emergency inspection. The check-up yielded a clean bill of health. He was back within ninety minutes. "Good news," he reported. "Everything seems fine. The mechanic found no problem."

Rather than sharing his father's relief, Marc immediately became defensive.

"Well," he huffed, "maybe I just imagined a big pool of a gallon of gasoline underneath the car!"

Jenny was startled by Marc's reaction. *Obviously it hasn't occurred to Marc that he might have parked the car over an oil slick and then wrongly assumed the source was David's car. I promised David I wouldn't intervene, but a few pointers on civility might be in order here.*

David ignored both Marc's words and his tone, and spoke as if nothing untoward had occurred. "We're going to eat out tonight. Why don't you invite Valerie, and the two of you can join us."

Marc met them at the restaurant that evening, but he came alone. Initially he said Valerie had gone off to have dinner with friends, then finally admitted that he and Valerie had broken up. "She ordered me to move out. Now I am on the street, so I have to move back into the house and stay until I leave for school in San Francisco."

David accepted this without comment. "Do you need help with the moving?" he asked.

"No," was the reply. Marc was sullen and distant for the remainder of the meal. Jenny was not happy about this sudden change of status, but she took her clue from David and said nothing.

"What happens now?" Jenny asked once they were home and could have a private conversation.

"The workmen still need Marc's old room as a staging area. The contractor estimated another two weeks to tile the basement floor. And I don't think we want Marc occupying Delphine's room. Until the basement's finished, her bathroom has the only functioning shower. Marc's tendency to sleep till noon poses an access problem, unless you're comfortable wandering through while he's buck naked."

"I'd rather not," Jenny acknowledged.

"So, for the time being, he's going to have to move into the guest room and sleep on the sofa bed."

The guest room was also Jenny's office. She kept her reaction to herself, but David understood, despite her silence, that this was not welcome news.

With efficiency but no enthusiasm, Jenny readied the office for occupancy, clearing her desk surface and filing her paperwork. Marc dropped off a load of belongings late in the morning. Much to Jenny's surprise, he presented her with a bouquet of flowers. *Is this an apology for my dead plants?* she wondered. Whatever the reason, she appreciated the gesture. "Thank you, Marc. These are lovely!"

Marc nodded wordlessly and shuttled boxes down to the office. David stuck his head in the kitchen as Jenny was putting her flowers in a vase. "I'm going to take Marc back to the apartment, then I'm off to buy some things he needs. Want anything?" he asked.

"No, I'm all set," she replied

Once they were gone, Jenny did a quick trip downstairs to check her e-mail. Marc had piled up his clothes, books and equipment in such a way that access to her computer was completely blocked. *Not good*, she steamed. *Not good at all.*

David returned with a full shopping bag and several bulging grocery sacks. "When is Marc coming back?" Jenny asked as she helped him carry things into the house.

"I don't know," David shrugged. "He didn't say."

"My desktop computer is totally walled in by all his piles."

"Do you need access right away? I can clear a pathway for you."

"No, it's not urgent. But we need to lay down some rules. I need regular access to it."

After lunch, David busied himself in the kitchen, making *boeuf bourguignon*, one of Marc's favorite dishes. Jenny spent the afternoon weeding in the garden, always a reliable therapy. Evening arrived with no word from Marc. "I'd like to put off dinner until Marc comes home," David said as they settled on the terrace for their *apéritif*.

"I really need to eat something," Jenny said when it got to be eight o'clock. "I can't drink two glasses of wine without some food to absorb it."

David resigned himself to the fact that Marc was not likely to show up, and he went in to heat up the bourguignon.

This is a no-win situation, Jenny muttered to herself. *If, at the same age, I had behaved the way Marc is behaving … well, I can't even imagine it. David shrugs it off, yet he's clearly worried about Marc. I know he loves him, but in my book that should include the possibility of administering a good spanking now and then.*

As they sat down to eat, Jenny searched for a way to express her annoyance without being confrontational. *I'll come at it sideways,* she decided. "When Marc didn't show up for dinner, I found myself wondering what my parents would have done if I had pulled a stunt like that. In our family, Mother was the one in charge of enforcing the rules. Punishment usually involved being sent to our rooms and having privileges revoked. My father rarely got involved unless Mother insisted he back her up."

David cracked a wry smile. "At my house, it was Dad who was in charge. He wasn't averse to applying a good swat to our backsides if we got rowdy."

"Did you ever do that with Marc?" Jenny asked.

"No," David answered. "Discipline was mostly Sandie's department."

"Do you think Marc's rudeness is a form of grief? If Sandie was the source of the rules, her death and the disintegration of the rules might be connected in some way."

"Marc has had a problem with rules and authority since the onset of adolescence. We're all still feeling Sandie's absence, but I don't think there's any cause and effect in terms of Marc's behavior."

"So, any ideas about how we should respond?"

"How *you* should respond is to keep a safe distance whenever possible. I'm used to his dark moods."

"Do you really think it serves anyone – us or him – to just stand by and do nothing?" Jenny questioned.

"I don't think of it as doing nothing. I think of it as being patient and trusting that he's capable of getting through to the other side. There's an American Indian myth I use in my classes about two youths who refuse to listen to the advice of their elders. They go out into the circle of life heading in the wrong direction. They've been instructed repeatedly to take the right-hand path; instead, they follow the left-hand path. They get into all sorts of trouble, but their misadventures give them experience and teach them about life. In the process, they acquire maturity and wisdom and finish their journey around the circle in a way that earns the admiration of the elders they initially disregarded. I'd like to see Marc take the right-hand path because it's a lot easier, but he seems to lean toward the left-hand one. I just hope his misadventures ultimately bring him the same maturity and wisdom the two Indian boys found."

Marc returned home in the middle of the night, started a load of laundry, and took off again early in the morning, before Jenny came downstairs. When she poked her head into the office, her computer was still inaccessible. Her tea was waiting for her in the kitchen. David was out on the terrace, smoking. She picked up her mug and went outside.

"Good morning," he said, rising from his chair as she appeared. They exchanged a quick kiss.

"It would be a better morning," she replied, trying to keep the frustration out of her voice, "if I could get to my computer."

"Sorry, Ducks. I'll go down and part the Red Sea for you."

"Did Marc say when he'd be back?"

"Nope."

"Did you ask him?"

"I did. He said he didn't know. Said he had too many effing things to do, and he had no effing idea how effing long it was going to effing take."

Jenny looked at David carefully. "You're upset," she concluded.

"Yup. Just a bit," he answered, the understatement clearly evident in his tone.

"David, we have a responsibility to hold Marc to a standard of civil behavior while he's staying with us. He's capable of destroying the harmony in this house in a matter of minutes."

"I'm working on it," David replied wearily. "Meanwhile, let's clear you a path to your machine."

The phone rang just as they finished shifting Marc's piles. It was the DuPonts, calling to invite them for an outing at their golf club. "Come by, and we will drive over together."

"Yes?" asked David, covering the phone's mouthpiece as he posed the question to Jenny.

"Sounds like a great idea," she answered. Jenny's capricious hip didn't permit her to swing a golf club, but she always enjoyed a walk. "It will be a relief to get away from the house."

The DuPonts' club had a lovely course, surrounded by fields with bales of hay and rows of crops that made patterns in green and gold. "Oops," David said as he extracted his clubs from the back of the car. "I forgot to bring my golf socks." After a quick stop in the pro shop, David returned fully equipped, and they set out under mostly sunny skies.

At the end of the round, they settled in for a drink at the clubhouse, and Josette commented on the socks David had to purchase that morning. "David has done the same thing before," she told Jenny, "only it was the shoes he has forgotten. He has arrived to play without his correct golf shoes. It was necessary to buy new shoes at the club. Sandie was very upset with him, because at the shop, the shoes are too expensive!"

If Sandie viewed a pair of golf shoes as an extravagance, small wonder five thousand Swiss francs worth of azalea landscaping sent her around the bend, Jenny mused. *How lucky I am to have reached a point where I don't have to keep track of every single penny!*

Jenny had managed a successful firm, saved carefully, and invested wisely. Combining her resources with David's salary, Jenny saw no problem in paying full freight for a pair of golf socks.

But how do I tell Josette that I like spoiling David, without sounding as if I'm one-upping Sandie? Maybe I can say he deserves it to counter the stress of Marc moving back into the house.

"What's the French word for 'spoil'?" Jenny asked, turning to David.

"Jenny's afraid I'm getting spoiled," David advised Josette in French.

"I am *not* afraid you're getting spoiled. That's not what I was going to say!" Jenny objected. "I *like* spoiling you."

"I like it too, Ducks," David rejoined in English, grinning at her.

Marc was not in evidence when they got back to the house, nor did he appear during the evening. The next morning, it was clear that he had not slept at home. On further inspection, Jenny noted that the laundry Marc put in the washing machine the day before was still there. She took a deep breath, hauled it out, threw it in the dryer, and started her own load.

Marc finally walked in at suppertime, sullen and scowling, no explanations, and no apologies. Hoping to generate safe conversation, Jenny smiled and pointed to the vase on the table. "Those flowers you gave me are still quite fresh and healthy," she commented.

"Yeah, that's pretty amazing," Marc admitted. "They were in the apartment for two days before I brought them here."

Aha – the truth will out, Jenny realized. *They weren't bought as a gift for me. They must have originally been intended for Valerie.* She made no further attempt to draw Marc out, and even David made little effort at conversation.

"You were awfully quiet during supper," Jenny remarked to David after Marc disappeared again. "You're not usually so preoccupied. Is this about Marc?"

"Yes," he conceded, "I'm deeply concerned about him, but that's almost a permanent condition. With only three weeks to go, I've also started thinking about the beginning of school. This always happens when the fall term looms," he advised. "My mind goes off in all directions, thinking about the things I have to do. Nowadays it's mostly a matter of getting back into the routine, but in the beginning, I had no experience with kids. In Paris, I only worked with adults. The first three years I taught here in Geneva, I really didn't know what I was doing. I practically lived at school, days, weekends, evenings, talking with other teachers, sitting in on classes, and trying to figure out how to be effective. It took me a long time to recognize that it was important to be with the kids where they were in their own development. The focus needed to be on them, learning, rather than on me, teaching. My colleagues were helpful and patient, but it was a really rough period for me."

"A rough period for *three years?* That must have been difficult for Sandie and the children," Jenny suggested.

"I was totally wrapped up in my teaching. They had to cope on their own," he said. "It wasn't fun."

This confirms Olga's story that Sandie felt abandoned during those early years in Geneva, Jenny concluded. *Did that set the stage for Sandie's affair? If Julien and Sandie met when David was neglecting the home front, Julien would surely have picked up on it and offered a shoulder to cry on — and then some,* she speculated.

The specter of Sandie's affair continued to intrigue Jenny, but the upheaval inherent in Marc's presence left her little time to dwell on it. Storming out of the house one afternoon, Marc left his father a note on the kitchen table, saying his college acceptance had been revoked because of a lack of US history credits. "Those American assholes think they have the only history that counts, and I'm not gonna waste my time to deal with some f***ing admission person."

"Have you seen this?" David asked Jenny in a tight voice after reading the note.

"Yes, and there has to be some mistake. I can't believe that lack of a US history credit would disqualify a student educated wholly in Europe," Jenny puzzled. "The computer probably processed his transcripts as if he had attended a US high school, since he's applying under his American citizenship. All Marc needs to do is contact the Admissions Office and explain the problem," she ventured. "They're not going to make American History a prerequisite for foreign students."

David just shook his head. "Solving problems is not Marc's strong point. He has little patience with the normal range of human error. I'll call them and see if I can straighten things out, but I'll have to wait until this evening. It isn't even dawn yet in California."

How much longer can we tolerate this dark atmosphere? Jenny wondered. She sought sanctuary in the garden while David read the paper and did some school preparation.

At five o'clock, he brought a bottle of wine and two glasses out to the terrace. "Leave those weeds alone, Woman. Time to call it quits."

Jenny washed her hands under the outdoor spigot and joined David beneath the awning. He poured the wine and raised his glass. "Let's go to Paris," he suggested. "Delphine is still in Spain. She won't mind our using her apartment. We can leave Marc to his own devices, stay for a long weekend, and inject some sanity into our lives."

Jenny was startled by the proposal, but only for a moment. "I'm still not used to the idea that we can just zip over to Paris at the drop of a hat. But yes, by all means. Let's get out of here!"

They took a Friday morning train and had a comfortable journey across the mountains and through the French countryside to Paris. They deposited their bags in Delphine's apartment and went back out immediately.

They crossed the Seine and wandered through some of David's favorite neighborhoods. "Oh, look! Can we get one?" Jenny asked, pointing to a street vendor selling fresh *crêpes* from a wheeled cart. They chose a *crêpe au chocolat* and shared sticky bites, licking the dark chocolate from their fingers as they walked. It had been a long-ago tradition between them, and the memories filled Jenny with nostalgia.

"There used to be a little *crêperie* on the Boulevard St. Michel, about half way between the Metro station and your apartment," she recalled. "I stopped there whenever I came over from London and treated myself to a *crêpe au Grand Marnier*. That was my reward for negotiating the plane-train-subway connections and doing the walk up to your place all by myself."

"Your reward?" David said in surprise.

"You know I'm not wild about being on my own in a city," she pointed out. "One of my tricks for managing my agoraphobia is to plan little treats for myself anytime I have to do something uncomfortable."

"But you never said a word!" David exclaimed.

"I didn't want you thinking I was a total wimp. And you were worth the trip. Of course, so was the *crêpe au Grand Marnier*. I always polished it off before I got to your building, so you never suspected I had a crutch for my travels."

The next morning, they breakfasted at a little bar across the street from Delphine's apartment. When David ordered croissants, the waiter hesitated. "I am sorry, Monsieur, the bar does not have croissants," he apologized, "but if you will wait one moment, perhaps it can be arranged." The waiter spoke briefly to the proprietor, who nodded and popped across the street to the bakery. He returned with two croissants, put them on a plate, and served them with a flourish.

"This is Paris at its best," Jenny smiled.

During the morning, they wandered the embankment, perusing the stalls selling used books and old prints. After lunch, they walked back across the Pont des Arts and stopped mid-bridge to gaze at the river and the Ile de la Cité.

"This is my favorite view of Paris," David commented.

It was predictable that David would reminisce about Sandie, given the significance of the Pont des Arts, but Jenny was surprised by his focus. "Sandie and I had a conversation," he began, "just before she went into the hospital for the last time. 'The reason we were able always to stay together through the rough times,' she said, 'is because you gave me my freedom.'"

"You mentioned that when you first told me you suspected an affair," Jenny reminded him.

"Did I? I've always presumed it was a veiled reference to Julien."

"But you never asked Sandie directly?"

"No. I didn't know how to ask. I wasn't sure what she meant at the time, and maybe I didn't really want to know."

Then he qualified his conjecture. "At least not then," he concluded. "Now I wish I *had* asked. I wish I knew what happened – *if* anything happened."

David had made no reference to the possible affair for some time. On the strength of Ross's advice, Jenny had been trying to keep her own curiosity within bounds, but she was intrigued that David was still actively thinking about it.

They resumed their walk. To Jenny's delight, there in the city of lovers, David put his arm around her shoulder and kept it there. She slipped her arm around his waist and gave him a squeeze in response.

"Thanks for this weekend, Love," she said, giving him a head bump. "I really needed this."

"*We* really needed this," he added, "and *you* earned it in spades. Sometimes I wonder how you put up with *me*, much less with Marc."

"You're not so difficult, though I probably shouldn't tell you that. Besides, you're really cute. Especially when you grin."

The weekend was blissful – a second honeymoon. "Here's lookin' at you, Kid," David said in his best Bogart accent, clinking their wine glasses as they sat in a little bistro.

In the evening, they strolled through the park that once housed the bustling market of Les Halles. They sipped a Kir at a sidewalk café, then chose a restaurant with an open terrace. Neither of them was a compulsive talker, but the relaxed ambience inspired them to non-stop conversation. "Sitting here brings back memories of the halcyon days when Sandie and I had good salaries, low rent and no responsibilities. We must have tried out half the restaurants in Paris. It was gourmet heaven."

"You really had a wonderful life in Paris," Jenny commented. "I've been trying to pull up recollections from the same time period, but most of the ones that have survived derive from my professional life, not my private life. I was married to Seth then. The marriage lasted fifteen years, but its unhappy ending rendered the era something of a black hole as far as happy memories go. There were some, I know, but they're pretty well buried."

Reluctant to pry, David's question was disguised as an observation. "I always wondered," he said, "why it was that your marriage foundered. It seemed so solid."

"Well, maybe you were just an impossible act to follow. I'm teasing, but there's an element of truth to that. I wasn't really in love with Seth. But then, he wasn't really in love with me either. I met him not long after I came back from London. He was intelligent, interesting and attractive. We had common interests, similar goals and similar values. I was still in love with you, but considered you a hopeless cause. You were a free spirit, and you were totally committed to Paris. Only in movies did a romance with someone like you work out. So I opted for a relationship that was solid and practical. That's what Seth was looking for as well. That's our Yankee ancestry coming to the fore," she joked.

"Seth and I were a team," she continued. "I loved him, but it wasn't what I'd call romantic. There was respect and cooperation and shared responsibility. I was happy living with him. We could have gone on that way to the end. But Seth had a roving eye. He had multiple affairs. You might call them flings, but they certainly lasted more than one night, so affair seems a more accurate term. I looked the other way for a long time, but the affairs got more and more blatant, and I got tired of all the lies.

"We agreed to divorce. I had to sell the home we had spent over ten years restoring and renovating. It was a place I really loved. The whole thing was a traumatic experience and left me feeling rejected and very hurt. Now, of course, I view it as a blessing in disguise. If Seth hadn't bailed out, I wouldn't have been free to come to you when you needed me."

"So, if Seth had wanted to preserve the marriage, and had shown his respect for you by satisfying his roving eye with a lot more discretion, would you still be together?"

Jenny speculated that this question touched on David and Sandie's relationship as much as on hers with Seth. "I take my promises pretty seriously," she replied cautiously.

"One of those promises is usually 'for better or for worse,'" David observed. "But I agree with you about the blessing in disguise. His loss, my gain. To us," he said, raising his wine glass in salute.

An hour after the meal was finished, they were still sitting and talking, David with a snifter of brandy and Jenny with one of Grand Marnier. "I love having you all to myself," she told him. "Usually when we go out, we're not alone. You're very generous with yourself, and you're very inclusive. You invite people to join us whenever we plan anything. It alters the dynamic. I'm not always enthusiastic about sharing you, so I am *loving* this visit and this evening."

David was surprised that it was important to Jenny to have one-on-one time with him. "Sandie used to get restless if we stayed home alone. It drove her nuts that I was such a homebody. She loved visiting and doing things with friends and was eager to be out and about. For me, it makes no difference. I can interact with one or several people to the same degree. I don't really consider whether I'm alone or part of a group."

"Well, you have nice friends, but I do feel possessive at times."

"It's helpful to know that," he said. "I'd never considered it before."

They had tentatively reserved Sunday for the Louvre, but the weather was too nice to spend their last morning indoors. They sat in the sunshine in the Tuileries garden like a pair of old pensioners, watching a trio of ducks paddling contentedly in a small pool, and had just enough time for lunch at Le Train Bleu before catching the train back to Geneva.

They walked in the front door to find the house reverberating with hip-hop music. "Back to reality," Jenny sighed. Marc emerged from the office, and Jenny felt herself bracing for whatever new crisis might be brewing. To her relief, Marc had good news. The problem with Marc's credits had been resolved.

"They cleared my admission," he announced.

"So we can go ahead and book the flight? When do you have to be there?" David asked.

"There's some orientation meeting for freshmen, but I don't care about that. Classes don't start until the week after, so I don't need to go until September 1."

"The orientation may be mandatory, Marc."

"Nah, they probably just hand out maps and stuff. I'll figure it out on my own."

Jenny kept still, but mentally she was shaking her head. *Marc really does like to do things the hard way.*

In the days that followed, Marc struggled to tie up loose ends. Unwilling to accept guidance or help, his progress was haphazard, and he was often in a foul mood. Jenny could feel her blood pressure steadily mount. She was blocked from using her office except in snatches. The workmen had yet to finish the tiling. Marc's car was still on the blink, and he regularly chalked up parking tickets using David's. His things were strewn all over the house while he debated what to take to California.

Delphine called from Paris, reporting that she had arrived back safe and sound from Spain, and would come to Geneva shortly for a quick home visit. This was good news, but it didn't erase the domestic tension. On top of dealing with Marc's behavior, David was doing a countdown for back-to-school.

"Do you want lunch?" David asked as Marc grabbed an apple in the kitchen.

"No."

Not, "No, thankyou." Just "No," Jenny noted with disapproval. David put together a tray laden with bread, cheese and paté and carried it out to the terrace. He also brought out a bottle of wine.

"Want a glass?" he asked as Jenny joined him.

Jenny usually passed on wine during the day, but this time she accepted. "This may need to be the first of many," she said, trying to joke but not succeeding.

"Why?" he queried.

"Why? Because this house is operating in a state of absolute chaos," she replied.

"It is what it is. Don't get invested in it."

David's tone was sharp. Jenny was startled by it, and hurt. *This is my home. This is my daily life. This is my marriage. Don't get invested in it?*

She was dangerously close to unleashing a caustic comment she knew she would regret. She stood up, withdrew without a word, went up to their bedroom, and lay down on the bed. Her mantra got her nowhere. She could think of nothing loving to do. She wanted Marc gone – out of the house and out of their daily life.

After fifteen minutes, Jenny heard David start the mower. Reason began to take hold. *This is ridiculous*, she thought. Marc was causing a serious strain on both of them. *It doesn't work if we're both upset at the same time. We have to take turns.* She got up, dabbed at her red nose with powder, practiced a smile in the mirror, and went back downstairs.

David was cutting the grass around the cherry tree. Jenny pulled out the edge-trimmer and went after the narrow stretches of lawn along the flowerbeds that were difficult for him to get at. When they finished their respective tasks, David wheeled the mower into the garage. As if nothing had happened, they sat down at the table where their lunch and their wine were waiting, exactly as they had been when Jenny retreated. David raised his glass to her. "Kind of hard to attempt motherhood with an angry twenty-two year old, *n'est-ce pas?*"

Jenny raised hers in response. "Right. So until he leaves," she said, "I'm replacing my usual mantra with 'This too shall pass.'"

They both expected rough sledding until Marc's departure, but neither anticipated the explosion that occurred the next day. Marc's recent birthday put him over the age limit for eligibility under David's family health insurance policy. Health insurance was mandatory in Switzerland. The insurance agency sent a form letter detailing this, along with a packet of policy options. Marc had to secure a policy in his own name before leaving for San Francisco.

David and Jenny were sitting on the terrace when Marc brought the packet out to show his father. "You're going to have to fill out these forms and send them in right away," David advised him.

Marc spat out something abrupt in French, and then turned heel and stalked off. Within seconds, they heard him yelling and swearing. For an instant, Jenny thought Marc had tripped and was just letting loose with his bad temper. Then there were sounds of banging and crashing.

"Goddammit!" David exclaimed. "Jenny, you stay put!" He counted to ten, and went inside. Marc shouted something, then suddenly everything went quiet. Jenny held her breath. She heard the front door slam as Marc stomped out of the house, cursing the sky and yelling obscenities at the neighbors' houses.

David emerged and Jenny went to him, wrapping her arms around him and pressing herself against his chest. "What happened, David? What on earth is going on?"

"Sad to say, he's basically having a tantrum. Marc hasn't learned to manage his anger, and when it reaches the boiling point, he explodes. I've seen him break chairs and smash china," David added grimly.

The shrieking continued from across the street. "Can you understand anything he's saying?" Jenny asked.

"The gist is that no one is helping him. He's all alone, and the only one who cared about him was his mother," David translated. "He hates me, he hates you, he hates Valerie, he hates the world, and finally, he hates himself."

By dinnertime there was still no sign of Marc. They ate in near silence. Afterwards, David poured himself a snifter of brandy and offered one to Jenny. "I think I'll pass," she said. "I am completely drained from the day's histrionics. About the only useful thing I can do is go to bed."

"I hear you, Ducks," he said.

"I don't know how you do it, David. I must have been born without any maternal genes, because all I want to do right now is strangle Marc. It drives me crazy that he is so rude to you and so hurtful and unappreciative."

David remained silent.

What can he say? Jenny pondered. *He's a father, and he loves his son unconditionally. I want to be out from under it, but David keeps on giving.* "You're a good man, Charlie Brown," she said, kissing his bald spot. David went and sat on the terrace, smoking his Gauloises and staring out into the garden. Jenny didn't hear it, but Marc arrived not long after and joined him.

"We talked well into the night," David reported to Jenny in the morning. "I think Marc's complete loss of control really frightened him. He apologized for his explosion. I'm hoping this incident may have released Marc's backlog of anxiety, and cleared the way for more responsible behavior. Nothing was resolved," David added, "but it was a good beginning."

When Marc appeared, he was contrite. Jenny accepted his mumbled apology and gave him a hug, but she wasn't optimistic about David's projection of "more responsible behavior." As a tension reliever, David scheduled a day of golf with the DuPonts. Jenny was invited to tag along, but when Marc expressed an interest in playing, she bowed out. "Since Dellie is arriving home tomorrow, I'd like to do some general cleanup and freshen her room," she said. *More to the point, this may be an opportunity for some further father-son communication. And in truth, I'm not eager to spend the day in Marc's company.*

David later described it as a very positive day. "Marc seemed relaxed and even content in a way I haven't seen him since Sandie died," he reported. "With luck, he's turned an important corner."

The following afternoon, Delphine arrived from Paris and bounced into the house. That evening, they had dinner *en famille*. Delphine told of her summer adventures in Spain. Marc described the courses he was considering. Everyone was cheerful and courteous, like a TV family out of the fifties.

Still processing Marc's tantrum, Jenny observed the dynamic with a cautious eye. *Has Marc really turned a corner?* she wondered. *After what Valerie said about drugs, is it possible that Marc's sudden calm is chemically induced? Or is Dellie's presence a factor? Is he on "best behavior" because his sister is here?*

Jenny watched as an animated Delphine talked about the Spanish markets, and was struck by how closely Delphine's expression and gestures resembled Sandie's. *Dellie is so much her mother's daughter that perhaps, in that sense, Marc feels as if Sandie is here with the family again. Maybe that's the source of the calm.*

Jenny's speculation gained some validity when Delphine returned to Paris two days before Marc was due to fly to San Francisco. The minute she was gone, Marc reverted to a bad mood. Saying, "Good Morning," was too much of an effort for him. He went about the house muttering imprecations as he packed for his flight. His father's attempts at assistance were summarily rejected. When David invited Marc to join them for lunch, Marc snapped at him angrily. "No!" he said. "I don't have time!"

"Well, don't worry about lunch," David replied, "but I do want to take you out for a special dinner on your last night in Geneva. Let me know where you'd like to go, and I'll make reservations."

"I can't be bothered thinking about things like that!" Marc barked.

He might as well have slapped his father in the face. "OK, we'll just have dinner here then," David said quietly.

The pain in David's eyes shifted Jenny's mindset back to strangle mode. *This too shall pass ... unless I wring Marc's neck first!*

Marc was absent all afternoon on his last day. The farewell dinner was scheduled for eight o'clock. Once the dinner preparation was under control, David and Jenny sat out on the terrace to catch the evening light. At seven o'clock, Marc was still absent. David started drumming his fingers on the table, a sure sign that he was anxious.

"You're worried. What are you thinking?" Jenny asked.

"I wish Marc would come home," was the reply.

"True, but I don't think that's the real answer. I think you're worried because you're afraid Marc might blow off this whole college venture."

"I'm afraid Marc might ruin his life," he sighed, "but I can't live it for him. All I can do is love him and hope he makes it."

Marc walked in just before eight. He said nothing about where he had been, and his father didn't ask. Jenny noted Marc's heavy eyelids and lack of focus, but she too held her tongue. Surprisingly, the dinner went well. Marc seemed to relax during the meal. He even expressed what Jenny thought was a rare insight. "I'll get up in time," he said, in answer to David's offer to wake him in the morning. "I have to. It's my last chance."

"Marc's comment at dinner, about this being his 'last chance,' was kind of a throwaway line, but I think he was both serious and accurate," Jenny said as she and David climbed into bed. "If he doesn't develop some personal discipline, his options will diminish at a rapid clip."

"I certainly hope he's serious," David commented. "Clearly he messed up when he went to San Francisco the first time, right after high school, and he hasn't done much that's productive or rewarding with his life since then."

"Do you think his 'tough guy' routine is a defense?" Jenny asked. "His hostile behavior seems to confirm what you once said – that he's frightened about going back to school."

"Yes. I think the bristling exterior is definitely a defense, but he's brandishing a sword in the wrong direction. The dragon he needs to slay is inside him."

It was still pitch black out as David prepared to drive Marc to the airport. Marc was so distracted he got into the car without his ticket. Jenny had to slip it to him through the car window.

When David returned, Jenny handed him a mug of hot coffee. He added some milk and took a long swallow.

"Marc didn't check the luggage restrictions and thought if he boarded with lots of small packages, there would be no extra weight charge," David said, shaking his head. "He also thought that he didn't need to carry any Swiss money with him. I had to cover the 400-franc surcharge for excess baggage."

Jenny was tempted to comment. *Marc will never learn to check on things, or plan for things, until he personally suffers the consequences of failing to do so – until you stop bailing him out.* But even though unspoken, she could hear the petulant tone in her words. *Nagging just backfires,* she knew, and chose to remain silent.

David shook his head and took another sip of coffee. "There were so many things I wanted to say to Marc," he lamented, "and I told him that, but there weren't words. It just wasn't the time and place. In the end, I simply wished him *bon voyage* and good luck."

Jenny reconsidered the advice she had just withheld and tried rephrasing it. "I agree with you that the airport check-in line isn't a good place for a father-son heart-to-heart," she said sympathetically. "Still, the fact that you told him there were 'so many things you wanted to say' gives you a great opportunity to start that conversation. You got the first sentence out. Now you can follow up, maybe with some comments on what happened. Given the screw-up about the baggage restrictions, Marc must have been embarrassed to seem so naïve and incompetent a traveler in front of both you and the agent. All kids want respect. This could be an opportunity to help him see that responsible behavior is one key to gaining that respect."

"Maybe," said David wearily. "We'll see. I'll think about it."

Your images – For Sandie

Your images are hung on walls within my mind,
Ageless since you left,
Since I strewed children's drawings around you
In the stillness of death,
Since I stroked your lifeless cheeks
And kissed your pallid lips so grimly drawn,
Since I called the guardian to seal the coffin lid,
Once I was sure you'd gone,
Not wanting those who paid respect
To see you as you weren't,
Not you, but your remains
Now shrouded in your nightshirt.
I knew that nightshirt alive, rising and falling
In the night air beside me,
I saw it, see it still, descending the stairs
To join me for coffee in the quiet dawn
Before school. I see you yet after your bath,
Clad in a skirt and lacy bra,
A towel around your head, no make-up,
Drinking your second cup of coffee.
Images have danced two years
Across my vision since you left.
Two years. To forget, not enough.

D.P. – September 25, 2002

Chapter 7

School reconvened, and David came home generally pleased with the opening-day dynamic. There were new faces among the faculty and a new Principal on board. The previous year's political angst over an accreditation evaluation had apparently receded.

"That's a relief. I know you were a little anxious about how it would go."

"Yup," he replied. "You want some wine?"

"I'll wait until we're closer to dinner."

David poured himself a glass and picked up the paper. Jenny retreated to her office to check her e-mail. There was good news from Graham. His latest scan indicated that the radiation and chemo treatments had apparently eradicated his colon tumor. Jenny dashed off a quick reply.

From: JWLongworth
To: Graham
cc: DavidP
Date: September 2, 2002
Subject: Re: Good news

Good news indeed! You're right, of course. One is never truly out of the woods with cancer, but I suspect you have sensed the majesty of those woods as well as the darkness that lies therein.

Be patient with the "cure." I still have after-effects from my radiation, but they are a small price to pay for the joys and exquisite agonies this gift of extra time has wrought.

Love, Jenny

When Jenny reported the e-mail to David, he quickly went to his own computer to read Graham's missive. He was slightly subdued, however, when he returned. "There's still no word from Marc," he commented with a frown.

"David, Marc is dealing with jet lag and registration and finding his way around the city and the campus. He's not exactly stellar about letting people know his plans, so it's hardly surprising that he hasn't been in touch."

"It's been a full day since he got there. We should have heard something by now," David replied, sidestepping Jenny's logic.

"If the plane had crashed, it would have been on the news," she teased. "I think it's pretty safe to assume he's on the ground and focused on figuring out the bus and rapid transit systems."

Her attempt at humor fell flat. David shook his head, refilled his wine glass, and remained edgy through dinner.

"Maybe Delphine has heard something," he said as they ended the meal. "I'll give her a call."

The conversation took place on the kitchen phone, but it was all in French. Despite Jenny's proximity, she understood only snatches. When David hung up, he summarized for her.

"Delphine hasn't heard anything from Marc, but she shares your opinion," David admitted. "She takes a 'no news is good news' point of view. For a twenty-year-old, Delphine has an astute understanding of human nature," David added. "She thinks it's a good thing for Marc to get out of Geneva and live someplace else for a while."

"How is she doing? When do her classes start?"

"Next week, apparently. She's doing okay, but she's feeling a bit down. September is a cruel month. The memories are pretty intense. There were three weeks between the time the doctor said there was no hope and the day Sandie died. During the deathwatch, Delphine went to the hospital with me three or four times a week. It wasn't easy for her to see her mother confused and in pain. Even though it's been almost two years now, the anniversary of Sandie's death brings it all back into sharp focus. Delphine doesn't feel quite ready to deal with it."

And you? Are you ready to deal with it? Jenny wondered.

The next evening, they ate supper early so David could attend a Neighborhood Association meeting. As they cleared the table, he said, offhandedly, "The meeting's at the Community Center. I wonder if they'll use the big hall where we did Sandie's Ceremony."

Jenny nearly dropped the plate she was carrying. The Community Center was where Sandie's memorial service had been held. David hadn't been inside the building in the two years since.

When he got home, he reported on the meeting. At the end he added, "The doors to the large hall were closed. The meeting was in the little room next to it." The pain and resignation in his voice launched Jenny. She went to him and hugged him with all her might.

"I feel so useless sometimes," she lamented. "So powerless to help."

They held each other for a long moment, and then David said quietly, "But you do help, Jenny. You do."

Jenny picked up the empty wine glasses and started toward the sink.

"Don't put mine in the dishwasher, Woman," he commanded, lapsing into folksy drawl. "I ain't finished yet."

Jenny handed him back his wine glass. David held up the bottle. "Want some more?" he asked her.

"No, I'm fine," she replied.

David refilled his glass, took out his cigarette pack, and flipped on the exhaust fan over the stove. "You go on up," he said, looking at the clock. "I want to set the table for breakfast."

She recognized this as a hint that David wanted some time on his own. An hour later, he was still puttering, making a stock and preparing a batch of pastry dough to be quartered and stored in the freezer.

"Are you planning to cook all night, or do you want to squeeze in a few hours sleep," Jenny teased, calling down to him.

"I'll be up in a minute," David said. He retreated to his computer and sent an e-mail to Jack Pogue asking for a status report on Marc.

As an old friend of the family, Jack had offered Marc housing in his rambling San Francisco Victorian until Marc found an apartment. The keyboard continued to click as David crafted a reply to Graham's update on his health.

Jenny became immersed in her reading and was surprised, when the clock chimed eleven, that David hadn't come up yet. One glance down the stairs, and she realized why. He was sitting in the dark, with a glass of brandy and his cigarettes, staring out the window. *Should I go down to him? But what would I say? There's been no word from Marc. Nothing I can say will change that. Delphine is grieving for her mother. Nothing I can say will change that either. The Community Center obviously stirred up memories, and now that he's back at school, David is surrounded by people who miss Sandie and probably want to talk about her.* Jenny picked up her book again. *Just keep yourself awake, Longworth, until he comes up.*

When David finally got into bed, he pulled up the covers, said good night, and turned away from her. *One step forward, two steps back. Let it be,* she decided.

David was up early, and by the time Jenny joined him in the kitchen, he sounded steady and positive. "Jack wrote back and said that Marc is fine," he told Jenny as he handed her a mug of tea. "I've forwarded his e-mail to you."

When Jenny finished breakfast, she descended to her office and checked her inbox. The forwarded message from Jack was simple but reassuring.

> *From: Jack*
> *To: David Perry*
> *Date: September 3, 2002*
> *Subject: Re: What's Happenin'?*
>   Hey, David, Marc told me he called you, but you Luddites don't have an answering machine. Anyway, he's settled in here and is fine. So stop worrying. I think everything will be okay. And frankly, I think he is in the right place right now. Jack

Jack was a man of few words, but his response to David's anxious e-mail was exactly what David needed to hear.

Jenny's in-box also contained a copy of the reply David had sent Graham the night before:

De: David
A: Graham
cc: Jenny
Envoyé: 3 septembre, 2002
Objet: Re: Good News

Don't know how you put up with all them medical folks pushing and prodding where the sun never shines. Jenny has been ragging me for the last year to do all sorts of exams. Got to admit Sandie used to do the same; it's a girl thing. So, being a docile husband, I did them. To the great disappointment of everyone but me, there's nothing wrong. No projected new expense for medical technology. I'm screwing up the local economy and not using my health insurance.

Howsomever, my wife has managed to corner me on the same issue that is dividing the Middle East. Terrorism you ask? No, water. Wants me to drink lots of water, flush out the bad doobies. I try to appease her by pointing out that coffee, beer and wine are basically water with taste, but no, that's not good enough. She wants me to drown myself in the Alpine stuff that filters through millennia and granite or some such shit. You wouldn't have a rejoinder handy, would you? I love to take showers, even the occasional bath, but drinking the stuff pure???

And you, dear Sir? How be's it in Beantown? David

Jenny's first reaction was to reply with humorous commentary, countering David's somewhat tipsy assertions that medical checkups were a waste of time. The water issue was harder to tease about. Right after Sandie's death, David drank heavily, anesthetizing himself against the pain. He had gradually moderated his consumption after Jenny's move to Geneva, and seemed back on an even keel until the shock of Graham's recent cancer diagnosis and the problems with Marc. Now, David was again using alcohol to cope with stress.

Graham was one of the few people with whom Jenny felt comfortable discussing her concern. David and Graham had shared nearly forty years of life's adventures, and supported each other through the dark days of Graham's divorce and Sandie's prolonged illness. Jenny had sought Graham's counsel about David's drinking two years earlier, when Sandie's death sent David into a dangerous tailspin. Given the current circumstances, she didn't want to wait until things got out of hand. *A stitch in time,* she told herself.

From: JWLongworth
To: Graham
Date: September 4, 2002
Subject: Water

Now that he has put it at issue, maybe David will listen to you on the subject of drinking something other than coffee, wine and bourbon. He, of course, will argue that he does: beer, scotch and brandy.

My tone is light, but the reality isn't. The alcohol consumption is creeping up again. This summer, he was back down to a normal level, at least what the Europeans consider normal, and I really thought I could check that problem off as solved. But your cancer scare was a shock, things have been difficult with Marc, and the anniversary of Sandie's death is looming.

The drinking is nowhere near the volume he consumed after Sandie died. He rarely gets inebriated in the way one normally associates with alcohol abuse, although clearly his language becomes more colorful. He doesn't try to hide his drinking. My guess is that he's fully cognizant and just "doesn't give a shit," as he would say.

You've known David as long as I have. He's stubborn and willful and disinclined to worry about other people's opinions. It doesn't work when I give cautionary counsel about drinking and driving. So I'm trying a back-door approach. I want to soften the impact by upping the intake of non-alcoholic liquid, preferably without caffeine.

Any ideas you come up with will be appreciated. In the meantime, maybe some light-hearted repartee about the virtues of water and fruit juice will help. It did, after all, take only a month for him to cave in on the question of vitamin pills. Now he even takes responsibility for buying more when his supply runs low. The man is full of surprises.

Meanwhile, how are YOU doing? Here I am going on about my concerns with nary a question about your progress. Hope all continues to improve for you.

Regards to Barbara. Love, Jenny

She read her draft carefully. *Am I overreacting?* She read it a second time, took a deep breath, and hit the send button.

David was in good spirits that afternoon when they set out for a farewell party for Laurent Barreau, a high-school student David had tutored in preparation for a British university program. Jenny was pleased that Graham's good check-up and Jack's reassurances about Marc had buoyed David's mood, but her own was subdued at the prospect of a party where she knew no one.

"It's just going to be a bunch of kids," David promised, knowing Jenny's reluctance to attend large gatherings. Most of the guests were indeed teenagers, but several adult family members were also present. David and Jenny went through the buffet line, filled their plates, and looked about for a place to sit. An elderly lady was seated not far away, with an empty chair on either side of her. David's southern manners immediately clicked in. "That's Laurent's great aunt. We should go sit with her," he told Jenny.

"I've been Laurent's tutor for the past year," David remarked as he introduced himself and Jenny.

Laurent must have accorded him enormous credit, because the great aunt expressed generous praise and gratitude for David's work. He responded with pleasantries while they ate.

"I'm going to go mingle with the youngsters," David said once his plate was empty. "You gonna be all right?"

Jenny was uncomfortable being left on her own, but she was still working on her salad, and she knew David was eager to talk with Laurent and his friends. "I'm fine," she said with a smile.

Having heard them conversing in English, the great aunt turned to Jenny. "*Etes-vous anglaise?*" she asked.

"*Non,*" Jenny answered, "I'm not English; I'm American. Unfortunately," she added, apologizing for her awkward French, "I have been in Geneva only one year, so my French is not yet very good. My husband is also American, but he has lived here for thirty years, so he is bi-lingual."

The great aunt repeated Jenny's last sentence. At first Jenny thought she was going to correct a grammatical error. Then Jenny realized that she wasn't reworking Jenny's French. She was puzzling out the logistics.

"Ah!" Jenny explained, "I am his second wife. My husband lost his first wife to cancer two years ago."

The great aunt regarded Jenny with heightened interest. "I, also, was a second wife," she said, describing her marriage to a widower. "Do you have children?"

"*Non,* but my husband has two. His son Marc attends college in San Francisco. His daughter Delphine is a student in Paris. Their mother was Parisienne," Jenny added.

"So, they do not live at home," the great aunt observed. "I too had no children of my own, but instead, two stepdaughters."

"Tell me, Madame, if I may ask. How long did it take your stepdaughters to accept your marriage to their father?"

The elderly woman looked at Jenny with a twinkle in her eye. "Oh, not very long." She paused. "Only twenty years."

Jenny's anxiety about her French disappeared. This spry octogenarian understood her even when Jenny couldn't finish a sentence. The woman knew from her own experience what Jenny was trying to say. David periodically checked to see if Jenny needed rescuing, but she wanted to absorb every bit of counsel the great aunt could share.

On the way home, Jenny related everything she could remember about the conversation. "I really appreciated talking with another woman who has been a second wife!"

David frowned. "There's something that bothers me when you use that term, 'second wife.'"

"Really? Why? It's a perfectly accurate term."

"Yes," he replied, "but it sounds pejorative, like 'fifth wheel.'"

"You're my second husband, and I love you much more than the first one!" Jenny teased.

"Yeah, but somehow 'second wife' sounds inferior. Besides which," he went on, "who is really the second wife in this situation? You and I started up several years before I even met Sandie."

Jenny looked at him in astonishment. "David Perry, if you count all the women you hung out with before you got married, they make a full harem!" He just grinned.

Does he really think of me as his first wife? For a minute Jenny delighted in the idea. *But that would make me first and third. It sounds like a baseball reference*, she decided.

Later that evening, Jenny received a reply to her appeal for Graham's advice.

From: Graham
To: Jenny
Date: September 4, 2002
Subject: Re: Water

Dearest Jenny, I'm going to have to give that some thought. David is such a steady-state drinker that most of the time he just seems like, well, you know, David. I remember how bad a shape he was in after Sandie died, and I did notice, this summer, that he seemed amazingly close to his old normal self. It's worrisome to think that he's starting to drink again. Even if it's tied to something specific, like the anniversary of Sandie's death, that doesn't mean he will automatically go back to his previous, lower level of consumption once he gets past it.

For your own sake, you have to have people to talk to, however much that goes against your stiff-upper-lip instincts and habits. I will think on this and will write more soon.

Much love, dear friend, Graham

From: J W Longworth
To: Graham
Date: September 4, 2002
Subject: Re: Re: Water

Thanks, G. Unfortunately, there is no one here I feel comfortable talking to about it. It's not just the language. All our Geneva friends are connected to l'Académie Internationale. David is a revered teacher, respected colleague and beloved friend in this community. The last thing I want is for this to become gossip at school.

It *is* worrisome, but we're not at crisis level - yet. As you say, he's just David. Alcohol doesn't alter his personality. He handles his wine well in public, and even when he doesn't, he's a lot of fun. Alcohol was never a problem (that I know about) before he lost Sandie, so I suspect this is a kind of "grief relapse." I keep thinking the mourning process is coming to an end, and I keep being wrong.

I'm looking for gentle ways to help him confront himself. He got this under control on his own before, and I'm hoping he can do so again. Humor and subtlety seem worth trying, whereas asking him directly to halve his alcohol consumption would be like asking him to halve his cigarette consumption. I can hear him now, in utter disbelief. "Get outta heah!"

Love, J.

With the following week came Jenny's first French class. She checked in at the Center's reception desk and was steered to a meeting room that held about thirty women. The large turnout obviously surprised the organizers. They were short of chairs. Ten minutes after the class was supposed to begin, the receptionist came in. "I'm really sorry. The teacher isn't feeling well," she reported, "and can't give a full lesson this morning, but she's here, and she'll stay long enough to outline your course requirements."

Jenny looked at the crowd that surrounded her. *This is not good,* she fretted. *Language classes need to be small in order to be effective.*

When the teacher walked in, she echoed Jenny's thoughts. "*Non!*" she said emphatically, "I cannot 'andle theez many student!" She did a brusque triage. Women with more than two years of academic French were classified as "Intermediate," regardless of how long ago the two-plus years might have been. Women with six months to two years were "Beginners." Women with no experience were told to find an elementary program elsewhere. "I cannot start from nowhere. We 'ave only zree class hevery week, and theez eez not enough for zee true *débutante!*" she asserted.

Since the lesson was cancelled, most of the women left as soon as the teacher dismissed them. There were some other activities going on – a quilting class, a bridge tournament – but Jenny was at loose ends. She had an hour and a half to kill before she was due to meet David. Her discomfort with unfamiliar places began to surface, so she occupied herself reading the notices on the bulletin board. *I just have to make myself keep coming until it doesn't seem so strange,* she told herself. *Rome wasn't built in a day.*

At noon, Jenny walked from the Center to l'Académie Internationale. David appeared promptly after his class. He dropped off a folder in the administrative office, once Sandie's domain, and then took Jenny into town to buy the books she needed for her French course.

"How did it go?" David asked.

Jenny described the problems that beset the first scheduled lesson. "The confusion was a little discouraging, and despite the triage, my class will have close to twenty people in it. Still," she concluded, "I managed to get there on time, by myself, without getting lost. That's definite progress!"

They arrived home to find a note from Graham.

From: Graham
To: David
cc: Jenny
Date: September 9, 2002
Subject: Health update

Well yes, Barbara has also ragged and nagged and finally converted me to the conviction that we don't drink enough of the pure stuff. I handle it by drinking Perrier and suchlike. And yes, I do feel better, in a number of ways, including intestinal process. I'm sure that's helped me these past months. Doc told me that I came thru chemo with "flying colors." I thought I'd had a hell of a time. Turns out I had no idea. So give it a try. You'll live longer and enjoy it more.

What do you hear from the young'uns?

Much love – Graham

De: David
A: Graham
cc: Jenny
Envoyé: 9 septembre, 2002
Objet: Re: Health update

Glad the doctors say you're on the mend. Ask Barbara if you can have a glass of *real* bubbly to celebrate.

Re the young'uns, I haven't spoken with Marc since he left, but we've swapped some e-mails, and he's apparently adjusting well to San Francisco. This isn't the most carefree time of his life, but that gives him a future to look forward to. Delphine is enjoying university and loving Paris. We plan to see her end of October, for *Toussaint*.

On the home front, Jenny is happy making to-do lists and pushing water. I'm happy declining her offer. The weather is still acceptable. My students are great. Beyond that, all's normal here in staid Geneva.

Kisses to Barbara. Love, David

Jenny was grateful for Graham's input. As a trained psychologist, he could add professional insight to the knowledge gleaned from his decades-old friendship with David. If anybody could plant a fertile seed in David's psyche, it was Graham. David trusted him the way Jenny trusted Ross.

Graham also sent a private note to Jenny saying, "I'm not sure your ruling out a direct approach is the best thing."

> *From: J W Longworth*
> *To: Graham*
> *Date: September 10, 2002*
> *Subject: Feedback*
>
> You have my super thanks for your response to David. The surface message is persuasive, and he may read the concern between the lines as well.
>
> Regarding a direct approach, I've been dancing around the alcohol issue in part because I'm a little afraid of rocking my own boat. David's reply to you was cheery enough, but despite his words, the next few weeks are likely to be tough. September 25 is the second anniversary of Sandie's death, and the major goal at the moment is just getting through it.
>
> David trusts me with his feelings and his thoughts about Sandie, but I am conscious of how huge the shoes are that I am trying to fill. I'm not yet secure enough to do something that might lead David to withdraw from me, like challenging his drinking. I can tease him about it, up to a point, but when David doesn't want to talk about something, he digs in his heels, and the conversation goes nowhere.
>
> Enough. Right this minute he's doing okay (laughing at some e-mail jokes!) so I'm doing okay too. I won't do this to you often. Someday I'll find a safe outlet over here. Or even better, someday I won't need one!
>
> Love, Jenny

On September 24, before he left for school, David reported an e-mail from Marc, asking for help in transferring the balance of his Swiss bank account to San Francisco.

"Why would he take money out of his Swiss account?" Jenny queried. "He has less than a hundred francs in it, and he'll have to pay both a wire and a currency conversion fee. He should be using the money in his education trust. That's what it's for, and it's already in dollars. All he has to do is write a check."

"I'm not sure he really understands how to use American checks," David suggested. "The Swiss pay everything by postal vouchers. It's a totally different system."

"Ah!" Jenny concurred. "I hadn't thought of that." While David was teaching, she produced a detailed explanation of how the American checking system worked and sent if off. "If there's anything you're not sure about," she advised Marc, "give me a call."

That evening, Marc called, but not to speak to Jenny. David answered the phone and within seconds, Jenny could see that David was struggling to control his tone and his words. When he finally hung up, he just shook his head. "Marc said that we're treating him like a baby who doesn't know what he's doing, and he doesn't want to use the effing trust money."

Jenny was astonished. "I don't understand. How can he *not* use the funds from his education trust? He's a full time student; he has no job; and he has no other money."

Looking at David's hurt, Jenny was incensed. *This, on the eve of the anniversary of Sandie's death?* Had David suggested that they let Marc sink or swim, she would have been tempted to root for the sharks. David, however, immediately composed a written reply.

De: David
A: Marc
Envoyé: 24 septembre, 2002
Objet: Your telephone call

I am upset by your call. I want you to know that, and I also want you to know why.

The last time you were in San Francisco, you had a problem with money. You have told me that it was very difficult and painful. Along with Jenny, I'm trying to show you that there are ways to avoid it happening again. The Education Trust comes from an arrangement Jenny and your mother worked out long ago. They planned it together for your education, including your living expenses while you're in school. That money is for you to use now, not some vague day in the future.

For the moment, you have little or no experience in using the trust funds. It has taken Delphine about a year to learn. You are just starting. It will take time. If you decide not to learn by not using it, that is your responsibility and, I believe, your loss, but I will love you whatever you decide. Dad

"Jenny, would you come take a look at this?" David called. "I'll put you in blind copy, but I'd like you to review it before I send it."

Jenny scanned the text on the screen. "I think it's a gentle and reasoned response," she said, "to a reaction that was puerile and unreasoned. I don't know what set Marc off, but he's behaving like a child." Jenny could feel her anger rising to the surface. "Is he offended because we thought perhaps he wasn't sophisticated about American checking? Or is it the trust money itself? Is he afraid he'll be beholden to me if he uses it? Maybe he thinks that accepting the trust money implies that he accepts *me* – as the family's new mother and his father's new wife. And maybe he wants to underscore that I am not acceptable in either of those roles."

David absorbed Jenny's words in silence. When it was clear she had nothing further to add, he simply asked, "Shall I change it, or send it as is?"

Jenny read the draft one more time and pulled herself together. "Sorry for the rant," she apologized. "I expect your approach is as good as anything. 'A gentle answer turneth away wrath' – isn't that the saying? So send it as is."

David was silent as he prepared supper. Jenny sat on a stool, watching him cut up vegetables. They managed superficial conversation during their meal, but Marc's angry telephone call left them both on edge, and the impending anniversary of Sandie's death lay like a shadow over the house. After supper, David returned to his computer, and Jenny went upstairs to read.

David finally came up to bed around eleven. They both slept for a time, but in the wee hours of the morning, David shifted onto his back, leading him quickly into repeated episodes of sleep apnea. His throat closed, he lay silent for twenty to thirty seconds, then suddenly gasped when his brain set off alarms that his body wasn't getting any oxygen. Jenny woke up with the first episode. After the second one, she nudged him whenever he went silent. He finally woke up enough to demand that she let him be.

"Dearheart," she said softly, "you're not breathing. If you would just shift onto your stomach or your side, you should be fine."

"Jeezus Christ!" he muttered, throwing aside the covers. "Stop playing your games, Jenny, and leave me alone!"

She was stunned. "They're not games," she said, her voice faltering.

He got up, grabbing his alarm clock and his pillow. Jenny realized too late how much was weighing on him, even in his sleep. Without looking back, David marched out to claim the bed in Delphine's room. Jenny's stomach went into a knot, and her eyes filled with tears. The only thing she could think of to calm herself was a hot bath. She went into the bathroom, plugged the tub drain and turned on the tap. As she lay in the steaming water, her mind was whirling a mile a minute. *There is no way I can go back to sleep.*

Finally she got out of the tub, put on her robe and slippers, and tiptoed down to the kitchen. It was 4:00 a.m. Using the stove light, she filled the kettle and set it to boil. She retrieved one of the memorial candles she had brought back from Boston, set it on the kitchen windowsill amid Sandie's miniature pitchers, and lit it. She made some tea, switched off the stove light, and carried her mug to the dining room table. Except for the brave little candle, she was in darkness.

Jenny sat in the chair David usually occupied, looking out to the garden and the streetlights at the far side of the field that backed up to the house. *I wonder if the view from David's chair might help me understand his vision of things.*

180

It didn't. She tried her mantra several times, but the loving thing to do, whatever it was, remained unclear. *Maybe I should call Bibi. It's only mid-evening in California. But what would I say?* she pondered.

She spent an hour in silent conversation with Sandie's candle, but not a single helpful thought came to her. *I know he's hurting, but so am I. And?* Several cups of tea later, she was still sitting there when David got up. He padded down the stairs, and gave her a ritual good morning kiss.

He spotted the flickering candle and asked where Jenny had put the reserves. He got a second candle, settled it next to Jenny's on the sill, and made himself some coffee. The room remained in darkness. "How long have you been up?" he asked.

She could hear the gentleness in his tone. *No point in doing battle,* she decided. "A while," was all she said.

"Sorry about last night," David apologized as he brought his mug to the table. "This is just a bad time on several fronts, and I don't handle it well." Jenny had no ready response, so she just pressed his shoulder in acknowledgement as she changed seats. He sat down and silently sipped his coffee. She remained silent also, staring out at the moon shadows in the garden. Neither of them was sure how to get things back to normal.

After breakfast, as David got ready to leave, Jenny confirmed her intention to try out a French conversation group that met Thursdays at the Center. "I'll walk up to l'Académie Internationale afterwards," she said.

Throughout the morning, Jenny dissected David's explosion of the night before. *Maybe I should talk to Rachel,* she thought as she waited for the bus. *Maybe an anniversary magnifies pain and loss beyond control.*

She stared out the window as the bus took her to the tram stop. *If I call Bibi, she'll yell at me and tell me to give David what for whenever he goes off the deep end. Maybe this is why David is so patient with Marc when he blows up. Maybe these fits of temper are genetic. David has them mostly under control, whereas Marc clearly doesn't.*

She gave up when she boarded the tram. *Maybe I should stop obsessing about this and concentrate on a subject I can do something about.* The French Conversation teacher had assigned some newspaper articles as preparation. Refocusing her mind, Jenny reread them until she neared her stop. At the Center, she joined seven other women in one of the classrooms. The teacher began the session immediately. There were no introductions. "*Bonjour, Mesdames.* You 'ave your newspapers, *oui? Bon.* We begin. We start at zee first page, from zee top on zee left. And we go zis way around zee room. You each read a paragraph."

As each participant read, the teacher corrected her pronunciation and had her repeat the relevant word or phrase. The entire session was geared toward helping the participants pronounce French properly, which was something Jenny could already do. Each time Jenny read, the teacher smiled, said "*Bon,*" and moved on to the next person.

When the class was over, Jenny made her way up to the school and met David. "How did it go?" he asked.

"To be honest, it was a letdown. I thought we would be discussing the newspaper articles, not just reading them out loud. I know these forays are also about becoming comfortable with public transportation and meeting English-speaking women, but as far as the French went, this was a waste of time. I'll just stick to my grammar class."

When they arrived back at the house, the memorial candles greeted them, bright even against the backdrop of a sunny sky. Their presence was not oppressive. They were simply dancing lights in the far corner of the kitchen.

Jenny opted for a nap. "Unless you need me for something," she said, "I'm going to go catch up on my lost sleep."

"I've got the newspaper to keep me busy. Sweet dreams."

Two hours later, when she got up, David was down at his computer, a tumbler of scotch in hand, reading e-mails from friends and family who shared sweet remembrances of Sandie. He sent off replies, then shifted into word processing. He stared for a moment at the blank screen, and then began to type.

Jenny watched him from the top of the stairs. She didn't have to see the words to know that he was writing a poem for Sandie. Face grim, fingers tensed over the keyboard, David tapped out line after line, with no hesitation and little editing.

This is where the grief will surface and find expression – an abstract of pain given form and substance in the written word.

If Jenny held a scintilla of residual anger from their spat of the night before, it vanished. Her heart flooded with love and concern. Still, David's poems for Sandie were always hard for Jenny, even though she knew they were therapeutic. *When he's immersed in the poetry, I can't reach him. I can't help him. I can only wait for him to emerge.*

Which, finally, he did. *Enrégistrer* (save). *Fichier* (file). *Arrêter* (shut down).

Suddenly the gears shifted, at least outwardly. "Do we need postage stamps?" he called up. It was late afternoon. The post office would close soon. They didn't need stamps, but David wanted fresh air and was looking for an excuse to go out.

After he left, Jenny checked her e-mail. There it was, sent to Marc and Delphine and cc'd to her: David's memorial poem for Sandie. "Images have danced two years across my vision since you left," he had written. "Two years – to forget, not enough."

Jenny read it carefully. *I don't want him to forget Sandie. I just want closure. I want the pain to fade and the happy memories to crowd out the sad ones.*

Marc called from San Francisco just minutes after David's return. The conversation was in French. Jenny inferred they were talking about Sandie, but given the apparent calm of David's tone, perhaps his missive about using the education trust had hit its mark. When he got off the phone with Marc, David immediately placed a call to Delphine. She wasn't home, so he left a brief message. "Hiya, Kid. Sorry you're not there. Just called to say I'm thinking about you and wanted to send my love. Talk to you soon. Bye."

The DuPonts paid a surprise visit around six o'clock with a bottle of Sandie's favorite Beaujolais. "Because there is no burial plot, there is no place to go to focus our sadness and our memories," Josette explained, "except that we wanted to be with David."

I wonder if they feel awkward coming here and making it clear, in my presence, how much they miss Sandie, Jenny speculated.

As David opened the wine, Jenny reminded herself that these were David's closest friends in Geneva. *They share his grief, they're demonstrating their support, and they're in need of comfort themselves. Mantra, Jenny! Be the kind of hostess you would hope for if the roles were reversed.*

"In this house," Jenny said with a welcoming smile, "Sandie is everywhere, but especially in David's heart. You were right that this is the place to come."

The conversation was subdued, but not somber. They raised a glass to Sandie and then chatted about school. It was a familiar topic, and one Jenny could follow for the most part, though she had nothing to contribute to the conversation. Michel and Josette had another commitment, so they only stayed an hour. The evening was going to be just David and Jenny. *He seems withdrawn,* Jenny decided. *Time for positive action.*

"If Sandie were sitting here right now, and her day had gone essentially as ours has, where would she want to go for dinner?" Jenny asked, looking for a way to get them out of the house.

"Le Borgia," said David, without hesitation. "It's a small family-oriented restaurant, not ten minutes from here, run by two Italian brothers."

"Sounds fine," Jenny responded brightly.

David called to see if they needed reservations. No problem. Within minutes they were in the car and headed toward the restaurant. En route, David offered another apology for the previous night's upset. His words were few, but his contrition was genuine. "You are completely forgiven," Jenny assured him. "Just promise me that you will never behave like that again."

"Oh, no," he said, "I can't promise that. You have to accept that I have a dark side."

"I know you have a dark side," she countered. "So do I. But you don't fully understand the impact your actions have on me. Tonight, you have more than enough on your plate, but some day, you're going to hear what happens in my head when you do something like that."

"Fair enough," he said.

David had described Le Borgia as "the local pizza place," but it was pizza to be consumed slowly, in the French fashion, pizza to be lingered over while sipping wine, discussing the merits of different mushrooms and debating which combination of cheeses made the best topping.

They were seated at a small table near the open brick pizza oven. David ordered a bottle of Chianti to sustain them as they considered the menu. After debating the choices, he ordered a pizza layered with thinly sliced ham. Jenny ordered hers topped with *champignons de Paris*. They toasted Sandie.

"To Madame," David said. Their glasses touched. Their eyes met. They each took a sip.

"Can you remember the first time you and Sandie came here?" Jenny asked.

"No."

"Not at all?"

"No."

"Well, then, what is your happiest memory of this place?" Jenny queried, working to bring David's thoughts of Sandie out into the open.

"Cast parties," he said. "Whenever we did a play at school, we had cast parties here."

Their pizzas were served. The conversation wandered as they ate. Jenny considered, then reminded David that this second anniversary of Sandie's passing was also the first anniversary of Jenny's arrival in Geneva as a prospective immigrant and his fiancée. The memory was burned in her mind, but it was news to him. "You got here on September 25?"

She paused. "I remember thinking it was symbolic. The beginning of a new year for both of us."

David cut another slice of pizza. At Le Borgia, the pizza did not come pre-cut. The Swiss ate it with a knife and fork, but David and Jenny reverted to their fingers.

"So," he said casually, curling a wedge of pizza into a mouth-sized roll, "The question is, are you up for another year?"

Jenny had to smile. *David can be wonderfully articulate – quick and witty, or utterly profound – but the language of romance is not his forte.* His question reminded Jenny of his guarded proposal, which began something like, "So, when are you coming back to Geneva?"

"Am I up for another year?" she echoed. "Dearheart," she replied, shaking her head in puzzlement that the question had even arisen, "I'm here for as long as you want me."

"Well," he said, backing and filling, "I want you here only as long as you want to be here."

Sometimes she wanted to throttle the man. She leaned across the table and looked him straight in the eye. "David Perry, you total turkey, do you not understand how much I love you?"

He was silent. A very light flush crept up his cheeks. *Have I embarrassed him? Or is it only the Chianti?* She pushed. "Or haven't you noticed?" she demanded.

He played with his napkin. He repositioned his fork on his plate. He leaned back in his chair. He looked at her. A slight smile played around the corners of his mouth. That impish look he sometimes got began to glimmer in his eyes. He nodded his head slightly. "I've noticed," he said. And he poured the last of the wine.

The next morning dawned cold and gray. Jenny went out to find a replacement rose for Sandie's vase, but the changing weather had taken its toll. There was no single rose that was unblemished. On the back trellis, however, in a more protected spot, there was a triple stalk, with three small buds. She cut it and brought it in, mindful of the analogy. David, Sandie and Jenny were also a threesome. It wasn't easy to keep everything in balance, but thus far, the juggling act was worth it.

Understanding

"Your poetry is trivial," she said,
"Like you and Graham talking."
She said she didn't understand.
It came out like that, off hand.
I don't understand either, he muttered to himself,
Wondering whether her objection concerned
comprehension or subject matter.
And which comes first, he thought,
Irritates her most?
And why is Graham mixed up
In her mind with things I wrote?
He asked her if she didn't understand the words.
She said she didn't get what lay
Behind the ones she heard;
She understood the English, not the chatter.
He tried to reassure her (himself as well)
That it didn't matter, and proposed she read
Some different ones, a choice he made,
Selecting subjects she might find
Appropriate poetically. She read, then shrugged.
"It must be beyond me. I didn't go to Harvard."
"Oh, Jesus!" he slowly hissed in feigned despair,
"What does Harvard have to do with my poetry?"
She couldn't say or wouldn't, but to her mind
It wasn't what you'd call lyric, (That it wasn't,)
Heroic or romantic. (Nothing truer.)
He said that was fine and,
Not knowing how to turn the trick,
Went back to writing, no sadder, no gayer.

D.P. – January, 1998

Chapter 8

October 1 fell on a Tuesday. The day brought good moments and bad – a kind of microcosm of their existence.

On the bad side, the postman delivered what Jenny hoped was the last of Marc's parking violation tickets. "God, I am so glad he's gone!" said David, shaking his head when he saw it.

Jenny was startled by his vehemence, although she certainly agreed with his sentiments. She knew David would pay the ticket rather than asking Marc to take care of it. It bothered her, but she saw little point in arguing about it. *Grant me the serenity to accept the things I cannot change.* She had told David before that he sent mixed messages, holding Marc accountable one day, then bailing him out the next. David recognized his inconsistency, but the pattern remained, and there was nothing new to be said about it.

In the good column, there were replies from friends to whom Jenny had sent a summary of her thoughts at the completion of her first year in Geneva. The summary contained a host of stories, some funny, some poignant, including an account of her pizza dinner with David at Le Borgia. She had closed with a philosophical observation:

> … I was in my office the other morning, and when I opened the window, I heard a rooster crowing. It brought back a memory of my first visit to Geneva, as David and Sandie's guest in what was then their brand new house. Then, as now, the office doubled as a guest room. My very first morning in that room, I heard a cock crow at dawn. My condo in Shawmut has lots of wildlife around

it, but there are no farm animals within range. Hearing a rooster, I was aware that I was in an unfamiliar world. There was a sense of adventure, but also a sense of being separate and apart. Much in my life has changed since that long-ago day, yet though I've been here a full year now, Geneva still feels foreign to me. I still get homesick. I still miss you all. But when all is said and done, the only place I want to be is with David.

From: BIBirnbaum
To: Jenny
Date: September 30, 2002
Subject: Re: An anniversary

You two are spinning a very complex emotional web! It sounds very full and rich. I am glad you are able to balance all of those conflicting emotions and find your way back to the core emotion: your love for this guy. What a jam-packed year!

All goes well here. I'm helping the grandkids make Halloween costumes. Boo!

Love, Bibi

From: Ross
To: Jewel
Date: October 1, 2002
Subject: Re: An anniversary

Well, your life does have poignancy and bouquet and inebriation. Ramon used to quote Don Quixote to me, and through you, I am at last beginning to fathom it. Kevin joins me in sending love. Know that we are over here cheerleading like mad for you.

Keep shining, Ross

Jenny well understood how much she needed friends like Ross "cheerleading" from back home. She also recognized the astuteness with which Bibi had analyzed her situation and identified the "core emotion: your love for this guy." Equally helpful was a note from Rachel, whose openness continued to enhance Jenny's understanding of grief.

From: Rachel
To: Jenny
Date: October 1, 2002
Subject: Re: An anniversary

Jenny, I love getting your e-mails. Anniversaries are hard and yet welcome. We are beginning to have family traditions around them. On Josh's birthday and on the date he died, my daughter Sarah and I take my grandchildren to the cemetery. They think of it as a park. We pack a picnic with as elegant a lunch as you can have with three children under four. Sarah and I clean the headstone with great care. And then, hopeless as it sounds, we tell Josh all the special things we have to tell him and decorate the headstone with stones and shells. In the evening, the whole family gathers for dinner. And yet, in spite of all this, the mist descends and each of us is alone with the sadness.

You are remarkable to understand David's need to grieve and remember Sandie while another part of him is able to love and begin a new life with you. As I enter the third year since Josh's death. I still want to talk about him. His likes, dislikes, foibles, and strengths continue to be very important. I like to laugh about the silly things he did. I sometimes think that people are afraid that if they bring up his name I will burst into tears. It's not like that at all, as you have learned. It makes me happy when people remember him.

Do keep in touch. Much love, Rachel

In addition to bringing welcome e-mails from the States, the first of October marked the anniversary of the luncheon Olga had hosted at her farmhouse shortly after Sandie's death. David's depression and withdrawal on that day had so frightened Jenny that she revealed her longstanding love for him, pleading with him not to succumb to despair. Re-enacting the long country walk in which that tearful conversation took place, David and Jenny left the house as soon as he returned from school, wearing light jackets against the early evening cool.

"It's such a special anniversary for me," she commented as they set out. "This was the day that changed my life."

"That's a very dramatic way to describe it," David replied. "It's more like this was the day that changed your address."

"No," she said firmly. "It changed my life."

Jenny slipped an arm around David's waist, and he put his around her shoulder. Once across the road, they followed the woodland path that bordered the narrow river. They stopped for a moment to watch two gray herons standing like statues at the edge of the field, waiting patiently for their dinner to emerge.

David stepped downwind and lit a cigarette. "I hope it was for the better," he remarked.

Jenny looked at him, puzzled. "What was for the better?" she asked.

David shook his head in mild exasperation. "When we started out, Ducks, you said that today was the day that changed your life. I'm just hoping it was for the better."

Jenny started to express reassurance of her love, but the slight breeze shifted direction and blew David's smoke directly into her face. She waved it away and tried to look sternly disapproving, but she had to laugh at David's stricken expression.

"Mostly for the better," she replied, "except for the fumes. If the air quality improved, my life would be practically perfect."

When he saw that she was teasing, he narrowed his eyes at her. "Woman, I ain't gonna give up my vices."

"I don't expect you to, Dear. You're like Churchill with his cigars and his brandy. You will never surrender."

"I don't smoke cigars," he insisted.

"No," Jenny conceded, "but your Gauloises are almost as bad!"

Over dinner, the mood remained light-hearted, but as they cleared the dishes, David lapsed into silence. He turned on the stove-hood exhaust fan so he could smoke, and poured himself a fresh glass of wine. Jenny eventually retreated upstairs with her book. She meant to stay awake but somehow dozed off. When she opened her eyes, the bedside clock said 11:50 p.m. David had not yet come up. She went to the top of the stairs. The only light in the dining room below was coming from the glow at the end of his cigarette and its reflection on a brandy snifter. *The anniversary of Olga's luncheon stirs different memories for him than it does for me,* she observed.

> *From: Graham*
> *To: Jenny*
> *Date: October 7, 2002*
> *Subject: Re: An Anniversary*
>
> Jenny, please know that my delayed response to what you wrote about David and Sandie, and about shoe-filling in particular, is due to my enervated condition and not any reluctance to be available for this kind of conversation. We share a long history together, a deep love for David, and now we share this cancer experience, which forms a special bond, one I know you had with Sandie.
>
> How I wish Sandie were still here to share it with us. Of course, she is, in one sense, and painfully not, in others, which you make room for so gracefully and graciously. That both costs you and nourishes you. In sharing David with Sandie, you have him as well, and he has you.
>
> So, about you and David and Sandie, and the enormity of the shoes you think you have to fill: no, you don't. And I don't see you doing that in reality. Rather, I see you leaving a generous, limitless space for Sandie still to be there, in her own shoes (and absent too, excruciatingly at times). Whether consciously or not, you seem quite wisely not engaged in shoe-filling.
>
> Nap time. I'll continue soon.
> With love always, Graham

It really does help to communicate with friends who have some perspective on all this, Jenny noted as she read. *I know I'm making progress, but my spirits get easily dampened with the days growing so short.*

Gardening season was almost over, sunshine was an increasingly rare commodity, and the thick cloud cover that darkened Geneva's skies through the winter was beginning to settle in. This made Jenny doubly grateful for Graham's encouragement.

From: JWLongworth
To: Graham
Date: October 8, 2002
Subject: Re: Re: An Anniversary

Thanks, G., for being such a thoughtful sounding board. I run my anxieties by David from time to time, but he seems to feel very secure about our relationship and our circumstances, so he doesn't understand why I don't. Yet when he is down, my emotions are roped to his like two mountain climbers. When he falls, I fall, and the worries run rampant: Is it me? Have I failed to dig my piton in firmly enough to secure a hold on this slippery slope? Is David growing impatient with my phobias, my torturous acquisition of French, my aversion to smoke? It's one of the few situations in which I'm the emotional one, and he's the epitome of logic.

Love, J.

From: Graham
To: Jenny
Date: October 9, 2002
Subject: More thoughts

Well, you're both right. I can understand that you have difficult moments, but I also know that David's commitment to you is absolute.

There's no small amount of *déjà vue* involved. Sandie and I had a sort of big brother/little sister relationship. It went all the way back to her anguished plea, must have been not long after you came back from London in 1970, that she was in love with David, and at a total loss to know how to get him to reciprocate.

Over the years, she and I always talked easily about what was happening in our lives. From those conversations and my own observations, I know that David and Sandie's devotion to each other was strong and unwavering, though it was not without its problems.

Sandie was deeply grounded and fulfilled by the relationship in a family way (she who had no father and had lost her mother so young,) yet at the same time unfulfilled in some painful ways. She felt the absence of romanticism and affection acutely, yet resignedly. She often, often spoke to me about that over the years.

As for David, I believe Sandie touched him in a unique way, with that waiflike side of her, the orphan side, which somehow sat together with her Parisian *femme-du-monde* side. She was very much both, but it was the little-girl-lost part that got under David's skin, and made Sandie his love in a particular way.

You don't need to feel anxious. David loves you. He always has, and now it's even stronger. It's a different love from his love for Sandie. Like many of us, he needs to be needed, and you fulfill that need. He can also be quite dependent. You address that by taking care of him in many ways, without his feeling diminished by your strength and competence (which, by the way, are considerable).

You may have longed, all these years, to be the love of his life and the mother of his children, but you are a different person. What you have done in life, much of it, Sandie could never have done. She knew that and admired you for your generosity, your qualities of heart and loyalty, which she saw and valued. I know because she told me, as she told me all the other things I'm saying here.

I don't think Sandie could have done what you're doing now, had the positions been reversed. That just wasn't Sandie. I believe she would have turned from David, (even after loving him from afar, presumably, if the positions were reversed,) rather than share him so completely, as you do.

With much love, G.

Jenny read Graham's words several times. She devoured his reassuring observations, but in the end, she kept coming back to the phrase, "She often, often spoke to me...." Jenny felt a little shiver go up and down her spine. *X = Y. If I'm like Sandie, Sandie is like me. I'm uncomfortable discussing my problems with anyone local, but I confide in Graham. It's clear from Graham's words that Sandie too aired her marital worries with him. Question is, did Sandie trust Graham enough to talk about Julien Charbonnet?*

Careful, Jenny. Phrase the question in such a way that you can dissemble if Graham proves unaware of Sandie's infidelity.

She took the plunge.

From: *J W Longworth*
To: *Graham*
Date: *October 9, 2002*
Subject: *Where to start?*

Many thanks for the encouraging words! I'm putting you at the top of my call list for any time I need a pep talk!

Now that I understand how openly Sandie talked with you, I feel more confident that I'm not compromising either her or David with my queries. As I've said before, I've been reluctant to engage Sandie's friends in sensitive conversation lest the subject matter become school gossip.

It would help me to know if Sandie ever felt the alcohol consumption was an issue. I see it as grief-inspired, so it may not have been.

It would help me to know what she said to David, if anything, when her need for affection and attention was not being met. I've gotten the sense from David that there were a lot of important things he and Sandie never talked about. Why?

And finally, it would help to understand what happened with Julien Charbonnet.

Having thrown that at you, I will share something that may change your view that Sandie couldn't have handled sharing David. After our wedding, Olga Gerasimova, one of Sandie's closest friends, told me a story.

Olga spent a lot of time with Sandie in her final months. They talked about what might happen to David and the children after Sandie's death. Sandie told Olga she didn't think David would be able to cope on his own. "But," Sandie concluded, "I do not worry for David, because I know that Jenny will come, and she will take care of him."

Sandie's blessing was incredibly important to both David and me, and it helped to know that it gave her some peace to envision David in my care.

196

There are still lots of things I want to talk about, but
you need to parcel out that slowly returning energy. I'll
stop here and save the rest for another day.
Love, Jenny

Jenny was buoyed by her exchanges with Graham, but David was
tense, withdrawn and sleeping poorly. When he got up at 5:00 a.m.
for the second day in a row, Jenny gave him half an hour on his own,
then joined him in the kitchen.

"What are *you* doing up?" he queried. He gave her a perfunctory
kiss and turned on the kettle for her tea.

"I wanted to make sure you're okay," she replied.

"Hanging in there," was his response. He lit a cigarette and stared
into space.

"You've been really down for the last couple of days," she observed
softly.

"Yup, nothing to do but get through it."

"Would it help to talk about it?" Jenny probed.

"Nope," he replied firmly.

When David wouldn't talk, it flung Jenny into a downward spiral,
despite Graham's soothing words. Because she wasn't sure what was
bothering him, her mind ran riot through all the possibilities. What
might, in fact, be only a cold gray day of the psyche suddenly assumed
the proportions of a blizzard, a flood, a hurricane, and a tornado, all
rolled into one.

David's mood was still subdued after school. He flicked on the
stove exhaust, lit a cigarette, and dialed Delphine in Paris. There was
no answer so he left a message. "Just called to see how you're doing,"
he said. There was no play in his voice.

As he poured their wine, Jenny suggested that they take their
glasses into the living room and sit in front of the fire.

"You're still in a gray space," she observed as they sipped their
drinks.

"Yup," he replied, moving his chair next to the fireplace so he could light up another Gauloise.

"Whatever your angst is, you should let at least some of it out," Jenny counseled. "I'm a good listener, and I'm a safe one as well. Besides, it's part of my wifely job description," she added with a smile.

David took a deep drag on his cigarette, but said nothing.

"Let's start with something easy," she continued. "What's happening in your life these days?"

David frowned. "Not a lot, frankly. I'm not very much together at the moment. I seem to be wandering, not knowing how to find my center. School is not that much fun even though the kids are wonderful. It's all too routine, and I don't know how to change that."

He paused, and Jenny thought the revelations might be over, but suddenly the words started to flow. "World news is depressing. Autumn is not my favorite season, and winter is coming fast. The kids are off living their own lives in San Francisco and Paris. You and I are here like a couple of old farts who go to bed at nine o'clock. Perhaps I've reached an age where only the spring is an acceptable period of life."

David's stated dissatisfaction with their life in Geneva set off alarms. *Are we reaching the stage I've always feared? Does he regret that he didn't choose a second wife whose social skills and vivacity mirror Sandie's – someone who enjoys being out and about with neighbors and friends – someone who doesn't mind a smoky café or restaurant – someone who isn't limited to movies with subtitles – someone French?*

Uncertain of how to respond, Jenny issued a simple, "Ouch!" Then she seized on a clue from David's attempted phone call.

"Have you ever considered that you might be experiencing a kind of empty-nest syndrome?" she queried, hoping to draw David out. "When the children left home, you were completely preoccupied with Sandie's death. I wonder if you're having a delayed reaction to the reality that they're no longer here."

David paused to consider "I don't miss their presence in the house per se. I'm glad they're off on their own, making their way. Where I'm shaky is that I feel inadequate trying to fill the role of mother as well as father. That phone call to Delphine – that's the kind of thing that Sandie always did. I would get on the phone at some point during the conversation, but it was always Sandie who made the call."

"Do you still feel you have to fill the mother role?" Jenny asked.

"Yes." The reply was emphatic.

"Did your father do that when your mother became ill?"

"He may have for my brothers, but I was out of the house by the time my mother's mind began to go."

"Did you ever talk to your father about it? About how he coped with his feelings?"

David was candid. "No. I was in my twenties. I didn't want to talk with him. I guess the harsh truth is, I didn't want to know."

When David made no further comment, Jenny searched for something to steer the conversation in a positive direction. "Our trip to Paris for *Toussaint* is only three weeks away. Paris always cheers you up, and it will be fun to see Dellie. You have a whole week for fall break. Why don't we extend the trip and go someplace in France that you especially enjoy?"

David absorbed the suggestion. "I'll think on it," he said, draining his glass. "Meanwhile, I'd best get dinner started."

David headed for the kitchen, and Jenny descended to her office to check her e-mail. She was rewarded by a note from Graham that surpassed her expectations.

From: Graham
To: Jenny
Date: October 10, 2002
Subject: Re: Where to start?

Dear Jenny – The story Olga told you is not a total surprise. At some level, I already sensed that Sandie was confident that you would come and take care of David, and that that knowledge gave her great peace and comfort. And not just take care of David, but also the kids. The fact that David is with you and okay means that they are free to go and live their lives.

About the drinking, no, Sandie never talked with concern about that. When she was alive, it was just at normal French standard. About communication, Sandie felt that David just wouldn't talk about certain things. Your pragmatism and direct nature may be yielding better results than she had.

And yes, Sandie talked to me at length, over the years, about her affair with Julien. I did not feel free to say that until you did. With Julien, she was seeking an affection and affirmation that was missing in her relationship with David. David is full of love, but he doesn't easily translate it into words or romantic gestures. He's an incredibly deep-feeling, expressive man, yet at the same time, not expressive in certain ways that can be so key to marriage. You of all people are aware of that.

You know my love for David, and my admiration for him. When I speak about his flaws or lacks, it's not from any position of judgment or superiority. It's as a loving friend, with flaws and lacks of my own! I look forward to hearing whatever you want to share.

Much love, Graham

Jenny had not only suspected it, but also presumed it, yet it was still something of a shock to see incontrovertible proof spelled out on her computer screen. Yet there it was: "Sandie talked to me at length ... about her affair with Julien." *Now what do I do?* Beyond her own desire to "know for sure," Jenny hadn't worked out exactly how to present the proof to David.

During dinner, her mind spun different opening sentences, but David's damp spirits deterred her. *There is no way I can spring Graham's tale on David when he's low,* she concluded. *Sleep on it, Jenny. Give yourself time to digest all this and weigh your choices. You'll make a total mess if you try to tackle this tonight.*

Once the table was cleared and everything put away, David headed to his computer. "I'm going upstairs with my book," said Jenny, inadvertently reinforcing his point about being an "old fart."

David had a restless night, and was up before dawn. "I have to get to school early," he announced when Jenny came down for breakfast.

"If you have time today, can you take the vegetable stock out of the fridge and put it on the stove at a low simmer for an hour or so? It needs to be reduced." A quick kiss, and he was out the door.

Jenny checked the kitchen clock: 7:30 a.m. 1:30 a.m. in Boston. *This six-hour time difference drives me crazy!*

> *From: JWLongworth*
> *To: Ross*
> *Date: October 11, 2002*
> *Subject: Help!*
> I need your wise advice, but you are doubtlessly sound asleep right now. If you open this before you leave for work, could you give me a buzz? I was handed proof last night of Sandie's affair. I haven't told David yet. He's low at the moment, and I want to wait until he's in a better frame of mind. Meanwhile, my own mind needs some sorting out.
> Thanks as always – Love, Jenny

She showered and dressed, then got out the pot of vegetable stock David had left in the refrigerator. Turning the flame to low, she put the pot on the back burner and went down to her office.

> *From: JWLongworth*
> *To: Graham*
> *Date: October 11, 2002*
> *Subject: Revelations*
> These e-mails are getting to be like eating artichokes. There is more on the plate when I finish than when I started!
> Let me tackle the affair with Julien first. It was David who alerted me. We got an invitation to have dinner with the Charbonnets, and he just blurted it out. He had no proof, but he was "99% certain," and felt the affair had probably gone on for several years.
> When he and I were in Paris in August, we did a pilgrimage to the Pont des Arts, where David scattered some of Sandie's ashes. While we were there, David shared the fact that Sandie once told him their marriage

201

had held together because David allowed Sandie her "freedom." He and Sandie never spoke directly about the affair, but David considers that a tacit admission.

On his side of the ledger, David admits to what he describes as a few "flings," when they were still living in Paris, but insists that they were one-night stands with no emotional content. To him, an affair involves duration and some level of commitment. A fling is meaningless.

Frankly, it was a real shocker when David first told me his suspicions about Julien. It makes me sad watching David berate himself for all the ways in which he "failed" Sandie, as if the affair were his fault. There is a lot of self-flagellation mixed in with his grief.

Now, about comparisons of Sandie's and my love for David, and his respective love for us: I don't think I'm fooling myself when I say I didn't begrudge Sandie the love David felt for her. Watching them together, it was clear that he made the right choice. David was a free spirit when he was young. I was intense and driven. Had David and I married thirty years ago, my guess is that we wouldn't have lasted more than two or three years before we started doing damage to one another.

But I do long to be the love of his life now, for this part of his life. Some of that is an ancient thirst. Some is simply an awareness that time is short. I don't feel morbid about it, but my reprieve from cancer is likely to be limited. Whatever David feels for me, I want him to express it *now*, not save it up as a lament that Wife Number Three will have to listen to.

I haven't yet shared your e-mail about Sandie with David. He's having a difficult week, but as soon as I think he can handle it, I'll tell him about it.

Meanwhile, I'd best go check on the stock I left simmering on the stove.

Love, Jenny

As Jenny finished lunch, the phone rang.

"Hello, Princess," Ross said when Jenny picked up. "I have ten minutes. You say you have proof of Sandie's affair?"

"Ross! Thanks for calling! Yes, I got confirmation from Graham. You know that Graham's a psychologist, don't you? He and Sandie were close, going back to the days when she first began dating David. He's good at getting people to talk, he's a sympathetic listener, and he understands discretion. Apparently, Sandie sought his counsel and confided in him throughout the marriage. She told him about Julien."

"So what is it you need to sort out?"

"All this time, I've presumed that getting proof of the affair would resolve everything. But I'm feeling very unresolved."

"And?"

"Ross, I love you dearly, but please don't 'And?' me right now. I need advice."

"About what?"

There was a pause as Jenny considered how best to answer his question.

"Jewel, I love you dearly too," Ross interjected, "but it's 6:30 in the morning at my house. What exactly is the problem?"

"The problem is that I have to tell David I've confirmed the affair, and I want to be able to focus on *his* reactions, *his* feelings, and *his* needs. I want to be in a neutral space, and I'm not."

"What space are you in?"

"I'm not really angry, but I'm certainly annoyed, at Sandie and especially at Julien."

"Why?"

"Isn't it obvious? For nearly a decade, they conducted a clandestine affair that – had it ever been exposed – could have had devastating repercussions for David's career, Sandie's job, and their children's education. On top of whatever seismic damage it would have inflicted within the family, it would also have created a major scandal at the school. The school board could have demanded resignations. The kids could have lost their scholarship status; they were at l'Académie Internationale only because of their parents' positions on the staff. David's entire social circle would have heard about it. His world would have been upended."

"For someone who's only annoyed, you sound a bit angry."

"Well, okay. Yes, I'm angry."

"Which is entirely reasonable, because this has to be hurting you too. I've heard you say a dozen times that you admired and respected Sandie, and appreciated the fact that she gave David a happy life. So, if it wasn't so happy, or if the happiness was a deception, you have to be disturbed by it, no matter what public face you put on it."

"*Mea culpa*," she admitted.

"Take it a step further," he said. "Suppose that, somewhere around a decade ago, you had discovered that Sandie had shifted her attentions elsewhere. Had you known, all those years ago, that something was amiss in the marriage, would you have considered having an affair with David? You loved him. You were divorced by then, and you were swapping vacation visits with the Perrys on a regular basis."

"I don't much believe in extra-marital affairs, Ross. And isn't this 'leading the witness?'"

"No," he countered. "It's just a phone conversation between two old friends. And so," he continued, "even if you had known Sandie was unfaithful, you would have stayed a spectator on the sidelines – saintly, resigned and sleeping alone?"

"I hope I would have stayed a spectator so long as they were married. But had there been a divorce, yes, I probably would have gone after David."

"There's at least one answer for you. Be grateful Sandie was so successful at pulling the wool over your eyes. If you'd raced off to Switzerland a decade ago, think of all the fun times with me you would have missed!"

"I'll give you that one, Ross. You were my favorite non-lover ever."

"Were?" he bridled.

"Are," she corrected.

"All right. Now I'll give you some advice gratis, and then I have to go: First and foremost, this is no longer a question of deciding guilty vs. not guilty. The affair is now stipulated. It's a finding of fact. What you're working on is deciding Sandie's sentence. Her penalty. I want you to think about whether such a thing is even within your jurisdiction. Do you have standing to punish her? If no, you have to let it go. If yes, you have to ask whether it's worth meting out a sentence, remembering that Sandie's friends aren't going to want to hear anything bad about her, and they're especially not going to want to hear it from you. Your motives will immediately be suspect. If Wife Number One's reputation is suddenly tarnished, who benefits more than Wife Number Two? Whichever way you go, you still have to achieve *your* closure, as well as helping David achieve his. Am I the only one you've talked to about this?"

"I've talked to Graham, via e-mail, but with caution *vis-à-vis* my own feelings. Graham loved Sandie like a sister. He's as protective of her as he is of David. That's probably why she felt safe confiding in him. Graham implied that Sandie felt justified in her actions, and he takes no issue with that."

"How about Bibi?"

"Bibi has no idea. Not even a suspicion. David wanted this issue well contained."

"Well, I suggest you get David's clearance to share this with Bibi. She has no connection to anyone in Geneva. She cares about your feelings, she's fearless, and she's direct. No doubt she will be happy to talk about this with you for hours, days, weeks and months, until the subject is threadbare and exhausted."

"Are you telling me that you don't want to talk about this any more?"

"I'm telling you that I have to go shave and get dressed for work."

"Okay, Ross. I hear you. Thanks for the call. Thanks a million!"

"Let me know how David handles it."

"Will do. Hugs to Kevin. You have a great day."

"You too."

The DuPonts joined David and Jenny for dinner that evening, precluding any possibility of discussing the affair. *I'll do it tomorrow,* Jenny told herself.

Saturday morning, the sky was clear and the weather crisp. After breakfast, David and Jenny tackled Marc's basement room, dismantling Marc's battered metal bookcases to make room for new shelving.

"Oh, Lordy. There's a mouse trapped in the window well," Jenny called out as David was removing bolts. She tried to capture it from the inside so she could set it free. Her first attempt failed, and she nearly fell off the stepladder.

"Woman, get the hell off the goddamn ladder and close the goddamn window before you bloody-well kill yourself!" David ordered.

Jenny retreated, went outside, and liberated the mouse by pulling up the grate and lowering herself into the well from above. The mouse scampered off into the garden without a backward look. "You're welcome," Jenny whispered.

She went back to the basement.

"Do you want me to carry up the bookcase sections as you finish with them?" she suggested.

"No," David replied. "I want to keep them together until I've secured all the hardware in a plastic bag."

"Shall I go find a bag?"

"Jennifer Longworth, stop being such a busybody! Go check your e-mail or something. Get outta heah!"

There was nothing hard in his voice. *He just wants to work at his own pace, undisturbed. He's actually enjoying the project,* Jenny realized.

When he finished the bookcases, David came upstairs and began to assemble leftovers for lunch. He poured himself a glass of wine and looked in Jenny's direction. "What do you want to drink?"

It's time. Jenny was nervous, but she felt there was no point in delaying any further. *Is this truly the loving thing to do?* she asked herself. *Yes,* was the answer.

Jenny usually opted for tea or water at lunchtime, but under the circumstances, she felt the need for something stronger. "I'll join you on the wine. There's something serious I want to discuss."

David looked at her with raised eyebrows.

"Over lunch," she clarified. She turned and began to set the table. David brought over a platter of cold chicken and *célérie rémoulade.*

"Shoot," he said as they sat down.

"You've said you wished you knew for sure about Sandie and Julien. If you still want to know, I have the answer. If you'd rather not hear it, I'll change the subject right now, and we can talk about something else instead."

David's face went still, but he voice remained calm.

"I still want to know, and the answer is obviously yes, or you wouldn't have offered an option to avoid it."

"Correct," she conceded. "Sandie had an extended affair with Julien Charbonnet. She was, she said, looking for a level of physical and verbal affection that was not present in your relationship. As you sensed, she did not perceive or intend the affair as a repudiation of your marriage. She was trying to take care of a need to which you couldn't or wouldn't respond, at least in *her* mind. She sought balance by taking care of that need with discretion and safety."

"How did you find out?"

"Graham."

David was flabbergasted. *"Graham?* How on earth did you get this from *Graham?* I figured Josette might know, or Olga, or maybe even Edie. But Graham?"

"It took a while," Jenny replied. She described the trail of newspaper clippings and photographs tucked in amid office supplies and musical scores. She told David about the Salève College brochure and finally, for her the clincher, finding Sandie's *Testament* suggesting Julien as the children's guardian.

"Based on those clues, I was certain the affair had taken place. It was then an absolute that Sandie must have told someone. She couldn't possibly experience something so emotionally significant, over the course of a decade, and keep it secret from every living soul she knew. Yet I found no way to ask her Geneva friends without running a great risk. If they didn't already know, even hinting at such a possibility would have been devastating.

"Sandie would only have turned to someone in whom she had total confidence. It was logical that she would seek an extra layer of protection and keep this information away from people connected with l'Académie Internationale and, if possible, Geneva. It was also logical that she would turn to someone who could defend her and justify her behavior, if you ever found out about the affair. Who better than Graham, who loved you both?"

David's face was a mask. Jenny couldn't read him. "I'm going to give you some room to absorb this," she concluded. "When you're ready, I want very much to talk about it."

David was restless and edgy for the next several hours.

"How are you doing?" Jenny inquired gently when it got to be five o'clock.

"Processing. I'm going to lay a fire. We can have our wine in the living room and talk there."

Jenny brought in some glasses. After he got the fire going, David selected a bottle of *Côtes du Rhône* and opened it.

"*Santé,*" he said, taking a sip.

"*Santé,*" she repeated, following suit.

"So, you said you wanted to talk," he opened.

"Yes. But mostly, I want to listen. When you first spoke of it, you said you were '99% sure' about the affair. Now you're 100% sure. How big a deal is the 1% difference?"

David was silent for a moment, then began. "More of a difference than I expected," he admitted. "I find myself looking back over a decade's worth of behavior and wondering how I could have missed what now seems so obvious. All the after-school meetings she had to attend. All the social outings she included him in. All the extra-curricular projects she had to help with. Not to mention all those trips we took to the States when Sandie had to fly over a week or two later than me, or return to Geneva a week or two ahead of me, ostensibly because, as an administrator rather than a teacher, she had a longer work year than I did.

"I can't really blame her," he shrugged. "Sandie craved romance – candlelit dinners and bouquets of roses. I've always been something of a loner, and I've never been what you'd call touchy-feely. This is something I simply accept in myself. My natural way of expressing affection flows through words and deeds, not hand-holding in the movies."

"Did you and Sandie ever talk about your differences?"

"Not in a productive way. Sandie sometimes complained, 'You never do this … you never do that …,' but no, we didn't really talk about intimate issues. Maybe that's a male thing."

"You talk about intimate issues with me."

"I think it's more that *you* talk about intimate issues with *me*," he offered with a half-smile.

"Perhaps. I've always felt I could talk with you about anything, provided the timing was right. What's hard for me to reconcile is Sandie's perception that you weren't showing her any affection. You don't send valentines, and, as you say, you don't hold hands in the movies, but you show your love in lots of little ways. Still, if Sandie couldn't recognize your affection as such, it might explain why she turned to Julien. And apparently, your guess about duration was correct. The affair began when Sandie was around forty. It's potentially a demoralizing age for women in a society with so much emphasis on youth and beauty, though I don't see that Sandie had much to worry about. She was attractive and elegant right up until the end."

"I always thought so," David agreed, "but I do remember that she worked at it. I didn't care one way or the other, but she insisted on dying her hair at the first sign of gray. She and Josette used to go to the beauty parlor every month to get their hair done and their nails manicured. Birthdays were always celebrated with a day at a spa."

"What's strange," Jenny interjected, "is that I recall you saying once that you and Sandie had 'one of the neatest and most successful marriages in town.'"

"That was certainly my take. And you have to remember, Ducks, that Sandie gave me Paris. She gave me a French family." He paused. "She was the one who turned my dreams of living in Europe into a reality." Jenny could see he was working to control his emotions. "But maybe my expectations of the marriage were different. Once you have children, your relationship with your spouse changes. The love becomes more familial. You're partners in the enterprise of parenting. The sexual attraction diminishes, and the focus of affection broadens to include your kids. Being 'in love' gives way to 'loving,' at least it did for me. I didn't expect violins and shooting stars. That stage of our relationship was long over, and it didn't bother me. I thought we had simply moved into a steadier, more mature kind of love."

"Do you remember the poem you wrote for Sandie, back in May, when I went to Boston for my reunion?"

"Which one?"

Which one? How many has he written that I don't know about? "The one where you talk about having lost your gardener and wishing you could be with her again. There was something about the Devil beating his wife, and you making Sandie suffer. The end line was 'I didn't know how much I loved you until you had gone away.'"

"This was May? You were in Boston? I was probably polishing off a large tumbler of scotch. My memory of it is vague."

"It was handwritten. I stuck it into Dellie's 'Maman' notebook. I can get it for you."

"Do I need to read it? What's your question?"

"What did you do to make Sandie suffer?"

David frowned and took his time framing his answer. "In retrospect, I think I took her for granted. I was content. I assumed she was. I never asked. But in confronting her death, in dwelling on our relationship and shared life, I fell in love with Sandie all over again. I realized too late just how much I had lost." He was quiet for a long moment, then added, "I've never told that to anybody before."

David refilled their glasses, and they sat for a while gazing silently into the fire. "I'd better do something about dinner," he said after a few minutes. "Anything else you need to talk about?" he asked as he stood up.

"The affair raises a lot of issues for me, but we've covered a fair amount of ground. It's time for a break. My turn can wait until later this evening. Or maybe even tomorrow would be better. I would ask one thing, though. I'd like your clearance to let Bibi in on this. When it was all just speculation, I kept her totally in the dark. Now that we know it's fact, not fiction, I feel as if I'm withholding part of myself when I talk with her."

"I don't mind if she knows. I'd just rather she not broadcast it."

"I'll make that a condition," Jenny promised.

Not surprisingly, David was up in the middle of the night for a cigarette and a glass of brandy. Jenny heard him descend the stairs, pour the liquid into a snifter, and flick his lighter. Given the international time difference, Jenny thought perhaps David would call Graham, but discovered later they exchanged e-mails instead. Copies awaited her in her morning in-box.

De: David
A: Graham
cc: Jenny
Envoyé: 13 octobre, 2002
Objet: Sandie's affair
Dearest G,

My feelings at the moment carom about with such speed and unexpectedness that I'm never in the same space twice. My mind is spinning with thoughts, but I don't want to undertake this journey with you over the phone. I'd rather do it in person. Perhaps our Christmas visit to Boston will provide a good opportunity.

Thanks for helping to choreograph this extraordinary dance we've all been swept up in. Jewel is one hell of a detective!

Love, David

From: Graham
To: David
cc: Jenny
Date: October 13, 2002
Subject: Re: Sandie's affair

I can imagine your feelings carom around. I love you, and I loved Sandie, and I love Jenny. All of us have loved each other for a long, long time. That's what counts. I feel that so strongly now, especially after this past summer. I'm so eager to see you both in December!

Just finished my follow-up scan. Doc says he can only find a normal rectum, and I'm to come back in six months. It's oddly anticlimactic, and even a bit sudden. Like, now I have to think about what I want to *do* exactly.

Much love as ever, Graham

"So," David began when Jenny joined him at the breakfast table, "I think I've figured this out."

To Jenny's surprise, David had been trying to chart Jenny's path to Graham.

"You and Graham obviously began independent communication after our visit to Boston back in July," he suggested.

"Yes," she confirmed. "There's a special relationship that develops among cancer patients and survivors. When they ask how you are, they mean it, and you tell them. These past several months haven't been easy. On top of the household disruption, there were the tensions created by Marc, your depression, and my anxieties, reinforced by little things that loomed large in my mind. When Graham asked how I was doing, I unloaded. Graham reassured me that your lack of attention didn't mean your affection was waning, and he backed this up by sharing things he and Sandie had talked about.

"Once I understood how fully Sandie had depended on him for support and counsel, I asked how Sandie had dealt with various problems, and then, knowing I had to be very careful, I simply said, 'It would help to understand what happened with Julien Charbonnet.' If Graham had been perplexed by the query, I was prepared to cover by shifting attention to Julien's selection as a possible guardian to the children. I would say I was confused, in light of Sandie's choice, by Julien's seeming indifference to Marc and Dellie. 'Why is he now so distant from the surviving family?' I would ask. I figured that would get me out of any hole I dug myself into."

"I'd like to see the e-mails if you're willing to share them."

"Of course. You can look at them on my computer, or I can forward them to you."

"And I'd like to understand what you mean by my 'lack of attention.' I don't want to make the same mistake twice."

"You want me to define lack of attention? It just means you're not handing out sufficient whatever-it-is a person needs in order to feel safe or attractive or happy or loved or appreciated. Some attention needs are legitimate; others have more to do with plugging up a hole in someone's self-esteem. I'll do my best to give you an orderly tour of the machinations of my mind, but all things considered, David, I'm likely to be all over the map. I've worked this issue like Rubik's cube ever since you first told me of your suspicions. I kept turning it one way and the other, trying to make all the pieces fit together, without success. One minute I felt anger at Sandie's betrayal, the next moment I felt sympathy for her dilemma.

"At first, I couldn't imagine Sandie being needy. To my mind, she had it all. Looks, poise, charm, elegance, *savoir-faire* – and you. I measured myself against her on several scales and always came up short. I presumed that you found it difficult to hold my hand or cuddle on the couch because it made you think of Sandie, and miss her. I assumed that Sandie was the reason."

"That's not the case," David insisted.

"Well, bear with me. The kind of attention I wanted from you was anything and everything that would salvage *my* self-esteem. I wanted whatever made me feel equal to Sandie. People sometimes wonder how I put up with your constant comparisons – the frequency with which you claim, 'You're just like Sandie.' But I've always seen it as a plus, as a backhanded way of you saying you love me, without having to use the 'L' word. The more I'm like Sandie, the better my chances are of keeping your love for the long haul, as she did.

"It didn't dawn on me until recently that Sandie and I shared more than just the same surface attributes. We shared similar anxieties. Your 'lack of attention' may merit some criticism, but the real culprit is the distortion with which you were viewed through the prism of

Sandie's insecurities. She interpreted your intense commitment to your students as a sign that you were losing interest in her."

"But I wasn't. I didn't," David protested.

"I know, Love, but Sandie's vulnerabilities moved her to misread you. And here's the thing. Now that I understand how far back Sandie's insecurities went, it seems possible that Sandie might even have wondered if *I* was the reason for your lack of attention to her. Olga told me Sandie was threatened by me in the beginning, and you said Sandie once asked if you were sorry you married her. You wrote me some very sweet letters and postcards over the years. I know Sandie saw them because she often added a personal note at the bottom. Your intentions were innocent, but Sandie may have wondered. It unsettles me to think I may have been a factor, way back when, in her decision to have an affair. It's just so bizarre. I sometimes worry that you may come to regret having married me. Yet now I wonder if Sandie worried that you regretted marrying her. She had the same anxieties that I have."

David looked at Jenny as if she had lost her mind.

"David, you have to understand. One of my chief frustrations is my inadequacy in helping you put your world back together again. There are so many things that Sandie did so well, and that I do so awkwardly, if indeed I can do them at all. I've told you this before, I know I have, but that doesn't mean I've laid it to rest. I was afraid when you married me that you were committing yourself too soon. I knew I could help you, but I also feared, when you finally found your balance again, that you might wish you had chosen someone French-speaking, more elegant and more cosmopolitan – basically, someone a lot more like Sandie."

David kept shaking his head, muttering, "*C'est pas vrai! C'est pas vrai!*" and berating Jenny sweetly for utter foolishness. "Ducks, if ever you need reassurance about my feelings and my approval, all you have to do is look at our relationship over, what, nearly forty years? If that's not approval," he hmpffed, "I don't know what is!"

"There, in a nutshell, is the perfect illustration of what I was just saying. I *do* need your reassurance periodically. You're quite correct that all I have to do is put forth a little effort and take a good look at our history. But being human, I like it best when the affirmation comes from *you*. Translation: affirmation from you constitutes attention. Silence on your part constitutes lack of attention. We delicate females look to our men to do some of the heavy lifting."

The conversation might have gone on all morning, but it was Sunday and the farmers' market beckoned. Later that day, David remarked that knowing about the affair brought important closure. It was clear that his mood was far more positive than it had been for weeks.

I'm glad he knows the truth, Jenny concluded, *and I have no regrets about being the one who found it for him. Still, I'm not sure exactly what's been settled. Some major issues remain. What's going to happen, for instance, the next time David and Julien cross paths? How do you deal with someone who has betrayed your trust and friendship to that degree? In the past, it was just a suspicion. Now there's proof. Personally, I'd just as soon avoid Julien altogether, but I don't see how David's going to manage that. I may have created a bigger problem than I solved.*

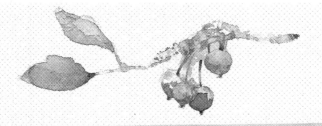

October, 2002

Melting frost on Toussaint

Loaded with melting frost, glinting, the last

Leaves dropped off the crabapple tree, spinning,

Like drops of water in line along the cornice, dripping

Off the roof after a summer storm has passed,

And the winter sun cast in the icy dew

Shadows and light, here green, there blue,

To let them float on the early morning grass.

Like frost, morning isn't meant to last, nor dew.

Chapter 9

From: J W Longworth
To: Ross
Date: October 14, 2002
Subject: Report

Quick report – I gave David confirmation about Sandie's affair with Julien. I think he's hurting more than he lets on, though we've talked about it pretty openly. He says the knowledge has brought him closure, but he indicated that he's reserving some private thoughts for Graham, whom we will see in December. I'll keep you posted.

We're stopping in Boston for a few days before going on to Chattanooga for Christmas. Mark your calendar.

Life goes on as usual here. One of David's colleagues is getting married, so we have a wedding to go to next weekend, and at the end of the month, we're off to Paris and Tours for a week, for David's fall break. Wish we could get you guys over to join us in Gay Paree one of these days!

Meanwhile, much love and many thanks for helping me wade through all this. J.

To Jenny's relief, the wedding on their agenda was low-key, and mostly anglophone except for the French ceremony at the *Mairie*. The bride, Alice Kramer, a Theatre Arts teacher at l'Académie Internationale, was an American, and the groom was British. At least half the guests were family and friends from England.

At the conclusion of the service, several of the attendees brought out packets of rice to throw at the newlyweds. Jenny turned to David.

"Oops!" she whispered. "I didn't know they do this at European weddings. I didn't even think to bring rice!"

How did I miss that? she puzzled. And then the answer came to her. *Because no one threw rice at David and me. There was no exuberant celebration at our wedding. Sandie's death still cast a pall over everything.*

As Alice and her new husband were being pelted with tiny white grains, Jenny felt a tinge of sadness that she and David had never been blessed with rice, but it quickly dissipated when Olga Gerasimova walked over to greet her. "I think David believes rice is only to cook," Olga commented mischievously, holding up a little bag. "Do you want to throw some of mine?"

Jenny took a small handful and joined in the fun. Olga took the last few grains and sprinkled them over Jenny's head. "I did not attend your wedding so there was no chance for me to do that!" she laughed as Jenny brushed the rice from her hair.

As the guests assembled for the wedding luncheon, Alice described plans for a honeymoon weekend in a little village in the Jura where neither bride nor groom had ever been before.

"How did you choose the place?" someone asked.

"Well," Alice hesitated and smiled in David's direction. "There's a small hotel there where Sandie Perry went several years ago, and she absolutely loved it. She kept telling me I ought to go. She wrote down all the information, but I never did anything about it. Recently, while I was reorganizing my closet, I pulled out a jacket and found a piece of paper in the pocket. It was the paper Sandie had given me about the hotel. That decided it." She nodded at David. "The hotel is Sandie's wedding present to us."

Before the gathering broke up, Olga took Jenny aside. "We must have another lunch," Olga declared. "We must make a date right now, so it will happen and not always become put off."

"My French class meets Monday, Wednesday and Friday mornings not far from the school. I could walk over afterwards."

"Then right after we all return from our autumn break," Olga insisted. "Come on that Monday. It will be good to continue our talk!"

When they got home late afternoon, David's malaise was apparent, but Jenny couldn't get him to talk about it. *I've seen him become emotional at other weddings, so it's possible it's just generic. Or maybe he thought about how much Sandie would have enjoyed seeing Alice get married. But why not say so?* And then it hit her. "A small hotel in a little village in the Jura – a place Sandie went several years ago, and she loved it," Alice had said. *What if it was a place unknown to David? A place where Sandie wasn't likely to encounter anyone she knew. A place where she went with Julien Charbonnet.*

Jenny could feel her anger mounting. *If this story about a hotel in the Jura has caused David even a moment's pain, I'm canceling my forgiveness of Sandie's past sins!*

Jenny glanced at her watch and subtracted nine hours from the time displayed on the dial. *I'm going to call Bibi,* she decided, descending to her office.

"Ahoy, California!" she exclaimed when Bibi answered. "How are those Halloween costumes coming?"

"I wish it were as simple as white sheets with holes cut out, but everyone wants to be a character out of Harry Potter. How's tricks on your end?"

"It's been an interesting week. We finally got resolution on a delicate and thorny question.

"Which was?"

"Well, it seems that not all is staid in Switzerland. Calvinist Geneva has its share of sin."

"Longworth, what the hell are you talking about?"

"Sandie had a decade-long affair with the Principal of the school."

"Say that again?"

"Not all is staid in Switzerland," Jenny repeated.

"The finale, Longworth! The punch line!" Bibi interrupted.

"Sandie had a long-standing affair with her boss."

"Holy shit!" Bibi exclaimed. "Are you sure? Does David know?"

"Yes to both. He's the one who raised the possibility to begin with."

"How did you find out? When did you find out?"

"Long story. There were a lot of little indications, and finally, last week, it was confirmed by someone Sandie used to confide in."

"This is unbelievable. *La Sainte Sandrine* was a closet sinner? My god, Jenny! Details! Details!"

For the next twenty minutes, Jenny laid out everything she had learned about Sandie's relationship with Julien. Bibi was uncharacteristically silent, except to seek an occasional point of clarification.

"Is David devastated?" she finally asked.

"He's had a long time to process this. He suspected it for years, so it's more a disappointment than a surprise."

"He suspected it for years but never did anything?"

"When it all came to light, I posed a similar question. He was surprisingly philosophical. 'Becoming aware of an issue, then becoming aware of how to deal with it, is an elaborate internal process. Why it requires the time it does remains something of a mystery, even to me,' he said."

"Your husband is so over my head sometimes," Bibi fired back.

"He just tries to understand things instead of shooting from the hip," Jenny replied, sensing her own position shift and feeling slightly defensive. "Frankly, I admire his tolerance."

"Tolerance, schmolerance. Where does this leave *you*? Are you pissed? Or pleased."

"Why would I be pleased?"

"Well, aren't there parallels with what was going on after Sandie's death? The contradictions? You were upset about her dying, sad for David and the children, but at the same time, you were bowled over by the possibility that David might ultimately become yours. So now, you feel distressed because David's been hurt by all this, but bingo, you're no longer in an impossible competition with the Late Great Perfect First Wife. Come on, Longworth. Fess up. You've gotta feel at least a *little* pleased about that."

"I won't pretend there isn't some relief discovering that Sandie wasn't perfect, but *schadenfreude* isn't my thing. I've suffered through my own insecurities, and it's pretty plain now that Sandie had her share of unhappy times. I admit to moments of anger. Frankly, I had a strong one this afternoon just before I called you. But when I'm being objective, I feel uncomfortable passing judgment. I guess, more than anything, I feel confused – annoyed with Sandie one minute, sorry for her the next."

"Actually *sorry* for her?"

"Based on what Olga said, Sandie believed for years that she had lost David's love. It's not true, but she believed it. Remember all those agonized poems David wrote after she died? The ones full of grief, whose heart-rending words left me fearing that David loved Sandie in a way that he could never love anyone else? Those poems are tragic beyond my initial understanding, because they're filled with the very words Sandie once longed to hear, but never did."

"So you're defending her? Where is it written that a decade of cheating is okay? Frankly, it's about time she got evicted from her Madame Goody-Goody throne, and it's fitting that it's her own behavior that's knocked her down a peg."

"That seems a little harsh, Bibi."

"Maybe Sandie deserves a little harsh. Where are those Puritan genes of yours when you need them? Are you going to let her get off scot-free after a ten-year spree of crimes against chastity, morality and decency?"

"It's a little late to embroider a scarlet letter on her clothes, Bibi."

"Couldn't you at least sully her reputation a bit? Send photos to the local tabloids? Something to tarnish the halo that her friends all think she earned?"

"Sandie's reputation is linked to David's. He wants this whole thing treated with serious discretion, and I agree with him. Exposing Sandie can only backfire and hurt David and the kids. Sandie's beyond feeling anything, but David isn't."

"And what's he going to do next time you guys cross paths with Julien? Pretend nothing happened? Give him a big hug?"

"I don't think he's figured that one out yet, but if and when it occurs, I'll give you the full scoop. Now enough about all this. I promise I'll keep you in the loop, and you need to promise to keep this mum. So let's pick a more cheerful topic. Tell me about the Halloween costumes. Which grandchild is going to be which Potter character?"

That was interesting, Jenny reflected when she hung up the phone. *Explaining Sandie and protecting David aren't so far apart,* she mused. *Maybe* nihil nisi bonum *isn't such a bad policy.*

The visit to Paris at the end of the month exceeded Jenny's expectations. They had dinner with Delphine and local friends every evening, but their days were their own, and they once again behaved like honeymooners. Thanks to the catharsis surrounding Sandie's affair, Jenny felt freer to take David's arm while they were walking, or to nestle against him in the bus. The affection flowed comfortably both ways. This was what she wanted from David, and she was getting it in spades. *How ironic,* she marveled, *that Sandie's affair has brought me closer to the intimacy with David that Sandie so craved.*

Still, Paris was not without its difficult moments. "There are some Buren sculptures in the *Cour d'honneur* at the Palais Royal you might enjoy," David suggested one afternoon. En route to the exhibit, they stopped briefly to listen to two college students playing chamber music on violin and cello. "They're good!" David exclaimed, tossing a Euro into their open instrument case.

As David and Jenny started to walk on, the students began a Bach cello suite. It was the piece David had chosen for Sandie's funeral. It stopped him in his tracks, and he needed a minute to gather himself. "I wasn't expecting that," he whispered.

Toussaint – Europe's Memorial Day – was just a few days away. The previous year, David and the children had observed the day in remembrance of Sandie.

"Is *Toussaint* on your mind?" Jenny asked.

"No," David replied, "it has no special meaning for me."

"It was special last year," Jenny argued. "You organized a ceremony with poetry readings and everything."

"That ceremony was mostly to reassure Marc and Delphine that, despite our marriage plans, I hadn't forgotten Sandie."

How could they think he might forget Sandie? Jenny pondered. *Surely they notice how often he still speaks of her.*

"In any event, with Marc in San Francisco, family ceremonies aren't really feasible. It's easier to write something and send it to the kids when the occasion calls for it. I'll probably do a poem for them when we get back."

After three days in Paris, they took a train to Tours and stayed in a small inn with a view of the Château d'Amboise in the distance and a broad stretch of the Loire in the foreground. They roamed the chateau country for two days, but devoted most of their attention to Sandie's favorite, Chenonceau. "I've seen lots of photographs of Chenonceau," Jenny said, "but they don't do justice to the incredible richness of the interiors. I can understand how Sandie would have loved it. It's elegant and very feminine. I like it too, because of the way it blends with the river."

As they strolled the paths, black swans preened on the lawns alongside the main promenade. A gentle fall breeze loosed colorful leaves that drifted down from the ancient sycamore trees. "The parks are beautiful too," Jenny added. "I've never seen a black swan before."

"It's very much a woman's castle," David commented. "Henri II gave it to his mistress, Diane de Poitiers, as a present. After Henri died, his wife, Catherine de Medici, wrested it away from Diane and sent her packing. It's been owned by a succession of women – wives and mistresses – over the centuries. There's quite a bit of romantic intrigue attached to it."

Is that another reason Sandie was drawn to it? Jenny wondered. She searched David's face, but decided that he was simply commenting on the chateau's history without any between-the-lines reference to Sandie's affair.

It was a restful vacation, and they were home in Geneva for the weekend with plenty of time to ease back into their regular routines.

"I'm supposed to have lunch with Olga on Monday, after my morning French lesson," Jenny reminded David.

"I'd give you a ride home," he said, reviewing the calendar for the week ahead, "but I have a meeting after my last class."

"No problem," she replied. "I'm gradually getting the hang of the transit system, and it's much less intimidating now that I've figured out I can walk different segments of the commute."

"So you are here!" Olga exclaimed when she and Jenny met in the school foyer the next day. "Good! Today I am not late, and also I have no appointments until 14:30, so we have no hurry. How does it go with your new French lessons?"

As they unwrapped their sandwiches, Jenny assessed her progress. "I was a good student in my youth. I presumed that once I got into a structured teaching environment, my French would improve rapidly, but I feel like a potato digger whose sack has a hole at the bottom. I memorize new words and phrases, but when I go to use them in conversation, I can't find them. By the time I come up with sufficient wording and grammar to create a sentence, the topic under discussion has gone off in some other direction.

"I've also discovered that I've been making some embarrassing errors. David's francophone friends sometimes ask if I plan to find a job. I don't have enough vocabulary to explain that my Swiss residency permit doesn't allow me to work, so I've been using a simple answer: 'Non, je suis en retraite,' 'No, I am retired.' At least, that's what I thought I was saying."

Olga smiled. Her French was fluent, and she could see what was coming.

"Everyone's been too polite to point out my error. It wasn't until I used the phrase in French class that I was corrected. 'En retraite means you are on a religious retreat,' my teacher advised the class, 'like a nun in a convent. To be retired, you must say instead you are à la retraite.'"

"At least now you have learned that expression," Olga pointed out.

"Yes, that one and one David taught me – *à un pas de tortue* – which is the rate at which my French is progressing."

"Well, over time it will come," Olga said reassuringly.

"But you speak *three* languages, Olga. It makes me feel like a real dunce that I'm not picking up French at a faster pace."

"I learned English as a teenager, and French as a young woman," Olga noted. "I think it becomes harder with age, and also, in America, one has so little exposure to anything except English. Here in Geneva, there is English, French, German and Italian every day, on TV, on the radio, and with all the advertising on every item we buy."

"Well, I need all the help I can get. I was at the grocery store the other day, and I had two ten-franc notes with me, plus a pocket full of coins from the kitchen 'penny' jar. The bill totaled 12.45 Swiss francs. I handed the cashier both bills, but I wanted to use up some of the coins. I pulled them out intending to say, 'I think I have exact change,' only I didn't know the word for change. I tried 'coins' in my mind, but again couldn't think of the translation. Finally I figured my meaning would be obvious, since the coins were spread across my palm. '*Sûrement j'ai 45*,' I said politely. I meant to communicate 'surely I have 45 centimes.'"

Olga burst out laughing.

"At least the cashier kept a straight face," Jenny remarked, giving Olga a wry look. "Then I realized that '*sûrement j'ai 45*' translates into 'surely I am 45 years old,' which surely I am *not*. The cashier cupped her hands signaling, 'Give me the coins.' She proceeded to count out the *entire* 12.45 in change. She handed me back my two ten-franc notes and nodded me off with '*Bonjour, Madame.*' I was mortified."

"I'm sorry to laugh, but everyone makes such mistakes as they learn. You must not be embarrassed."

"It's okay. When I told David the story, he laughed too. 'You'll get there, Kid, you'll get there,' he told me."

"Are you making new friends through your French class?"

"My classmates seem like nice women, but the socializing has been very limited. Our teacher usually invites us to join her at a nearby café for conversation after class. I've tried to participate a couple of times, but I'm hypersensitive to smoke. Inevitably some customer lights up at the next table, and I have to abandon ship."

"Ah, yes," Olga shrugged. "There is always smoke. And how does it go with David? My office is away from the classrooms, so I haven't seen him since Alice's wedding."

"He can still be up and down." Jenny described David's agitation over the event at the Community Center where Sandie's memorial service had taken place and his reaction to the Bach cello piece they overheard in Paris.

"Yes, I can see that would be difficult," Olga sympathized. "Don't you feel alone at such times, when David's head is occupied with the past?"

Jenny considered the question. "Sometimes. Of course I do. But I know that when he's remote, there's a reason. In the beginning, I worried that maybe I was the problem, that maybe I wasn't up to filling Sandie's shoes. David's not obviously affectionate, and if you're feeling insecure, as I was, it's easy to overlook his ways of expressing love."

Olga paused and gave Jenny a searching look. "David is very lucky that you see so easily beneath his surface. Sandie had no instinctive understanding as you do of David's way of showing love and affection."

Jenny waited for more. For a moment, Olga said nothing. Then, in the face of Jenny's silence, she resumed.

"I don't think you know how deeply romantic Sandie was. She wanted for her life to be like a movie from Hollywood. She wanted romance in everything. With David this was not possible. It is not who he is."

Jenny's antennae went out. The conversation was moving into a sensitive area. "Still," Jenny said, choosing her words carefully, "whenever I saw them together, Sandie seemed cheerful and happy."

Olga regarded Jenny with unblinking eyes. "Perhaps that is because she didn't rely only on David for her happiness."

Olga had always enjoyed a deep friendship with Sandie, and before she became Director of Human Resources, she had been Julien

Charbonnet's personal office assistant. *Could the affair have happened without Olga knowing, or at least guessing?* To Jenny, Olga's phrasing was a test. *She's trying to figure out how much I know. It's what I did with Graham, asking a question that invited discussion of the affair, but that also allowed me an escape route. Olga is where I was, not wanting to expose Sandie's secret to someone who may be unaware of it. My move.*

"Sandie seemed to appreciate her life on many fronts," Jenny agreed. "She obviously adored her children, liked her job and had many special friends. And," Jenny added, keeping her tone as normal as possible, "I understand that she was particularly close to Julien Charbonnet, the school Principal."

Olga held her gaze absolutely steady as Jenny spoke.

"Yes," Olga said, nodding. "She was *particularly* close to Julien. Your understanding is correct." For a moment, there was silence. "Does David understand this also?" she finally asked.

There it was. *There's no other way to interpret what she's saying,* Jenny concluded. *Olga knows about the affair.*

"David knows about Julien," Jenny stated candidly.

"I thought so, but I wasn't sure," Olga commented.

"He readily admits he didn't give Sandie the kind of romantic attention she wanted," Jenny offered.

"That much is clear," Olga replied. "Once David became obsessed with his teaching, Sandie believed the marriage was failing. It did not fit her picture of what a romantic marriage should be. She slowly withdrew emotionally from David. But she had grown up fatherless. You know this, yes?"

Jenny nodded.

"Sandie was determined that her children would not suffer the same fate," Olga went on. "The marriage would continue as a partnership, and she would take care of her emotional needs in other ways. The affair with Julien began. She was both flattered and excited by his attentions. Julien is not a perfect human, but their affair was far more than a relationship conducted only for sex. Sandie had a warm and affectionate nature, and I believe Julien became involved far beyond a merely sexual interest. I think he came to trust her. As he revealed his private worries, his unguarded self to her, she, in turn, became emotionally committed to him."

"I have to admit," Jenny responded, "that I couldn't understand why Sandie chose Julien. He strikes me as a womanizer and a wheeler-dealer, but there has to be more to him than meets the eye."

"In some ways, you are right," Olga confirmed. "He is a politician who will save himself when he is in a corner, but that is not to say that he didn't love Sandie," she cautioned. "Because he did, as she loved him. Julien showed her his vulnerable side, which was real, and that is what she responded to. Sandie was also drawn by Julien's power and position. She sometimes viewed David as too feminine."

That's an odd comment, Jenny thought. *I wouldn't choose the word "feminine," but then, English isn't Olga's native tongue, nor was it Sandie's.* "David is certainly very nurturing, if that's what Sandie meant by feminine. He sometimes jokes about his 'feminine side,' citing his love of cooking, flowers, art, music and poetry. But in my view, that simply makes him a kind of Renaissance man. He's cultured. He's literate. He's also perfectly comfortable doing housework. He's certainly not someone who feels bound by narrow opinions about gender roles. And thank heavens for that!"

Olga cocked her head and studied Jenny. "I think what Sandie meant was that David does not display the normal male traits of competition and desire for power or control. He is not aggressive. He has no wish to climb over others and sit at the top."

"True," Jenny acknowledged. "Despite his colorful language, David's a real gentleman. It's one the qualities I really appreciate in him."

"That is understandable, but perhaps because of the poverty of her childhood, Sandie was drawn to Julien's drive – his ambition. I don't think she saw the calculating elements in Julien's personality," Olga stated, "because those elements were not obvious when they were together."

Jenny frowned. "This is a lot to digest."

"Yes, but it is good that you know. I have seen you worry that you are not perfect for David. But I think you are. He is a very unusual man, and you see the whole of him. You love the whole of him, even the parts that are weak."

"There are elements in David's personality that are challenging, but I'd be hard pressed to define any part of him as weak," Jenny countered.

Olga smiled. "Your husband is a lucky man. Tell me, and be very honest. Did you ever think the time would come when you and David would be back together again?" Olga asked frankly.

"No," Jenny answered without hesitation. "I had some wistful moments over the years, but David seemed genuinely happy with Sandie. She was younger than me, and I always assumed she would outlive me. I loved David, but it wasn't a jealous love. I wanted him to have a wonderful life, but I didn't need to be a daily part of it. I had a life of my own."

"You were wise to take such a position. Sandie accepted you only when she was sure she could trust you with David. Sandie and I discussed you many times, Jenny," Olga admitted. "Sandie was careful at first, but finally concluded that you were not a threat. Still, I must tell you something. I knew from Sandie that you and David were together when you were young, and that your affection for him continued. But the first time I saw you with him, I was *étonnée* – astonished – by how deep was your love. It seemed so present," she said, "so clear and so strong. As if it had always been and would always be, no matter where you were or who you were with."

"You're right about that," Jenny replied with a smile. She could feel a slight blush start up her cheeks. "When David and I parted long ago to lead separate lives, I wrote in my journal that we had a love that surpassed all things. Time has proven that to be true."

"We must talk more of this, but now I think we should end our lunch. I have an appointment, and I must prepare some papers. We will do this again soon."

The two women embraced, and Jenny headed for the tram stop. Olga's words were whirling around in her head. *How do I reconcile*

Olga's story with the one Graham told? Graham said nothing about Sandie withdrawing emotionally from David. Or being drawn by Julien's power and ambition. Does Graham even know? Did Sandie tell him that? And what should I say to David?

By the time she got home, Jenny accepted that reconciliation was neither possible nor necessary. *My own 'story' has as many different versions as there are days in the week, depending on whom I'm talking to. I can be happy and upbeat one day, then gloomy and discouraged the next. Perhaps there's no such thing as a single absolute truth. I shouldn't be surprised that the gospel according to Olga is not the same as the gospel according to Graham. I just regret there is no gospel according to Sandie.*

"How was your lunch with Olga?" David asked when he returned from school.

Tell him, Jenny. If the roles were reversed, you'd want him to tell you.

"Interesting. She's very perceptive, and very observant. She's also very discreet. Remember when you said you thought she might know about Julien? You were right. But it took half our lunchtime and some very careful linguistic maneuvering before the cards were laid on the table. She was protecting not only Sandie, but also you."

David's visage remained neutral. "What did she say?"

"Essentially the same thing Graham said, that Sandie was trying to strike a balance between her personal needs and her family life. I didn't ask Olga specifically, but I'm sure she would be willing to talk with you about it, if you wish."

"We'll see. I'm going to get started on dinner. Want a glass of wine?"

Jenny accepted the wine and waited for further comment. None was forthcoming, and the subject did not reappear during dinner. *He will do with it whatever he chooses*, Jenny concluded.

Jenny turned her attention towards Thanksgiving and enlisted David's help in finding a turkey. Europeans didn't normally cook whole turkeys. The local butchers generally featured only birds that had been filleted or turned into paté. "If all else fails, we can always substitute wild duck or pheasant," David suggested. "It's hunting season in France, so they're easy to come by."

Jenny wanted a traditional meal, however, and David devoted several phone calls to tracking down two small turkeys, eight pounds each. Jenny was pleased that she could present a classic New England Thanksgiving feast, but when the day came, she felt oddly peripheral to the celebration. She and David were the only Americans present, and the dinner table conversation was heavily francophone.

I suppose, she decided, *it must have felt equally odd to the Indians who attended the first harvest festival at Plymouth Colony and had to listen to the pilgrims chattering away in an unintelligible language.*

The following week, David had a routine check-up with his urologist. To Jenny's relief, he was given a clean bill of health. "Hallelujah!" she chirped. "Now the only thing left is setting up an appointment to see why your knee is giving you trouble."

"Don't push me on this medical stuff, Jenny," he warned. "The only reason I do it is for you. I'd just as soon step out in the street and get hit by a bus. That would suit me fine."

Wham! Jenny turned away from the kitchen, where David was working, walked to the far side of the dining room, and stood for several minutes looking out over the garden, breathing deeply until she had herself under control. *Why is getting hit by a bus suddenly appealing? Is this a delayed reaction to the revelation that Olga knew of the affair? Or that Sandie genuinely loved Julien? But David always assumed that, so why would it matter?* Jenny could come up with no explanation. She forced herself to refocus on their upcoming holiday plans and sent an e-mail to David's siblings about their projected arrival date in Chattanooga. As she typed, she heard David get on the phone and wearily start making calls about school matters. He also made a call to Dr. Payot to schedule an appointment regarding the pain in his knee.

The December weather was relentlessly cold, wet and gray. David sounded okay when he spoke on the phone to Delphine and Marc, but he had little enthusiasm for routine domestic activities. Even cooking, which he normally loved, seemed like a chore. *Hopefully things will perk up when we get out of Geneva and head to the States for Christmas*, she thought.

From: JWLongworth
To: Bibi
Date: December 3, 2002
Subject: Follow-up

Some bright California morning when you're up really early, give me a call. For some reason, David's back down in the dumps again, and I could use a pep talk. He usually gets home between 5:00 and 5:30, so it would be best if you rang before 7:30 a.m. your time. J.

The phone rang late the next afternoon. Jenny answered with a clearly articulated American "Hello," rather than the Genevan "*Ahlo*." She wanted to alert people at the outset that she might not understand a barrage of French.

"Don't I even get a *Bonjour*?" the voice at the other end queried.

"Hi, Bibi!" Jenny exclaimed. "Thanks for calling!"

"What's with the e-mail about a pep talk? Is there a new scandal? More skeletons in the closet? Has David taken a potshot at Julien?"

"No, no scandal, no skeletons and no potshots. It's just same old, same old. David's down in the dumps again, and I'm not handling it well. I think maybe I need a new mantra," Jenny said.

"What's the old mantra these days?" Bibi asked.

"The old mantra is, 'What is the loving thing to do?'"

"You're tired of doing loving things?"

"No, but I'm tired of … how can I describe it? I'm tired of the recovery being so slow. David is still struggling, and it's not just Sandie's affair. Ever since we got back from Boston in August, it's been one thing after another. There are good moments – good days and good weeks, even – but then, bam, something happens to knock him down. Just the other day, he had to attend a memorial service for the mother of one of his students. I asked him about it, and he said the woman had succumbed to breast cancer. 'She was about the same age as Sandie was when she died,' he added. Then his voice caught, and that was the end of the conversation.

"Winter is here with a vengeance, which I know gets to him. On the turn of a dime, he can become distracted and discouraged and depressed. His optimism disappears, and he withdraws. I want to help, but I'm running out of ideas."

There was silence on the other end.

"Bibi?"

"I'm here. I'm just thinking."

There was another pause.

"Maybe you should stop trying to help," Bibi finally suggested. "Or at least, stop trying to help David. Maybe you should start trying to help yourself."

"What do you mean?"

"Well, it seems to me that all this time, you've been incredibly sensitive about not disrupting David's space and David's routines, and that goes for his kids too. But who's looking out for your space? Who's caring about your routines? Does David have any idea how much you've turned your life inside out for him?"

"He knows that life here isn't easy for me. Yesterday, he was on the phone with his brother Nate, and I heard him say, 'Jenny is well, or at least well enough to put up with me for the time being.' So he knows it's tough for me sometimes, even if he can only acknowledge that in a roundabout way."

"Yeah, but that's my point. If a subject isn't comfortable for him, he doesn't talk about it, even though it might really help you to hear his thoughts. Yet he expects you to listen to Sandie this and Sandie that. He's obviously still in mourning, and he won't countenance anyone bringing her to task for her misdeeds. Maybe his enduring love for Sandie is admirable, but Jenny, there's something to be said for selective silence. When you told me about that wedding poem he gave you back in January, I had to bite my tongue. If a man handed me a poem on our wedding day about how his love and grief for his dead wife trumped any joy he might feel about marrying me, that is one marriage that would never take place, guaranteed."

Jenny was taken aback. "David has gone through a devastating emotional loss, Bibi, and I'm including the infidelity as well as Sandie's death. You've only seen him in snatches, during the roughest period of his life. He didn't used to be like this. You don't know his layers and subtleties the way I do," Jenny went on. "I love this man. My commitment to him is total. Beneath the folksy language, the jokes and the profanity, he's a deeply sensitive and wonderfully thoughtful human being."

"Yeah, yeah, I get that, but I'm waiting for the day when you can tell me that he loves you with the same passion and total commitment you have for him. I understand that love and rational choices don't always coincide, but from where I sit, I'm getting nervous that you've settled for half a loaf."

"I don't feel it that way, Bibi," Jenny insisted, rising to David's defense. "Maybe it looks like half a loaf to you, but I see a whole loaf that David is giving me in slices. In time, the whole loaf will be accounted for. And some day," Jenny's tone turned mischievous, "well beyond that loaf, I have every confidence that David will present me with a full gourmet dinner and a totally decadent dessert!"

"I'll bet you believe in the tooth fairy too."

"No, but I'm right. Though I'll grant, I'm more than ready for this feast to arrive at the table."

"And what about the new mantra?"

"You're a great therapist, Bibi. You've succeeded in clearing my head. Instead of asking 'What is the loving thing to do?' I just need to recite the answer: 'The loving thing to do is be patient.' Thanks, Bibi!"

"I'm not sure you're welcome, but I gotta go to work soon, and I'm not dressed yet. Keep me informed about those incoming slices of bread."

During breakfast, Jenny asked David for his input on their upcoming Christmas visit. "We have to decide what presents we're getting here and what presents we'll pick up in Boston," she advised him.

David just shook his head. "I wish we weren't going to the States," he replied. "It's gonna be exhausting."

"Well, think on the gift list, and we can talk about it tonight at dinner," Jenny replied, sensing she would get a better response over a glass of wine. When she checked her e-mail after David left for school, she could see why David's mind wasn't very focused on Christmas presents.

De: David
A: Graham
cc: Jenny
Envoyé: 4 décembre, 2002
Objet: Where you at?

We're headed to Chattanooga for the holiday hoopla, but we'll spend a few days in Beantown first. I wanna make sure you and your lady are around. I'm looking forward to the conversation we talked about.

I'm feeling pretty stressed at the moment. Too much to do in school, for school and outside of school: grades, papers, travel plans, dinners, visits, medical appointments, etc. All bullshit, but it has to get done. The prospect of Christmas Crazies in the US ain't thrilling, but it will be good to see you folks.

Bises, David

Jenny decided that David's stress could use more than just patience. "Dearheart, you are stretched too thin. You never say no to anyone or anything, and it's running you ragged. Please, please, let's implement some 'do not schedule' days. Let's clear the decks and make this weekend an in-house retreat. Just us. No visiting, no calls, no guests."

David yielded without protest. Saturday morning, they had a leisurely breakfast. David ventured out mid-morning to pick up fresh bread. Jenny had her camera ready when he returned, and she snapped a picture of the crusty loaf so she could send it to Bibi with an appropriate caption.

Late afternoon, David laid a fire and lit it, then went to the kitchen and made tea. He set cups and saucers on a tray and brought everything into the living room. It was exceptionally civilized. He sat next to the fire so he could smoke, and Jenny curled up on the sofa, enjoying the coziness of the room. When he finished his cigarette, he moved to join her on the couch. He kicked off his shoes and reached over to remove Jenny's as well.

"Don't want to risk tearing up the couch," he said.

When she saw where this was headed, Jenny resettled her teacup on the far side of the coffee table.

"Don't want to break up the tea service either," she replied.

Jenny was wide awake after their lovemaking, but David slept for over half an hour. "Hiya, Kid," he said when he opened his eyes and regained his bearings.

"Good nap?" she asked.

"Better than good," he replied with a grin.

Later, he traded in the tea tray for a bottle and two glasses. "Cheers, Jewel," he said as he toasted her.

"I love you too," she smiled, settling back to enjoy the last of the fire.

Once the weekend was over, Jenny began to organize for their upcoming travel. She was scheduled to leave for Boston a week ahead of David. Much as she disliked their being separated, she looked forward to the intimacy and playfulness that always suffused their communications when they were apart. On departure day, she drafted an e-mail for David to find once she was on her way. Just before they left for the airport, she hit the send button.

David walked her to the security area, kissed her, hugged her, kissed her again, then kissed her a third time. She passed through the checkpoint and blew him a final kiss through the glass.

Awaiting next year – December, 2002

In warm and sunny Florida

Sandpipers scurry back and forth

Between the waves for bubbling fare,

Seagulls bitch and scream

Without concern for time or others' care,

Pelicans glide and plunge regardless,

Gulping fish as gulls fly near,

And we watch languidly

Awaiting next year,

Hoping for a new and happier tune,

In which we all will share.

Chapter 10

From: JWLongworth
To: DavidP
Date: December 15, 2002
Subject: WARNING: Love Letter

You would interrupt me if I tried this in person, but with an e-mail, I know you'll read it all the way to the bottom, even if it makes you squirm!

You may not be very good at expressing love in words, face to face, but you have a lot of indirect routes. You rarely bring me flowers. You rarely give me presents. But you have looked out for me and taken care of me. You're patient with my foibles, and you respect my phobias. You tease me and fuss over me, and I feel your love in that process. You are splendid in my eyes, warts and all. As I told you long ago, it is a love that surpasses all things.

May we both have safe crossings. May this week that we are apart pass swiftly. May you behave yourself coming through customs.

Je t'adore, Jenny

Ross met Jenny at the airport. In the back seat of his car were cartons of Chinese takeout, plus milk and orange juice for the morning.

"Bless you, Ross. You take care of me almost as well as David does," Jenny remarked as she buckled her seat belt.

"Perhaps," he said wryly, "but only in certain departments. How fares your Lord and Master, given the recent startling revelations?"

"Actually, he's handling it with exceptional grace. It has to be hurtful, but he blames himself for not paying enough attention to Sandie. David was raised with a southern tradition of chivalry. When a lady is involved, if there are two possible explanations for questionable behavior, he automatically leans toward the kinder one – at least as far as I can see."

Ross deposited Jenny's luggage in the hallway, they opened the cartons of takeout, and Ross caught Jenny up on his life with Kevin. "Generally things are good," he reassured her. "Our biggest challenge is the cultural divide. The correct temperature for Guinness is a major issue. But other than that, we're doing pretty well."

"Adjusting to new patterns at our age takes some doing, even little things," Jenny observed. "David teases me about my on-going resistance to the metric system. He constantly has to translate the temperature for me, from Celsius to Fahrenheit. Fortunately he has no objection to my American measuring cups and my American bathroom scale."

Ross laughed. "Speaking of temperature, finish the moo goo gai pan while it's still hot, and then I'm going to let you go to bed. I'm marking you and David down for dinner on the twenty-third, okay?"

"Okay. And Ross, thanks. Really. For the ride, the dinner, and the company. I miss hanging out with you. I adore David, but it's lovely to have this time with you. And oh my god, it feels *so* good to be home!"

> *De: David*
> *A: Jenny*
> *Envoyé: 15 décembre, 2002*
> *Objet: Re: WARNING: Love Letter*
> DON'T BRING YOU FLOWERS, LONGWORTH!!!!! You've got a lot of damn gall, Woman! I always want to get flowers, and every time I do, I hear "No! We've got them in the garden." Lotta bloody gall. JEEEEzus! No flowers.... Bullshit!
> *Bises*, David

From: JWLongworth
To: DavidP
Date: December 15, 2002
Subject: Re: Re: WARNING: Love Letter

I know that there exists a correct response to this serious distortion of whatever it was I said, but I'm too tired to tell you about my trip even, except that flying in over Boston harbor was lovely – green water, blue skies, and sun so bright that I had to root around in my bag for my sunglasses.

Love you, J.

De: David
A: Jenny
Envoyé: 16 décembre, 2002
Objet: Re: Re: Re: WARNING: Love Letter

Mornin', Jewel. Up early. Have been correcting papers to pass the time before I go out and buy myself flowers.

Bises. David

From: JWLongworth
To: DavidP
Date: December 16, 2002
Subject: Freshman Psychology

Here is something to keep you out of trouble until you get here:

Course description: **ROMANCE 101** – The Meaning of Flowers

Read the following and be prepared to discuss the questions below in class:

Scenario 1: David and Jenny are at the market. They pass a flower stall. David asks, "Shall we get some flowers?" Jenny replies, "We have lots in the garden that I could cut." They buy potatoes and broccoli.

Scenario 2: David and Jenny are at the Mall. They pass a florist shop. "Do we need any flowers?" David asks. "The daisies in the kitchen are still fresh," Jenny answers. They buy photo frames and computer paper.

Scenario 3: David and Jenny stop by the supermarket on the way home. *Why are we stopping?* Jenny wonders. *We've done all our shopping.* "I have to get some special markers for my class," says David. He buys her a surprise bouquet of flowers.

Questions for discussion:

1) In which scenario(s) is Jenny most likely to swoon?

2) In which scenario(s) does David imply that a consultation about "needing" flowers has the same romantic value as surprising a lady with an unexpected bouquet?

3) Discuss the relative romantic merits of broccoli, flowers and computer paper.

4) Is this couple dating? Or married? Justify your answer.

Good luck on the exam. Professor J.W.L.

PS, I forgot my US checkbook. It's in the black file cabinet in my office, in the top drawer. I would be enormously grateful if you would bring it with you.

De: David
A: Jenny
Envoyé: 17 décembre, 2002
Objet: Re: Freshman Psychology

Found your checkbook. Lotta damn good it does some people, who shall remain nameless, to make lists.

Working on my term paper for Romance 101.

Kisses, Your humble student

From: JWLongworth
To: DavidP
Date: December 18, 2002
Subject: Sunday Brunch

It *does* do a lot of damn good to make lists. The only thing I forgot was the one item that never made it onto a list.

I spoke with Barbara Wells. We'll have brunch with Graham and Barbara in Cambridge on Sunday. Meanwhile, I think it's wonderful that you're working so hard on your term paper.

Miss you. Love, J.

David's plane arrived mid-afternoon on Saturday. "The rental car is a blue Toyota," Jenny told him as they walked to the central parking area, "but I forgot to memorize the license plate number. All I remember is that it's on level four."

"Over there, maybe?" David guessed after scanning the parked cars. Jenny aimed her key, pressed the "open" button, and a blue Corolla winked its lights.

"What would I do without you?" she teased.

"Hmpff," was his reply.

"How was the last week of school?" she asked as they drove to Shawmut.

"Pretty much straight bullshit. There wasn't much in the way of education going on. Assembly with Wassail, Wassail. Clean up the lockers, drink a glass of port with the colleagues. I was glad to wave Ho, Ho, Ho and get the hell out. How was your week here?"

"It's always an interesting experience being back on my own. I revert very quickly to my independent Boston persona, including my old bad habits regarding meals. Lunch is eaten while standing at the kitchen sink watching the birds through the window, and dinner is usually in front of the TV. I may assemble a handful of grapes and a hunk of cheese, or I may just stare at the contents of the fridge until something clicks. I am very spoiled by your haute cuisine!"

David adjusted quickly to the time change and was alert and ready to go the next morning when they drove up to Cambridge. They had last visited Graham while he was still undergoing chemotherapy. It was a relief to see him with real color and some flesh on his face.

After a leisurely brunch, Graham suggested a walk. Jenny knew David wanted to talk with him about Sandie and Julien so she, who normally enjoyed a walk, declined. David, who normally eschewed walking, readily accepted the invitation. "I'll stay and keep Jenny company," said Barbara, who must have known or sensed that the men wanted some private time. The two women did the brunch cleanup then settled on the couch with mugs of tea.

Like Jenny, Barbara was a second wife. Her marriage to Graham was barely two years old. Jenny had met her for the first time during their summer visit, when there was little opportunity for one-on-one conversation. Now, with just the two of them, they had a chance to talk.

Jenny got out the photographs she had promised Barbara. They included several shots of David and Graham during their college days, plus a copy of the classic photo of a young David and Jenny taken in Paris.

Barbara loved the early pictures of Graham. He had grown a moustache after graduating, and then added a beard, which he sported well into his thirties. He finally reverted to being clean-shaven, but Barbara had never seen a youthful picture of her husband without at least a moustache. "Oh, this is wonderful!" she exclaimed.

She smiled at the picture of David taken junior year, with his tousled hair and devil-may-care grin. And then she saw the Paris photo, a copy of which both David and Jenny had mounted, poster size, and hung on their walls through the decades of their lives apart. "Oh, my god," Barbara whispered. She looked at Jenny with her mouth wide open in astonishment. "To say Sandie was tolerant is putting it mildly. She must have felt incredibly secure to allow this picture in her house. It's so intensely ... intimate!"

Jenny hadn't thought of it as intimate, but when she considered Barbara's description, she could see she had a point. The young couple was obviously in love. "Well," Jenny clarified, "Sandie did admit that she was nervous about me when we first met. She could see that I loved David, but she could also see that I respected her role, and that I appreciated her for taking such good care of him. Eventually we were able to joke about it, so it worked in its odd way."

I wonder if Graham has told Barbara about Julien. Best to check that out before I say anything, Jenny decided.

The men returned. Barbara and Jenny gave each other a to-be-continued look and rose to greet their respective husbands. An hour later, they said their farewells. "It was great to have this time together,"

Barbara said as Jenny reached for her coat. "I love the history that the three of you share, and I appreciate that I'm so warmly embraced and included."

"Good talk with Graham?" Jenny asked as she and David walked to the car.

"Yup. I'll fill you in when we get home. But he did tell me that I've managed to find a goddamn saint for my second wife. One of the sexy kind, fortunately."

One slice at a time, Jenny smiled to herself.

They lit a fire when they got back to Shawmut, and David recapped his conversation with Graham. "I've already done most of the sorting out on my own," he said at the end, "but this added some perspective. Sandie was clearly trying to find a safe balance in a frustrating situation."

"That seems consistent with what you told me about Sandie's comment that your marriage worked because you gave her her freedom. I expect part of her really did want you to know the truth. What better way than a gentle reference in the context of a sweet review of your life together?"

"Sweet review, bullshit! It was nothing of the sort. Those words were said in anger. It was Sandie's last week at home, and she was debilitated, nauseous and devoid of hope. We were in the kitchen. I dropped a greasy spatula and let fly with my usual temper and profanity. Sandie was not amused. In no uncertain terms, she told me that the only reason she had stayed married to me was because I gave her her freedom."

Jenny was taken aback. Even allowing for Sandie's exhaustion and pain, her words must have landed harshly on David's ears. David observed Jenny's surprise. "There was a side to Sandie that could be very hard," he said simply, "but even so, I can see it from her point of view. I have a lot more trouble with Julien's behavior," he continued. "I really went to bat for him back when some of the school board members wanted to fire him. I thought we had a friendship based on solid trust that went both ways. Guess I was a pretty poor judge."

"More likely that Julien was a pretty skilled dissembler," Jenny countered.

David made no further comment, and Jenny posed no further questions. *He and Graham must have covered a lot of ground. I expect there's more than enough for him to digest at the moment*, she decided.

Two days later, they flew south. "Off to Klan Land for the Yule Celebrations," David jested. He joked about his Chattanooga connections, but Jenny knew he relished family gatherings.

David had invited both his children to spend the holidays with his siblings, but Marc chose to stay in California. When David and Jenny proposed adding a west coast visit to their itinerary, Marc discouraged them, saying he had plans to drive down the coast with some friends. "I wish we were going to see him this trip, but he sounds okay," David reported after his phone conversation. "He has some complaints about school, but he's sticking with it."

"That in itself is a major plus. I know you were worried that he'd drop out if the going got tough. I'm keeping my fingers crossed that encountering new people and new ideas will help Marc open up," Jenny commented. *Still, it doesn't sound as if he's very eager to see his family*, she concluded silently.

Delphine accepted the ticket offer happily, and flew in from Paris. Despite her jet lag, she was bright and cheery when they met her at the Atlanta airport. "What do you want for Christmas?" David asked as they drove north to Chattanooga.

"I thought the ticket was my present," Delphine replied.

"That's your big present," David agreed. "We wanted to have something special under the tree here too, but since you have to fly back to Paris, we didn't want to burden you with extra weight or bulk. We thought you might like to choose something you could get when you're back home."

"I could really use a rug," Delphine said hopefully. "That's kind of a medium-sized present. Would that be okay?"

"Sure," her father answered. "We can pick one out with you next time we visit."

"Where did you find the rug you bought for the living room?" Delphine asked, turning to Jenny.

The rug in question was a thick wool Berber that Jenny had installed soon after her arrival in Geneva. Both Marc and Delphine had initially viewed it with suspicion and resentment.

"We bought it at the Migros home furnishings store," Jenny answered.

"Well, that's exactly the kind I want," Delphine said firmly.

Jenny was delighted by Delphine's belated approval of her choice. *That's a slice of bread from Dellie's corner. Bibi will have to credit that one too,* she thought. "When you get back to your apartment, Dellie, send us the dimensions. We'll pick up the rug in Geneva and drive it to Paris," Jenny promised.

When they arrived, Jenny was again impressed by the warmth and affection that eddied through the Perrys' free-form reunions, despite the political differences that stretched the three brothers from one pole to the other. From the minute David walked through his brother Nate's front door, it was clear that he was happy to be there.

He's more relaxed and upbeat than he's been in months, Jenny noted. *Is it the family setting?* she wondered. *The cathartic talk with Graham? Being away from Geneva?* The mood of the holiday was definitely more cheerful than Jenny's first Christmas with David's family, just three short months after Sandie's death, but it was not without difficult moments.

"It looks like Dellie still misses Sandie badly," Margaret observed when she and Jenny were alone in the kitchen. "Particularly her motherly concern and interest," Margaret added with some emphasis.

Jenny hesitated. *Is this a criticism? I know I'm not good at being "motherly."* She was instinctively defensive, but clearly Margaret had Delphine's best interests at heart. She posed a careful response.

"Yes, I expect Dellie will miss her mother for a long time. I'll never forget the statement Dellie read at Sandie's memorial service, recapping moments they had shared: '... we used to laugh and argue ... I told you about my boyfriends, my worries ....' Each line of the recitation closed with, 'C'était bon.' 'It was good.' And at the end, Dellie simply said, 'I miss you, Maman.' Everyone in the auditorium was in tears."

"It might help if you asked Dellie more personal questions about what she's doing and who she's seeing, like her mother used to," Margaret counseled.

Yes, this is a criticism. Dellie once told David that she didn't feel she could talk "girl talk" with me. She must have said something similar to Margaret, Jenny suspected.

Jenny wanted to explain herself, but she was fearful of seeming argumentative. Margaret had regarded Sandie with the affection of a sister. *If I don't handle this right,* Jenny worried, *I'll seem like a cold Northerner without a maternal gene in my body.*

"My heart goes out to Dellie," she began diffidently, "but her relationship with me will never be like the one she shared with her mother. My personality is very different from Sandie's. So is my role. Sandie related to Dellie as a mother to a child. To me, Dellie is an adult – a young adult, granted, and still maturing, but an adult nonetheless. I think my best contribution is to counter-balance David's protectiveness and push Dellie gently but firmly toward independence. I can only hope she'll understand someday that this is an expression of my confidence in her, not a lack of concern."

"That may be real helpful down the road, but right now, she needs a mom," Margaret advised bluntly.

"To be honest, I don't think Dellie wants *a* mother so much as she wants *her* mother. I've attempted some simple 'motherly' tasks that I quickly regretted," Jenny confessed. "When Dellie was home this past spring, for example, I took her clothes out of the washing machine and put them in the dryer. She didn't say a word to me, but she told her father, in no uncertain terms, that she didn't want me touching her laundry. 'Sandie always hung things on the clothesline to dry,' David pointed out, but it had to be more than that. I must have stumbled onto sacred ground. There were major issues with both kids over furniture and decorating in the beginning. Ever since then, I've been more than a little nervous about unwittingly crossing whatever lines Marc and Dellie have drawn."

"But I got the impression from David that the kids welcomed your arrival."

"When David first talked to them about our getting married, he said they seemed surprised, but happy for his sake. In retrospect, they were more likely *so* surprised that they couldn't marshal a coherent response. Once I arrived, it became clear that they were conflicted about my presence and opposed to the marriage. Our original plan was a quiet wedding in October, after a year's mourning had been observed. But with tears streaming down her face, Dellie pleaded with her father not to go ahead with the wedding. 'There is only one Madame Perry,' she wept."

"That must have been real difficult for David as well as for Dellie," Margaret observed, shaking her head.

"It was," Jenny concurred. "David and I agreed to give the kids more time to adjust. It was obviously still hard for them to hear a woman's tread on the stairs, to have that instinctive expectation of Sandie's appearance, and to find their hopes dashed when it was me who walked into the room instead of their mother. David figured that their emotions would settle down once we passed the anniversary of Sandie's death, but he seriously underestimated the amount of time they really needed."

"I remember y'all had trouble choosing a wedding date, but I thought that was just a problem of paperwork and bureaucracy."

"There were some bureaucratic problems, for sure, but the primary issue was helping Marc and Dellie accept the necessity. The only way I could get a permit to live in Switzerland was by becoming David's wife. We ended up getting married less than a week before my visa was due to expire. Otherwise I would have had to go back to Boston and wait three months before returning to Geneva on a new tourist visa."

"Did things settle down after that?"

"Sort of. David thought it would be a lot easier for the kids to relate to me as a longtime family friend, rather than as a stepmother. He felt Sandie's maternal role should be absorbed by him, not by me. David was the one who ran errands with the kids, spent solo time with them, and served as point person on all communication."

"Maybe that was a mistake, David's not letting you be the mother."

"Maybe," Jenny said uncertainly. "There were so many contradictory feelings flying around. When David told the kids we had to go ahead with the wedding despite their objections, I remember his saying, in essence, 'We have no future in wanting Sandie to be with us, except in our minds and hearts.' It was a 'damned if you do and damned if you don't' situation. There was this awful hole in the family. Everyone felt the vacuum. But the kids didn't want any part of that hole filled by someone else trying to take Sandie's place. They were strongly resistant to any merging of my role with Sandie's."

"Still, that was nearly a year ago. I'll bet they're in a different space now that they can see how much you've helped David."

"Margaret, you've always been great with Marc and Dellie, and I know they feel close to you. If I had half your mothering skills – or Sandie's – I might feel confident attempting a more maternal role, but I don't see a pathway to it."

"Then how do you show them that you care about them? Kids need to feel loved."

"The way that's most comfortable for me is helping them find their way through adult issues. With Dellie, for example, she has lots of older women around her, you included, who can be motherly and inquisitive. My focus is on teaching her self-reliance. I want Dellie to develop the strengths and capabilities that can keep her afloat in rough times, and ensure a modicum of control as she journeys through life."

Margaret shrugged. "She's still real young for that. Someone acting like a mother might help her feel more confident, less like a half-orphan."

Jenny had no answer for that. They shifted to other topics, but she felt uneasy. *Is Margaret right? Should I push more on the personal front even though it's not an area I'm comfortable with. Am I really doing the best I can do, or am I chickening out? Accountants don't like making mistakes, and the truth is, I don't deal well with rejection.*

Jenny knew herself to be reticent by nature, and she had been raised in a social environment in which it was considered impolite to ask personal questions or gossip about others. Moreover, on the few occasions when she had posed specific questions to Delphine about her life, she received only casual responses, with no suggestion that Delphine wanted to discuss anything further. *But that's not really rejection,* she admitted. *The hesitation might exist on both sides. And Dellie did just give me a major vote of confidence regarding the rug. One thing is for sure. This stepmother business isn't simple.*

Jenny was mulling this over when David called Marc to wish him Merry Christmas. Jenny joined the conversation briefly, then handed the phone to Delphine. Jenny was aware that Marc still resented the timing of the marriage. In his mind, their "haste" was disrespectful to Sandie. Marc wanted his father to be happy, but, in defense of Sandie's honor, not as happy as he had been with Sandie. Marc had come to respect the fact that Jenny was good with logistics and finance, but he still held himself aloof in all other areas of his life.

Give it time, Jenny counseled herself. *Both directions. Things with Marc aren't great, but they're certainly better than they were at the beginning. A un pas de tortue.*

David's Christmas gift to Jenny, delivered as they sipped homemade eggnog in Nate's living room, was a "post-it" note on which was written, "To Jenny, 25, From David." He refused to explain, except to say that her "big" present wouldn't be ready until the next day.

Having overheard him ask Margaret to recommend a florist, Jenny suspected that a bouquet was in the works. Her guess was right. David disappeared briefly the morning of December 26 and reappeared with twenty-five white roses, still furled, and not a single blemish to be seen. With one fell swoop, he sought to demonstrate how misguided Jenny was in her perception that he rarely gave her flowers, and he succeeded. Within a day, the plump buds opened into luscious globe-shaped blooms the size of magnolia blossoms, taking pride of place in Nate and Margaret's living room for the rest of their stay.

"Now listen, Bro," Nate scolded. "That bouquet's impressive as hell, but it's stealing the thunder from our Christmas tree! And do you get what an insensitive, unromantic cad all this Covent Garden stuff makes me look like?"

David just grinned. He was unabashedly delighted by his coup.

Jenny watched this exchange and smiled to herself. *Something has shifted,* she concluded. *David seems calmer, more stable. Right this minute, he's like Ferdinand the Bull, happily smelling the flowers. Since our arrival in the States, his alcohol consumption is down, his energy level is up, and he's in good spirits. Dare I believe we have finally turned a corner?*

Their last week stateside was spent in Florida. Delphine's classes didn't resume until mid-January, so she was able to go with them. They stayed at the beachfront condo that Jenny and her siblings held onto after their mother died, reserving it for family use in December and January, then renting it out the rest of the year.

Delphine occupied the bedroom on the inland side of the apartment. David and Jenny took the larger ocean-side bedroom, furnished with twin beds. "Let's push these twin units together to create a king-sized surface," Jenny suggested, but her solution was not without drawbacks. On one occasion their amorous exertions drove the two beds apart and them, in a tangle of sheets, down into the widening gap. They were laughing so hard they could barely negotiate themselves out of the twisted linens and clamber back up to finish what they had started.

When David did a grocery run, he came back with fresh vegetables, a fat chicken, and a bouquet each of asters, goldenrod and baby's breath. Jenny took charge of the flowers while David put away the chicken and vegetables. She could find only one vase so she combined the three bouquets into a single arrangement. "Where do you want them?" she asked.

"They're your flowers," David pointed out. "You decide."

They took full advantage of the warm sunny weather, visiting wildlife preserves, paddling about in the pool and watching sunsets from the apartment's balcony. When David played golf, Jenny and Delphine took long walks on the beach. Jenny thought often about Margaret's comments and the issue of girl-talk, but their beach conversations, though animated, centered on the seabirds they saw or memories they held of past beach experiences. Their last afternoon, Jenny and Delphine sat out on the balcony, waiting for David's return from the golf course.

Don't be shy about this, Jenny. It's now or never. Just do it.

"It's five o'clock," Jenny pointed out. "Would you like a glass of wine? David should be back any minute."

"Sure," Delphine answered. "Do you need help?"

"No, thanks. The bottle's already open."

Jenny poured two glasses and handed one to Delphine.

"*Santé*," she said.

"*Santé*," Delphine responded.

"You know," Jenny began, "Margaret mentioned something in Chattanooga that I wasn't quite sure how to deal with. She was concerned that your mother's death has left a big hole in your life that you haven't been able to fill. She suggested that I should try to be more motherly."

Delphine's eyes widened slightly, but her face remained still. She said nothing, covering her silence with a sip of wine.

"I told her I had no experience with parenting," Jenny continued with a half shrug, "and even if I had, I could never hold a candle to your mother's maternal instincts and skills. I remember your lovely speech at Sandie's memorial service, the one where you described how you and your mother used to laugh and argue and talk girl-talk – the one where each line ended with '*C'était bon.*'"

Delphine's eyes were beginning to glisten. *Back off*, Jenny told herself. *Keep it light.*

"Well, I certainly envy Sandie her mothering skills, but envy is as close as I'm ever going to get. I'm also really limited in the girl-talk department. What I can do, however, is what I think of as 'women-talk' – sharing experiences and thoughts on balancing life's demands, dealing with life's setbacks, and sustaining rewarding relationships. You already know I'm the consultant of choice when it comes to financial issues and travel schedules and what your father wants for Christmas. I just want to be sure you know that I'm also here for you on the women-talk front – not as a mom, but as an adult friend."

Delphine's lip was quivering. "Yeah, I know. Thanks," she said, and immediately put her glass up to her mouth.

"Hello, Ladies! Into the wine already?" said David as he walked in.

"Hi, Love. How was your golf game?" Jenny asked, giving Delphine a chance to steady herself.

"I didn't play worth a damn, but I had fun."

"That's all that counts," Jenny replied. "Would you like a glass of wine?"

"Soon as I wash up," he answered. "Hi, Delphine. What did you two ladies do all afternoon?"

"Nothing much," Delphine replied. "We just walked the beach and chatted."

"Ah. An afternoon of girl-talk," he commented.

"More like women-talk," Delphine corrected. "We *are* grown-ups, Dad."

One - For Jennifer on our First
Wedding Anniversary

One by one, like crystal beads
Dropping into a glass of champagne
Or grains of sand stirred in a child's pail of water,
Your moments fill my space
And make me choose to drink the tears
Or let them overflow the place
And, soaking through the sand, reach others,
Whose more recent claim to sadness
Needs them more than I to quell their fires of grief.
You in time flowing through me
Now let me hear Bach's Suites in measures
That bring me solace and gentle joy.
Boisterous it isn't yet, yet I find sublime relief
In teasing your measured intellect,
Knowing all the while the ripe mind
That nurtures it will, with time,
Produce in us a riot of shape,
Unruly vines of variegated flowers
Blooming through our autumn
Late enough for folks to ask the secret,
Unknown to us, for them to find.
One more year, if we count the celestial clock,
Out of thirty-eight;
An eternity behind us! Yet before us
Still another seems to lie in wait.

D.P. – January, 2003

Chapter 11

Their first full day back in Geneva, David went grocery shopping and returned with three long-stemmed roses – one red, one yellow and one orange with crimson tips – plus a large bouquet of white roses and another of mixed blue and yellow blossoms.

"Look at all the flowers!" Jenny exclaimed.

"Well," David shrugged off-handedly, "Now that I know...."

She proffered a hug and a kiss. "You're my hero!" she teased.

"Hmpff," he replied.

A week later, there was a repeat performance. David made a dash home from school during a break. "Just thought you might need some more flowers," he said, handing Jenny three more roses, similar to the previous week's array. Over the weekend, he presented her with a perky bunch of red, white and blue anemones.

On Sandie's birthday, David brought home five ivory roses to honor her memory. He and Jenny observed the birthday as they had marked the September anniversary of Sandie's death, with dinner at Le Borgia. During the brief drive home, David tuned the radio to Geneva's classical station. Bach's First Cello Suite filled the car. "Aha!" David proclaimed, "I expect Sandie arranged that."

"Did Sandie like the cello suites?" Jenny asked.

"Yes," was the reply.

Jenny was surprised, but kept her thoughts to herself. *The cello suites seem awfully somber for Sandie's taste. I wonder if Julien liked them.*

When they got home, David headed for his computer. Jenny heard him tapping on the keyboard. *He must be composing a birthday poem for Sandie,* she presumed. By the time he finally came upstairs, it was nearly midnight.

The next day was the anniversary of David and Jenny's "first" wedding, the one conducted a month prior to their legally sanctioned *Mairie* ceremony. When Jenny checked her in-box to see what David had written for Sandie, she found instead a poem titled *For Jennifer on our First Wedding Anniversary.* "One by one, like crystal beads dropping into a glass of champagne ... your moments fill my space," it began.

She devoured it, then went back and reread it slowly. *What a difference one year has made!* The poem David had given her on their original wedding day was wistful and sad, underscoring his still-dominant grief and his chagrin that he could not summon the rejoicing the occasion deserved. It was not an easy composition with which to launch a marriage.

This new poem was so dramatically different that it was hard to believe only a year had passed. David spoke of "sublime relief," but the relief was Jenny's. This poem was filled with hope and wonder and love. These were words Jenny had longed to hear, and now they were there in front of her.

David appeared and acknowledged Jenny's rapture with a hug and a kiss. At lunch, he presented her with twenty-five long-stemmed red roses. "Don't want my woman telling folks I rarely give her flowers," he teased. Echoing the timing of their original wedding ceremony, he summoned Jenny to the dining room in the late afternoon for champagne and a slice of *Gallette du Roi,* a traditional January pastry with a small trinket baked into it symbolizing the gifts of the Magi.

"Aha! My slice has the trinket," David exclaimed, extracting a tiny plastic camel from his wedge. "That earns me the right to crown myself King." He donned the gold paper ringlet that came with the *gallette,* then produced a second ringlet, also part of the tradition, and crowned Jenny his queen. They toasted one another with happy smiles.

Halfway through his glass of champagne, David paused to pick up a pen and a notepad. He looked at Jenny thoughtfully, tilting his head slightly in concentration. She held her breath, expecting some sweet expression of love. "When we go to the market tomorrow," he asked, "do we need to get carrots?"

"David Perry, you are outrageous!" she laughed. *What else can I do with a man like this, except love him to pieces? How could Sandie not see what I see?*

Jenny spilled her delight into countless e-mails. She recapped the playful correspondence before Christmas, detailed the barrage of flowers that left a trail of petals across two continents, and ended with a description of the *gallette* and its two crowns. With special friends, she also shared David's poem and was rewarded almost immediately by a call from Bibi.

"Okay, okay! You were right," Bibi admitted. "You got your decadent dessert!"

In mid-February, the sky suddenly cleared and the weather hinted at an early spring. As Jenny and David emptied a trunk-load of paper and bottles at the recycling center, Jenny stood for a few seconds studying the accumulation of winter mud and salt that covered the car.

"You know," she started, "now that we have a sunny day, it would be really nice to...."

"Yes, I know, I know," David interrupted, cutting her off.

"You know what?" Jenny asked.

"I know what you're about to say," he replied.

"How can you know what I'm about to say?" she frowned, highly skeptical.

He stretched out his index finger and, on the car window, wrote, WASH ME.

"That's impressive," Jenny conceded. It was precisely what she was going to suggest.

David shrugged. "Sandie was always after me to get the car washed as soon as the weather turned warmer."

"Great minds…," Jenny observed.

"No," David rejoined, "I'm inclined to suspect transmigration of souls."

He's joking, she decided. *Mostly, anyway. It's a big leap from being "just like Sandie" to being her Medium. But hearts and minds often work in the same way, so I suppose that souls, however one understands the term, might also run on parallel tracks.*

Jenny hardly needed David's observations or the notion of transmigratory souls to keep Sandie in mind. *My relationship with Sandie has become deeper and far more complex now that she's dead than it ever was when she was still alive. Back then, we shared vacation adventures, but we led separate lives. Now I know Sandie's deepest secrets, her hidden desires and feelings, and her sins.*

As she started on her spring-cleaning, Jenny found a damaged photograph of Sandie in her mid-twenties. *She really was a beauty,* Jenny acknowledged silently. *This must date from when she and David got engaged. I ought to have it restored and reproduced for Marc and Dellie.* She set it aside and later went looking for the negative. She pulled a carton marked PHOTOS off a high closet shelf and started going through the folders inside. The top folder was filled with pictures from Sandie's childhood. The second folder held packets that were clearly of more recent vintage. Jenny opened two of them. They all featured Sandie with Julien. Shaking her head, she put them back, and shoved the folder into the bottom of the carton.

My admiration for Sandie has increased, but I'm still uncomfortable with her infidelity, Jenny admitted to herself. *This quandary isn't likely to disappear any time soon. Maybe the best way to deal with it is to recognize that. There are a lot of people who would judge me harshly for sharing David's bed so soon after Sandie died. Maybe even Sandie would. Maybe I should just accept the moral confusion and shift my focus to something more useful. Like tidying Dellie's room.*

Jenny had asked Delphine's permission to use her room periodically as a guest room, so Jenny wouldn't lose access to her office computer when they had overnight visitors. "Sure. And thanks for asking," Delphine added. "Dad would have just stuck people in there as needed."

The permission included clearing the top of Delphine's desk so guests would have a place to put their things. Jenny took up two storage boxes and began to pack the pictures, books and notebooks stacked on the desk surface. As she worked, she uncovered a sheaf of drawings. *Is this artwork from Dellie's childhood?* Then she realized she was looking at letters and drawings done by the children at l'Académie Internationale as memorials to Sandie. Delphine had already put together an album filled with sympathy letters – the "Maman" binder – but she had not yet created a second album for the student offerings and the overflow.

"Sandrine Perry, if I were superstitious, I'd suspect you arranged to put these directly in my path today," Jenny called out to the empty air. *Lordy, I feel like a yo-yo!* After a moment's hesitation, she started through the messages from the children:

> I am really sorry about Mrs. Perry. I will miss her. She was a great lady.

> We are so sad you have gone. Your sweetness was never ending, no matter what your mood, because you cared so much about others that you wanted them to smile.

> Mme Perry was so radiant, lovely and kind that when God needed an angel, he chose her.

> When we would trudge into school in the mornings and see those awful gray walls, then we would see Mrs. Perry sitting in her office, and we would get a smile and a wave.

After the pages of children's tributes, there was a draft of Delphine's eulogy, enumerating sweet memories and declaring, after each one, "*C'était bon.*" Then, near the end of the pile, Jenny encountered her own farewell letter to Sandie, written ten days before Sandie's death:

September 15, 2000

Dear Sandie –

I have had a wonderful time with Dellie visiting campuses in Boston and Cambridge. Thank you for entrusting me with her care during her college research.

This is yet another example of the graciousness you have shown over the years by sharing your family so generously with me. Please rest assured that I will always do my best to be there for them, wherever they are and whatever they need.

It has been a privilege to be counted among your friends. I shall think of you often and remember you always. Have a gentle journey.

With much love, Jenny

Jenny's eyes were so blurred that she couldn't go on. Every word was a reminder of the pain that Sandie's loss caused. One child had summed it up in a single sentence: "Everybody likes you, Madame Perry."

Jenny placed the letters and drawings in the storage box and closed the lid.

How can I be resentful of behavior that was the result of Sandie's mistaken but nonetheless genuine belief that David had turned away from her? There's the confusion again. He's not the kind of man to send Valentines, but he gives many a gift in his own time and in his own way. Sandie might have longed for more conventional expressions of love, yet I find no difficulty in spotting David's alternative communications. How sad for Sandie that she couldn't see it!

"Five o'clock. Sun's over the yardarm." David called to Jenny when he arrived home. "You want some wine?"

"Be right there," she called back, heading to the kitchen to join him.

The traditional gray weather had returned, but crocuses were beginning to open up in the garden. They sat where they could look out the window on the burgeoning patches of color before the tiny flowers disappeared in the fading light.

They clinked their glasses. For a moment they sipped their wine in silence. It was Jenny who spoke first.

"Who would ever have thought, back in the days when we were trudging through the snow to class or staying up all night to finish term papers, that you and I would end up here, in this place, together at this moment and this stage of our lives," she mused.

"Yet amazingly, looking back, you can see the pathway," David rejoined, "despite all the zigzags. For me, it was life-changing to come to Europe, but at the time, I didn't think it was going to be permanent. I arrived in Paris with only a hundred dollars in my pocket and no safety net. It was sink or swim. It was all up to me. Nobody else was going to do it for me, so I swam like hell."

"And you made it. You've had a wonderful life here."

"Until Sandie died," he said bluntly. "Although now that some time has passed, I'm beginning to accept even that as a late-life rite of passage. Once I knew she was dying, there was a critical moment of decision for me. I had to make a choice about whether to die, figuratively or literally, with Sandie, or to survive and go on with my life. I couldn't have articulated it at the time, but I understood the issue before me, and I chose to survive."

"You had a lot of people rooting for you," Jenny said.

"I know." He reached over and squeezed her hand. "I know," he repeated.

In the pause that followed, David glanced at the mail sitting on the table. "Anything important?" he asked.

"Bills, advertising, and one letter addressed to you," she replied, reaching over to the pile and handing him an expensive looking envelope.

"This'll be interesting," he noted wryly.

"What is it?" Jenny asked as he opened it.

"It's a wedding invitation. Julien's son François is getting married on February 23. I need to note this in our calendar."

"David, February 23 is our anniversary."

"Only the legal one at the *Mairie*," he countered. "We just celebrated the January one. That's the one that really counted."

"Even so," she protested. "Are you actually thinking of going?" she asked in surprise. "If his son is getting married, Julien will obviously be there. Why not plead another engagement?"

"François was one of my students," David replied simply.

"Have you had any contact with Julien since, uh …?"

"Since Graham confirmed the affair? No," David said bluntly. "I haven't seen Julien since the night you and I had dinner with the DuPonts and the Charbonnets last spring."

"Do you absolutely have to attend?"

"I really should. It won't take long. We can still do something for our anniversary."

"Do I have to go too? Julien has fluent English. I can't use my bad French to avoid speaking with him, and I really don't want to."

"I'll come up with an excuse to get you off the hook, but I have to be there for François's sake – something about not visiting the sins of the fathers on the sons. I'll attend the ceremony, but I only need to stop by the reception briefly to offer my congratulations."

After dinner, Jenny called Bibi and told her about the wedding invitation.

"My god! Are you going?"

"I'm not, but David is."

"Why?"

"François, Julien's son, is a former student of David's, and he feels obligated."

"Does this mean he's forgiven Sandie?"

"As best I can tell, yes. I think that was resolved with Graham's help, if not before. But he's still working on the question of Julien."

"And you?"

"Me what?"

"Where are *you* on the forgiveness scale?"

"I guess I've pretty much forgiven Sandie too, but I'm a long way from having benign thoughts about Julien. There's no way I would willingly be in the same room with him."

"Unless maybe you could sneak in a packet of poison and slip it into his champagne glass," Bibi suggested. "With Ross defending you in court, I'm sure you'd get off. Justifiable homicide or something like that."

"Ross would tell me we shouldn't even joke about such possibilities. Remember the old rule about 'Judge Not.'"

"'Judge Not' isn't that old a rule. It's New Testament, which makes it your problem, but not mine. I think poison sounds just dandy."

"What about 'Thou Shalt Not Kill?' Is that old enough for you?"

"What about 'Thou Shalt Not Covet Thy Neighbor's Wife?'"

"Okay, enough, enough. And, Bibi, David's calling me, so I need to cut this short. I'll be back in touch as soon as I have something to report."

"Promise?"

"Scout's honor."

As they came closer to the wedding date, the specter of David confronting Julien nagged at Jenny as well as David. When David spoke about getting a wedding present for François, Jenny used the occasion to take a reading. "Any thoughts on how you're going to handle the meeting?"

"I want to be completely free of the whole thing, but I don't yet see a clear path."

David made no further mention of it, so Jenny didn't bring up the subject again until the night before the event.

"Have you figured out what you're going to do?" she asked.

"I'm still having trouble with it. Julien was a core member of our social circle. I stood by him when he was involved in political battles with l'Académie Internationale's Board of Directors. Yet all the while I was defending him, he was betraying our friendship."

"He was betraying a lot more than your friendship," Jenny interjected with more vehemence than she intended. "As the school

Principal, it was egregiously unprofessional for Julien to have an affair with Sandie. She was an employee whose position depended on his approval. You were also an employee, and Marc and Dellie were students there, making Julien's self-indulgence unconscionable!"

David held up a cautionary hand. "One thing I do need to be careful about, however this plays out, is the kids. Whatever I do or say, I'll have to be circumspect. I don't think Marc and Delphine could ever handle the knowledge of their mother's infidelity."

"They might be able to manage it some day, when they're older and married and have lived long enough to discover that love isn't simple."

David looked skeptical.

"No, really, David. Have you ever seen *The Bridges of Madison County?*"

"Doesn't ring a bell. There aren't a lot of American movies showing in Geneva," he answered.

"There's a powerful scene at the beginning of the film, when Meryl Streep's two middle-aged children are meeting with the family attorney after her death. Going through their mother's papers, they discover evidence that she had an affair when they were young. The daughter is shocked. The son is devastated. Then they find a letter she has left for them. In it, she explains her decision to tell them about the affair, saying something like, 'It would be terribly sad to die and have the people you love most never really know who you were.'

"Some day," Jenny continued, "when Marc and Dellie are in their thirties or forties, it might help them to discover that their parents were complex people who didn't have a perfect marriage. Then their own won't suffer by comparison. But I agree that in their present state, yes, they would feel hurt and betrayed. Others would too, including any of Sandie's friends and colleagues who aren't in the know. And then there's Julien's family – his children and his wife, Dominique."

"Sandie liked Julien's children," David sidetracked, "but she didn't have much respect for Dominique. She didn't think Dominique was terribly astute," he added.

Jenny was tempted to comment, but thought better of it. *How could Sandie have had respect for Dominique? Respect for Dominique would have interfered with the affair. Respect for Sandie certainly kept me on the straight and narrow regarding David, despite numerous opportunities over the years for a discreet tryst. Sandie's assessment of Dominique could well have been self-serving rather than accurate,* Jenny suspected.

The following day, Jenny wrapped the wedding present while David dressed for the ceremony. She could sense the tension, but he attempted a casual air. "I'm off," he said, bidding her farewell.

"I'll be thinking about you," she promised, handing him the present as he kissed her goodbye.

Will he chat politely with Julien? she wondered. *Will he pretend there's nothing wrong – that he doesn't know anything?*

Jenny was aware that sexual fidelity per se wasn't something David felt strongly about. *Nor do I,* she decided, *at least at a theoretical level. But I do care deeply about honesty in a relationship, and all indications are that David does as well. Julien's behavior translates into a serious lack of respect for David and the marriage. I don't see how he's going to get past that.*

She tried to imagine a civilized interchange between David and Julian, but she was stymied by vivid images from her own past confrontations with her ex-husband over his flagrant and hurtful deceptions. She busied herself with domestic chores, but when she heard the car pull in, she raced to the door.

"How did it go? What happened?"

"Let me get us both some wine, and I'll fill you in."

They settled in the living room, and David lit the fire.

"I finally managed," he began, "to initiate the conversation I've been contemplating for such a long time."

"You actually had a conversation?" Jenny asked with astonishment.

"I've told you, haven't I, that Julien was so upset by Sandie's death that he couldn't attend her Memorial Celebration? Dominique came in, but Julien sat outside in the car for over three hours."

"Yes, you've told me," she confirmed, nodding at him to continue.

"Well, I opened the conversation by saying that I knew Julien couldn't bring himself to participate in Sandie's final ceremony. I told him I hoped he had found some way to process his grief. I then said that Sandie had loved him very much, that their relationship was very special and very important to Sandie, and that this was okay with me." David's voice was full of emotion as he related the story, but he kept an even keel.

"After Sandie died, I went through her wallet. Mixed in with her credit cards, I found a haiku poem and half of a dollar bill. They obviously had some significance to her, but she had never mentioned them to me. I assumed they were connected somehow to Julien, so I put them in a sealed envelope. This afternoon, I gave them to him."

"What was Julien's reaction?"

"He didn't react visibly, but then, I didn't really give him time to. We were standing there in a crowd of people, in the middle of the wedding reception, and there was no further opportunity to talk."

"He must have been stunned. Blown away! But I can't believe you told him it was okay with you. Is that true?"

"I didn't say that what *he* did was okay. I said that Sandie's loving him was okay. There's a difference. It doesn't threaten me that she loved Julien. It *is* possible to love two people at one time. Look at Sandie. It didn't threaten her that I loved you from afar at the same time I loved her. Look at you. It doesn't threaten you that I still love Sandie."

Jenny's mental reaction was that David was greatly oversimplifying the issue, but out loud she said, "I'm impressed by the way you've handled this. Very few men could do what you've done with such civility."

He shook his head, frowning. "It's hardly a noble act, Jenny. I don't feel I'm in a legitimate position to judge. I never saw my flings as a violation of my commitment to Sandie, but she may have. I never intended to hurt her by directing so much of my passion into my teaching. I'm not happy that she had an involvement with Julien, but I've got to admit that I failed to provide her with the romantic element she was looking for in our marriage. I have to blame myself before I blame anyone else. If she had walked out on me and run off with Julien, I'd have a real case, but everything suggests she was doing a balancing act on a high wire, trying to be loyal to me and our marriage, yet keeping herself happy and whole at the same time. I'm sorry it happened, but that's hardly reason to let the affair eclipse all the good things we had.

"And as far as Julien goes, if he truly loved Sandie, I don't need to take him to task for it. He's more than paid the price with the pain of her death – a pain he had to suffer in secrecy and silence. Sandie was a very perceptive woman. The affair would never have lasted if Julien had been exploiting her. I think he grieved as much as I did when she died."

"I hadn't considered that," Jenny admitted.

"In any event, forgiveness isn't about denying your feelings. It's a simple recognition that resentment takes your focus away from the people and things that matter, and directs it to those you disdain. Someone once asked Nelson Mandela why he wasn't angrier with the white separatists who jailed him for so many years. 'If I thought it would be useful,' he replied, 'I would be.' I've reached the point where I feel pretty much the same way as Mandela. Anger isn't useful."

"So, are you saying that you aren't angry with Julien any more?"

David lit a cigarette and moved next to the fireplace. "You know how much I admire the works of Joseph Campbell. Campbell used to recount a well-known Buddhist tale about two Tibetan monks who suffered imprisonment and torture at the hands of the Chinese communists. When they met one another many years later, one monk asked the other, 'Have you forgiven our jailers?' The second monk replied, 'I will never forgive them.' The first monk considered this and said, 'Then it seems they still hold you in their prison.'"

They sat silently for a moment while David finished his wine. "Time to do something about dinner," he said after a few minutes.

"You didn't eat at the wedding?"

"Nope. Butterflies," he shrugged. He rose and started to head for the kitchen, then detoured to the front door. "Forgot I left something in the car," he explained.

Jenny returned to her office and turned on her computer. *I wish I'd been able to get all that down on tape*, she thought as she contemplated the e-mails she needed to write to Ross and Bibi.

When she joined David in the kitchen half an hour later, David handed her two fresh roses. "Here," he said. "One's for you and one's for Sandie's vase."

Happy Legal Anniversary to you too, Jenny thought, suppressing a smile. *He's forgetting his Romance 101 lessons, but this is not the time to remind him.* She chose the orange rose for herself and allocated the yellow one to Sandie. On inspection, she found that the current rose in Sandie's vase was still fresh, as was her own rose, in her office. She selected a slender bottle from the collection on the kitchen shelf and slipped the two new roses into it so they would keep until the old ones needed replacing.

She set the bottle on the counter, trying to decide where to put it. Each rose stood out, yet they enhanced one another. *Sort of like sisters — a sibling rivalry*, she felt, *different, independent, yet still family.* She had to smile. Unwittingly, she had made a floral statement that mirrored the thought that had been slowly evolving in her mind: the palpable degree to which Sandie's existence and hers had become fused by their relationship with David, however complicated, and his with them. She let the flowers stay where they were.

C'était bon. It was good.

Printed in the United States
By Bookmasters